Lines on the Mirror

An m/m Romance
Lynn Michaels

Copyright © 2015 Lynn Michaels & Rubicon Fiction
Blue Eyed Dreams, LLC
All rights reserved.
ISBN: 1517017254
ISBN-13: 978-1517017255

DEDICATION

To the CB girls group - the best bunch of mm romance fans on Facebook. Thanks for your support! Ya'll rock!

TRADEMARK RECOGNITION

The following trademarks or brand names appear throughout this novel. The author acknowledges any trademark or brandname items that are solely the property of the respective owners. Use of brandnames, trademarks, or any other copywrited items are solely in a fictional context and do not represent the views of any organizations or individuals.

Spotify, Michael Kor's, Ralph Lauren, Macy's, Kenneth Cole, Hanes, Armani, Canadian Mist, Wild Turkey, Hugo Boss, FaceBook, Clarks, Red Bull, Jack Daniels, Nickelodeon Network, American Express, Star Wars: Darth Vader, Seven Jeans, Joe-Boxer, Aviator, Berber, 2(X)ist, Emporio Armani, Levi's, American Eagle, Timberland, Saab, Volkswagon, Mazda Miata, Toyota Celica, Rolls-Royce, Puma, Matinique, Tommy Hilfiger, Google, Avian, Astroglide, iPod, NASDAQ, Rolex, Tootsie Roll, Vans, Mattel: Ken doll, Converse, Dior Homme

Sirenia, Theory of A Dead Man, The Who, Marilyn Manson, Royal Blood, Metallica, Megadeth, In This Moment, Van Halen, Band of Skulls, Starset, Kasabian, Stone Sour, Manchester Orchestra, Puddle of Mudd, Machine Head

DISCLAIMER

This is a work of fiction. Any similarities to the real world are imagined. All brand names are used with the utmost respect and are used fictitiously. This is an erotic m/m romance with 18 and older type scenes and recommended for mature audiences only.

ACKNOWLEDGMENTS

Special thanks to my cover artist Jay Aheer, my editor Devil in the Details, Editing Services for Writers and my Beta Readers who I could not do this without: Maggie and Amy

Chapter 1 - Graduation Day

Graduation day should have been a happy occasion but I couldn't bring myself to feel celebratory in the least. Aside from being done with college, I couldn't think of one damn thing to celebrate. Since I couldn't do anything about it, I sat in my chair on the lawn as the ceremony commenced and tried not to focus on the acid churning in my stomach.

The cap and gown added extra weight to my shoulders, dragging me down in the heat and making me want to escape whatever future my father had planned for me. Obediently, I waited for the Dean to call my name. "Martin Hannan." I stood and made my way across the stage.

Despite the wiggling worms burrowing into my stomach lining, I stood straight and forced a smile on my face. This two seconds, walking across the stage, shaking the Dean's hand, taking the symbolic scroll that had my name printed on it—my name, not my father's—etched itself into my memory. The diploma represented the last two seconds of my childhood. All grown up now, done with college, done with any rebellion I might have gotten away with; I sucked in a deep breath and readied myself for whatever the future could throw at me.

Just as I released the Dean's hand, it happened. I tripped

over a non-existent line on the stage. One heel of my shoe sticking, while the toe of the other smacked into it and I went flying. My hands splayed out in a useless attempt to stop my fall. I could just imagine my father burying his face in his hands and wishing he'd had a different child.

"Are you alright?" the Dean's assistant asked. She seemed nice enough, but my embarrassment required me to remove myself from the premises as quickly as possible. I shook her off as she grabbed my arm to help me up.

"Fine. Really. I'm good," I muttered and marched down the far side of the stage, making a point not to make eye contact with anyone, not wanting to see pity and disbelief looking back at me. It shouldn't have bothered me; I didn't really know any of these people anyway. Four years of classes in a public university, and I didn't know a single person. Sure, I had acquaintances. I knew their names. That was it. They didn't know me, or even want to know me.

This wouldn't be any different than my obsession with the dancer I'd met at the one party I had ever attended. After never ending weeks of pursuing the man, it ended like everything else in my life, with slipping grades, a broken heart, and an embarrassing story that I'd never tell anyone. Ever. Especially my Dad. Chasing after a guy that's not interested and having him tell you to fuck off in no uncertain terms in front of an auditorium full of people is beyond humiliating, even worse than falling across the stage at graduation. Nothing in my life could ever be normal. Could it? Just once? No, guess I was resigned to that.

Making my way back to my spot on the lawn, I stood in front of my chair with the other graduates, feeling my eyebrows tense with brooding and reflection. We waited there with reverence and joy all wrapped up together. Tomorrow I would start the next chapter of my life. It would be different, yet sickeningly the same. I stuffed my hand in my pocket searching for my last antacid tablet.

My elbow and hip started aching before every graduate had their scroll and they let us sit back down, but my pride had taken the worst of the fall. I wondered if anyone noticed my blush and if it would still be smeared across my face the next time I looked in the mirror.

After the ceremony, all the graduates milled about the auditorium, slowly making their way out the doors after connecting with their loved ones. My eyes skimmed the faces with the unrealistic hope of overlooking my parents and stuffing that wish to see Daltrey's face in the audience down like I was choking myself on his memories. With Dad watching me, expecting things from me, I couldn't think about Daltrey, the past, and what might have been.

"Martin! Martin!" I couldn't miss my father's voice. Steven Hannan was a small man, not reaching my own diminutive five-foot nine. Yet his voice called loudly through the auditorium as if he were ten-feet tall. He wore shoulder pads in his tailored jackets to ensure his stature was presented in the most flattering and powerful manner possible. His Armani tie was a glimmering red silk, dark hair slicked back from his forehead, and thick glasses hid his deep sapphire eyes. On his arm, a tall blond bombshell, six inches taller than him in her heels, tottered along. She wobbled and clutched at Dad's arm. Mother was drunk. Again. Still.

"Dad," my voice scratched. I wanted to crawl under the chairs, run out the back doors, or just sink into oblivion. He reached out his hand to me and I shook it.

"Come on, Son. Let's get some dinner. My treat." He clapped his hand on my shoulder, beaming with pride.

I should have been happy. Who the hell didn't want their father to be proud of them? I did want that, but it felt plastic. Even emotions like contentment and love felt cold with him. His approval centered on his own expectations. It bothered me, more than I wanted to admit, but I was used to it, like those worms eating away at my intestines. I should have been relieved that he didn't bring up the fall I took on stage. Why couldn't that just be enough?

Dinner turned out to be just me and my father. I kissed my mother goodnight and she headed up to her hotel suite.

She could barely stand. She was getting worse and I wanted to talk to my father about it, but what could I say that hadn't already been said? Dad had eyes, he could see.

He ordered steak for both of us, medium rare with a baked potato—butter, no sour cream. I wanted sour cream, but I choked down the dry potato loaded with salt and pepper instead. "So, what are your next steps, Martin?"

"Job, a place to live." I shrugged, waiting for him to tell me what my next steps were supposed to be. He knew better than I did, didn't he?

Sure enough, he slid a set of keys across the table. I picked them up. "Upgrade. You deserve it." They were Saab keys. Fucking Saab.

"Thanks." I shoved them in my pocket to keep company with my roll of antacids and forked through the remains of the potato on my plate.

I barely saw him reach inside his jacket pocket and set the piece of paper on the table. "Here's your itinerary for next week," he said, shoving the paper toward me, dishing out the directions as if this were any other business meeting. My life dictated down to the second, listed in black and white on the paper sitting between us. I wanted to cram the paper down his throat.

My voice cracked a little when I asked, "What's this?"

Dad smirked, as if disgusted that I couldn't figure it out myself. He resettled in his chair, schooling his features back to neutral before answering, confidently. "Job interviews. See which one you like best. Research the firms before you go in so you don't sound ignorant. You can do that much, right?" He ended his orders with a question, as if he wasn't sure I was truly capable of taking on adult responsibilities. Maybe I wasn't.

I didn't need his job interviews. I could get them on my own. "Yes, sir," I responded flatly. My voice sounded so much calmer than the anger boiling just beneath the surface. "Thanks."

"It'll save you time." He shrugged it off and went back to

his food. Prescribing my life was nothing more than another task on his to-do list. "Can I count on you to find your own place to live? Get something nice? Maybe close to where you end up working?" He waved his hand at the itinerary that I still hadn't picked up off the table.

What a fucking mess my life was. "Yes, sir. No problem. I got it." Reluctantly, I picked up the paper and stuffed it in my front pocket to keep time with the new car keys and the antacid.

"Uh, one more thing, Martin." He reached in his jacket again.

"Sir?"

He pulled out his wallet and flipped through it. Finding what he was looking for, he looked up, meeting my gaze with blue eyes the color of mine, yet looking completely different. He reached out to me and I tore my eyes away from his glare to see a card in his outstretched hand.

"What's this?" I asked, taking the metal card. It was black and shiny with numbers on the bottom and a shiny security emblem in the corner. It was the mother-fucking Darth Vader of credit cards. I half expected my father to whisper in husky voice, "Martin I am your father." I swallowed hard and scowled at him, sitting self-righteously across from me.

"For whatever expenses you have until you get your first few paychecks tucked away." He waved his hand around dismissing the gift and stuffed his wallet back in his pocket. He had just slid me an American Express black card as if it were nothing. "You have to eat."

"You don't think this is too much?" I held the card in my fingers, as if it were fine china instead of titanium.

Dad flipped that hand around again, dusting off my concerns like the lint off his ridiculously expensive jacket. "Pick yourself up a few new suits, too. For the interviews. You want to look your best."

What could I say? My dad loved me and wanted the best for me. I knew that in my heart, but the anger at his control and his assumptions that I couldn't take care of myself rubbed me the wrong way.

"Martin?" I looked up at him again, away from the shiny black card that meant so much between us and yet meant nothing. "Most kids would be ecstatic. This is a great graduation present. You deserve it. Relax. Enjoy it. Soon enough you'll be doing your own thing."

"Sure, uh, I don't know what to say. Thanks, Dad." I still didn't put the card away. My brow creased over my eyes. Fire burned in my gut. I wanted to throw the card back at him and walk away, but he was right. Dad was always fucking right. I stood to fish my wallet out of my pocket and hide the blasphemous card from my sight.

I pulled out the roll of antacids, peeled back the paper and slid a chalky pill in my mouth before sitting back down to enjoy the rest of the stunted conversation with my father.

Chapter 2 - My New Place

Several weeks later, I started my day by hauling boxes back and forth to my new apartment. It was moderate for an upscale building. The front had a stucco finish of desert sand tan with painted white balconies climbing the building. The apartments all opened to the inside and the four stories were navigated by an enclosed stairwell. On the ground floor, they provided a club house area as well as a work out center that was partially inside and partially outside by the pool.

I went up the stairs with a few more boxes and rested the big one I had against the door jamb as I fingered the keys into the lock.

"Hey neighbor! Whatcha got there?" A young woman with a tight, compact body and long auburn locks flowing over petite shoulders stood by the stairwell. She trailed one hand along the wall. "I heard someone was moving in. I'm Wendy. I live upstairs." She pointed up, as if I didn't know what the word meant. Her makeup was heavy, accentuating sharp cheek bones and her dark eyeliner brought out the mossy green dancing around in her hazel eyes.

"Nice to meet you. I'm Martin." I managed to get the key in the door and shove it open. "Come in?" I nodded to her, not really caring if she followed me in or not, but figuring I should meet the neighbors, despite my lack of social skills.

Wendy swept in to my apartment as if she were my personal welcoming committee. "You don't have much here. Is this all? You need help? I can start unboxing while you get more."

"I'm gay." Blurting the words out there seemed like the fastest way to prevent her onslaught.

She laughed, "I'm not trying to pick you up. For real. Just being neighborly." Her fingers were red-tipped and long like a piano player's. They drew shapes all over the taped up boxes and the table I'd already brought in and played over the built-in breakfast bar separating the kitchen from the other living spaces. I couldn't help think they would dance over any surface she was near, including my own body. They seemed to follow her eyes around the space, taking in the dark wood paneling of the kitchen and the boxes stacked up against the long wall across the living room from the balcony.

I stuck my hand in my empty pocket, searching for my familiar roll of antacids. Since accepting the job offer from Apex, the one LGBT friendly organization on my dad's list, I hadn't had a hard time with my stomach issues. Accepting the black card, the new Saab, and everything else felt easier by taking the one job I felt I could live with. Plus, Dad hadn't been calling every night since I told him I took the job, either.

It wasn't the highest paying job; it would take care of my bills and let me save up money, but for what I had no clue. The job would start on Monday. I just needed to get through one more weekend. So, why was my stomach churning again?

Wendy stared at me with a smirk on her face, greenish-brown eyes sparkling mischievously, obviously waiting for my next move. I nodded to the kitchen. "You can start in there, I guess. I have a few more boxes to bring up. That's all. Not much."

My new neighbor smiled at me. "All right, Martin." For the first time since descending on me, her words were slow and pronounced. I couldn't help search for meaning in that, but how the hell would I know what she thought? I was completely out of my element with Wendy and had no idea what she could ever want with me.

I dropped the box in the middle of the living room and made my way back to the car for the last few things. By the time I returned Wendy was well into unpacking the kitchen boxes. She had the glasses and plates stacked in the dishwasher. I lifted an eyebrow to ask her what she thought she was doing.

"After being packed up, you need to wash them before using. Duh." Her red lips smiled at me, laughed at me. "It's all good, Martin. Seriously. I have a boyfriend. Alec. He lives with me." She lifted her eyes to the ceiling and back, presumably to indicate her own apartment upstairs.

"Do you live directly above me?"

"Yeah."

"Great." I smiled, but I wasn't too happy, wondering how sound proof the ceiling/floor would be and whether or not Wendy was a screamer. I didn't want to be kept up listening to them having sex all night. I bit at my bottom lip, knowing I was assuming a lot. What the hell did I know about hetero-couples? "Uh, thanks for the help." I turned and started looking for the bathroom box. My stomach gurgled, demanding I find a new pack of antacids quickly.

I worked quietly in the bathroom and by the time I actually found a pack, I didn't need them. I'd been listening to Wendy work in the kitchen. She'd been humming to herself, so I didn't put on any music, despite my laptop already set up for it.

"Hey, when you getting more furniture?" she asked leaning up against the doorway.

I shrugged. "When I get to it." Other than the table, my bed, and a small dresser, I didn't have any other furniture. The few pieces at my old place were garbage, not worth moving.

"I can help you shop," she said, hopefully, practically bouncing up and down with excitement.

I gave her another eyebrow move. "What would your

boyfriend think?"

She smiled brightly. "Thought you were gay? Why would it matter?"

"I'm still a guy." I spread my arms wide as if to show her I still had all the proper equipment and silently wondered what she thought of my body. I'd hit the gym some in the past few job-searching weeks and even though I was still as lanky as ever, I knew my shoulders had bulked up a bit more and my stomach was flat. Taking care of my body was another expectation of my father's, but finally one I had to agree with.

Wendy's laughter was like champagne bubbles going to my head, and the sound was contagious, making me laugh with her. "I like you. Come upstairs and have a drink with me? Alec should be home soon." She added the last while looking at her watch that graced her delicate wrist.

"Okay?" I followed her up, though hesitantly. I thought about grabbing the pack of the antacids I'd found, but wondered if it'd seem rude. Why did I care? Well, I'd always cared way too much about what others thought of me, yet this was on a different level. I wanted Wendy to be my friend, something I'd never had a lot of in my life. Not since Daltrey, anyway.

Wendy and Alec had decorated their space in a homey palette of beige and brown. They'd painted their walls an indistinct shade of tan, but compared to my standard issued white, it was nice. They had a huge brown leather sectional sofa and I wondered if it was faux. Colorful throws in red and orange sat on the back of the couch invitingly. Artwork hung scattered on the walls, some in black and white and some in color.

One grouping in particular, on the wall leading to the bedrooms, caught my eye. Several photos of a young man were framed in black. The man was attractive with lean muscles making him skinny but not scrawny by any means. His brown hair was short, buzzed around his ears, but there were distinct highlights through the longer top. In some, his big dark eyes stared out like they knew more than anyone else in the room.

"Hot, huh?" Wendy interrupted my ogling of his half-naked form. "That's Alec. I do his hair. That's what I do. Professionally, I mean."

"Shit. Um, sorry. I mean, he is. Hot." What did I mean? Alec looked spectacular, but it didn't get my cock throbbing or anything. In L.A., he was just another pretty face.

"Alec is a model. He's been working a lot lately. I'm sure you'll see him in a magazine or two soon. Come on." Wendy grabbed my sleeve with a little chuckle. "Drink." She pulled me into the kitchen area. They had a table, similar to mine, set up in front of the breakfast bar, just like mine. I pulled out a chair and sat, waiting for her to join me. She put a bottle of Canadian Mist and two shot glasses on the table. "Not my fav, but it'll work." She winked at me and filled the glasses.

I wasn't much of a whiskey drinker. Who the hell was I kidding? I wasn't much of a drinker, period. Seeing my mother living in her bottle all these years generally gave me a distaste for alcohol. Maybe I was afraid I'd end up just like her. Not that I had many invitations to drink over the years. None of that stopped me from lifting the shot glass to clink against hers.

"To new neighbors!" Wendy toasted.

"Neighbors!" I watched Wendy shoot the drink back, her mossy eyes on me the entire time.

I copied her, tossing the drink to the back of my throat where it burned like hell and left me coughing. Wendy guffawed, as she refilled the glasses. I narrowed my gaze at her. Who liked being laughed at?

"Relax. It's all good, Marty!"

"Martin. Just... Martin, please." I wanted to leave, but wrapped my fingers around the glass instead.

Keys crunched in the front door and the living breathing version of the hot guy in the pictures peeked in. "Hey! Who the hell is this?" The rest of his body followed his head through the door. He was even hotter in real life, with big brown doe-eyes and a forthcoming smile. Of course, the warmth in my chest and my head from the alcohol probably influenced my first impression.

"New neighbor. Martin..." Wendy started to introduce me, but I'd never given my last name.

"Hannan. Martin Hannan," I provided, reaching out my hand.

Alec grabbed it and gave a quick shake. "Hannan, huh?" His eyes scanned up and down, taking me in, judging me. "I'm Alec Randall. That's Alec, like in Trebeck."

"Uh, I think his name is Alex, dude," from someone following Alec through the open door.

"No? Fuck, whatever. Why the hell didn't you tell me, Wendy?" Alec laughed and Wendy joined him, as did the nice looking guy who'd commented. It felt like a long-running inside joke that I didn't understand. "Oh, this is Seth," Alec tagged on, pointing his thumb at the other guy.

"Hello," I squeaked out. Seth smiled and shook my hand. It was all I could do to keep my mouth from hanging open. Seth was gorgeous with long blond, messy hair and eyes as blue as any summer sky. He wore a T-shirt with a Theory of A Deadman band logo on it. Perfect.

"You like, man?" Seth asked, noticing that I was staring at his shirt.

I felt stupid and my tongue felt thicker than normal. I nodded, barely. "Uh, yes, great music." I slammed back the second shot before I could stick my foot any farther into my mouth. Comments about his broad chest should not be falling from my mouth two seconds after meeting the guy, but I was oh-so tempted.

Seth smiled. "They're alright, I guess." When he smiled, his teeth looked like a supermodel tooth paste ad. The man couldn't have been any more my type. His bulky shoulders had me salivating and his close proximity had my cock twitching. "So, Tia will be here to pick me up soon. Grab another glass, Wend."

Well, he could have been gay—that would've been more my type. "Tia?" I asked, tentatively, my stomach burning with alcohol and unquenchable desire.

"My girlfriend, man."

Oh. Enough said. I leaned back in the chair, feeling just a bit lightheaded, and watched Wendy pour out four shots. Alec came back in the room, though I hadn't realized he'd left. He'd exchanged his nicer button up shirt for a plain gray Tee while out of the room. He grabbed a glass and lifted it up. "To new neighbors. Let's have a fucking party this weekend, Wendy!"

"Cool!" she agreed as everyone shot back the whiskey, including me. "You have to come, Martin. Meet everyone else. We'll make it your special night!"

I heard myself answer, "Okay." It felt surreal. I hadn't been in my new apartment one whole day and I already had a buzz going with my new upstairs neighbors who had invited me to a party. Suddenly, I was living an alternate life, one that didn't include my father's constant dictation. It was mildly disconcerting.

"Sure," Alec seemed to agree with her, though I wasn't sure why they were so interested in me. "It'll be our welcome to the neighborhood bash. Just for you." He pointed at me, but his words didn't sound friendly, it felt like sarcasm. Why did this have to circle around me? I wasn't sure I liked being the center of attention. That was a place I'd never really been. "Bring a date. You seeing someone?" He cocked an eyebrow, as if daring me to be in a relationship. Alec's mixed signals felt strange, or maybe I just didn't know how to read him. Socially inept, I was out of my comfort zone completely anyway.

I shook my head. "No, no. I, uh..." I didn't want to talk about my lack of relationships. My stomach twisted with the mere mention of needing a date.

"No girlfriends? Dude, I can't believe that." Seth put his two cents in.

Wendy snapped quickly, "No boyfriends? I'm sure you have guys begging for a date."

I just shook my head and stared into the empty shot glass, watching the remains of the bitter brown liquid sliding back to the bottom. She had just outed me to everyone in the room, including—especially—surfer-Seth. The heat of a blush rolled over my face and neck.

I didn't generally discuss my sexual orientation with anyone. Just thinking about it had my stomach burning like a roaring campfire. Thoughts of the hot dancer in college who rejected me so publically rose like bile in my throat. My parents knew, though they just ignored it. Daltrey had known, all those years ago, but that was in the past. How the hell would I deal with this? I certainly wasn't planning on living in a closet or dating girls. I shrugged, pretending that it didn't bother me, yet most likely failing.

"That's cool," Alec said. "We'll have some single guys here, I'm sure." He turned away from me as he spoke, gesturing to Wendy with his empty shot glass.

"For real, man," Seth added, matter-of-factly. "I know a few guys we can invite. Lots of guys that model are gay."

Seth was definitely a model like Alec. I should have known. I couldn't help but frown, knowing I was way out of my league with these people. Fear dug into my stomach as I waited for them to turn on me, then Wendy filled the glasses again.

"Super! Here's to hooking Martin up with a hottie this weekend. Those models are gorgeous." She winked at me again.

I slammed back the shot. How many had that been? My head was starting to spin, or was that the room? "No... No. I don't—"

"Oh, come on, Martin," Wendy complained. "It'll be great."

"I don't do, uh, I mean, I'm not..." Damn, I was stuttering like a nervous high school dweeb.

Alec laughed, mocking me. "Surely, you're not a virgin. I mean you're, what? Twenty-one, twenty-two?" It really started feeling like high school all over again. Wasn't I beyond that? Did he have to pick on me?

"I'll be twenty-four in a few months and no, I'm not a virgin. I just haven't ever been in a relationship. Not a real one." Gay guys could get sex, even socially awkward ones like me. You just had to be in the right place, and willing to take it, in more ways than one. I didn't want that, but I didn't want to discuss it with my new straight neighbors, either.

"Not one?" Wendy asked, eyes all big and begging me for more information or more likely gossip. Apparently, I was the evening's entertainment.

"Well, I mean. I had one. Back in High School, but I guess that probably wasn't real either. You know? What the hell did we know in High School?"

The whiskey helped the words fly out of my mouth. I regretted them the minute they fell off my tongue. My heart pounded, wanting me to defend myself and not put all my pathetic dreams on the table for these strangers to imbibe like alcohol in a shot glass.

Alec laughed again. Really, it was a bit irritating and I glared at him, hoping the daggers would hit their mark, but he ignored it. "So, what? You're still in love with this guy? What's his name?"

I lifted a shoulder, not really wanting to play this game, but what else was I going to do? Seth leaned over and nudged my shoulder encouragingly. At least they weren't bashing me. "Uh, Daltrey. His name was Daltrey."

"Daltrey?" Alec's nose crinkled as if the name disgusted him.

"Well, his mother was a bit of a hippy. She named him after that guy, you know?"

They stared at me.

"From the band, The Who? Roger Daltrey? You know?" I waved my hand in the air as if that would grant them the knowledge I wanted them to have.

"Oh!" All three said with heads bobbing. I still didn't think they knew what I was talking about.

"Hey, what's his last name?" Alec asked, as if it mattered.

"Uh, I don't know. Don't remember." Alec glared at me. Why did it bother me so much to tell them? "Boxbower, Boxwood...something." I knew damn well what his name was, but I was more concerned with getting out of this conversation.

"Boxbaum?" Alec asked.

My head shot up, eyes wide. I couldn't deny the recognition. "That's it."

"Fuck, I know him!"

"What?" How could he know Daltrey? They'd moved across the whole fucking country to New York at the end of our junior year of High School.

"For real," Alec elaborated, "I don't know him, like personally. My mom does. She's into all this artsy-shit. He's like an artist."

I stared at him. I hated the *it's a small world* bullshit, but what could I say? Daltrey had always been into art. He was always sketching in his notebook; most of his pictures were of me. Was Alec right? Had he become famous?

"So, right, maybe I'll just call Mum tomorrow and see if she can hook you up with his digits. Lover boy!"

"Uh... Thanks, Alec." I gestured to Wendy to hit me with another shot. I couldn't even think about the possibility Alec was putting on the table.

Seth leaned across me, reaching toward Wendy with his own glass, bumping his shoulder into mine again, sending shock waves of lust shooting up through my arm and straight to my dick. "You should totally look him up on Facebook, man. If he's an artist, you know, he should have a page, right?"

I'd never thought of that. Actually, that was a lie, I'd just never been brave enough to do it. Perhaps the whiskey let me believe the lie easier. "We never broke up. He just, like, moved." Why I volunteered that gem, was beyond me, but it was true, at least.

"Sounds romantic," Wendy sneered with an eye-roll. I felt my forehead tightening. I didn't know what I'd done to make her suddenly adverse to me.

"For sure," Alec agreed. "So romantic. Sounds a little pathetic. Still hanging on to your first crush. What? Is this your first job out of college? Your first apartment? Hell, how can you even afford that ride I saw you pull up in? Did your daddy buy that for you? What kind of job do you have, anyway?"

I couldn't look him in the eyes; couldn't look at any of them. He was right, what did I really have to offer Daltrey, or anyone. I sucked my bottom lip between my teeth, wishing for another shot and not sure if I should ask for one. My legs bounced up and down a little, begging me to make a run for it. I knew it was coming. They weren't really interested in friendship. They'd just wanted to check out the new fag upstairs and see how they could torment him. I didn't want to be that guy. For once in my damned pathetic life, I wanted to be one of them—the cool kids.

"Ah, leave him alone, Alec. We'll still have your fucking party. It doesn't have to be all about Martin." Seth came to my rescue, but I wasn't sure why. I didn't want to be the guy that needed a hero either, yet I was certain that need reflected in my eyes when I looked at him.

The conversation moved on to what supplies were needed and who would be invited, and Wendy opened a second bottle of whiskey. Somewhere along the way, I stopped worrying about every damn thing that was said.

Chapter 3 - Hangovers Suck

The sun stabbed me in the eyes like a prison inmate with a shank, waking me from the solitude and peace of sleep and into a painful morning. I grabbed my pillow and rolled over, pulling it over my head. I really needed to get curtains.

What an unbelievable turn of events. I'd told complete strangers about Daltrey. Ugh!

I hadn't thought about Daltrey this much in a long time. My first day on my own and I was getting drunk and spilling all my life secrets. Well, maybe not all of them. I sure as hell didn't tell them about how many nights Daltrey had spent in my bed all those years ago. We'd started out as friends when we were kids, so sleepovers were no big deal, but the closer we got emotionally, the closer we got physically as well. Those sleepovers entailed a lot of discovering each other's bodies, hot mouths, lingering kisses, and hands touching fevered skin. Thinking about those nights had my morning wood throbbing in a way that rivaled the pounding in my head.

My hand wandered down my chest and abs and finally stroked my dick as I thought about Daltrey. He'd been the ultimate love affair. I'd never be over him. In the solitude of my own bed, I could admit it.

I missed the freckles splattered across his nose and cheeks and the way his brown hair flopped over his dark eyes. He had the longest, thickest eyelashes in the world. I wanted to push that silky hair away from that perfect, angelic face, just one more time.

Closing my eyes, I thought about Daltrey's hot mouth and plump lips and imagined him taking my dick inside his mouth, swallowing me down. I stroked harder, remembering how many times we'd gone down on each other. I tugged at my sack, thinking about his fingers there and maybe his tongue, licking my balls, feeling his hot breath against my sensitive skin. It didn't take long for me to shoot off, messy cum spraying on my stomach and rubbing into my softening cock.

Most of our sleepovers had been at my house. Daltrey's mom was always too interested in what we were doing when we were at his house, but my parents didn't give a shit. Mom was usually drunk and ready to pass out by eight and Dad was always working. That was the only time in my life that I could honestly say I was thankful for their crappy parenting skills. They left us alone and we were pretty damn happy about that. Until he moved.

I needed Tylenol, coffee, and a hot shower, but I couldn't stop thinking about Daltrey. After getting the coffee machine set up and rolling, I opened my laptop, and clicked on Facebook. I'd set up my Wi-Fi the previous day. Hell, that was the first thing I did. Living even one minute without the internet was just not going to happen.

It only took me a moment to type Daltrey's name in the search bar and only a second to bring up his profile. There was only one Daltrey Boxbaum, after all. In seconds, my heart stopped beating as I stared into his face again. His profile picture was in black and white, his face turned slightly to the side, obviously done professionally. The monochromatic image didn't show the depth of Daltrey's eyes or the gleam of his hair or how soft it was beneath my fingers, but it was definitely Daltrey: his face, cheeks a little sharper than I remembered, his angled chin, those same lips that were shaped just right, thick and pouty. Oh God, that mouth! How many times had that mouth been on my skin, my cock? I wanted him just as much as I ever had. We'd shared so much back then, even beyond sex.

Daltrey knew how I felt about my life, my parents, my hopes and dreams. I knew how he escaped his parents fighting inside his sketch book. I escaped my parents in Daltrey. We were inseparable. We stayed up late watching old B-movies like *The Incredible Shrinking Women*, and *The Thing from the Deep*. We'd laugh and make fun of the bad acting and horrible props. We stuck together in school as much as possible, looking out for each other and keeping people from picking on either of us. We had other friends, but at the end of the day, it was just us. I missed him more than I could dare even think about. The hole he'd left in my heart ached for him.

I made my way into the kitchen to get a cup of coffee and shore up my confidence before looking at the rest of Daltrey's profile. I wanted to let myself hope we could reconnect and at least be friends or pen pals. Daltrey still lived in New York, according to his Facebook status.

I sipped my bitter black coffee, thinking of how the taste matched how I felt reminiscing about the past. Our glory days had been ruined when Daltrey's family abruptly moved. At seventeen, he might as well have moved to a different planet. He had taken my whole world with him when he moved away, leaving me in a dark hole that I couldn't climb out of. I'd never been accepted by any others like Daltrey had accepted me.

I spent long days through the rest of high school, avoiding bullies and keeping to myself and that same trend carried over to college.

With a sigh, I clicked on Daltrey's photos. Pictures of his art filled the screen as I scrolled down, until one made me stop, jaw falling open. I put my mug on the table and leaned forward to get a better look. I clicked on the picture, making it larger and stared into my own face. Suddenly, that hope for more Daltrey in my life seemed a lot brighter. I still meant something to him. He'd put a painting of me on his Facebook page.

Didn't that mean something?

Unable to take any more emotional revelations with this crappy hangover, I shut my laptop and headed for the shower. The relief of hot water felt like salvation washing over me. I just wanted to stop thinking, if only for five minutes.

After the steamy shower, I dressed and headed for the grocery store a few blocks over. They had an attached liquor store and I felt compelled to replace the bottle I'd drank my share of the night before. Plus, the party was supposed to be for me, or so Alec claimed, which made me determined to help out. That black, metallic Vader-card in my wallet would buy some party trays as well as some groceries and Dad wouldn't look twice at a statement from there.

A few hours later, I took the trays and the booze up to Wendy's apartment to escape my own pathetic musings. I set my mind on keeping everything in perspective and refused to let myself dwell on Daltrey anymore, because I had stopped and peeked at his profile picture nearly a dozen times while I was supposed to be unpacking more boxes.

I'd played my favorite playlist on Spotify, hoping to change my mood, but even the raucous sounds of Machine Head and In This Moment couldn't pull me out of my funk. I blamed the hangover, but thoughts of Daltrey and longing for him had more to do with it. Seeing his picture on Facebook brought back all of my teenage dreams and fantasies and left me feeling like some insipid schoolgirl, mooning over her first crush. Damn, I hated feeling girly, especially over a pipedream.

Wendy opened her door and gave me an odd look. "What's this?" she asked, staring at my armful of party food. I held a bottle of Wild Turkey and a bottle of red wine by the necks in one hand and balanced the trays with the other. I couldn't believe I hadn't dropped the load coming up the stairs.

"You know? I'm, uh, helping?" I answered with a decidedly effeminate squeak.

Wendy shook her head and grabbed the alcohol. "Come in, you nut."

I followed her in and put the party trays in her fridge. Another woman was sitting at her table, looking at me with curious eyes. "Hey," she said in a breathy voice. She looked like a grown up version of a cheerleader, not unlike my mom on her better days, though much younger. My mother had been a cheerleader, so I knew all about them, and everything about this girl from her rail-thin body to her straight brown and very shiny hair to her perfect makeup job screamed Rah! Rah! Rah!

"I'm Tia," she said with a quirk of the head.

Oh-my-fucking-god. Seth's girlfriend. They'd talked about her the night before, but I'd left before she showed up. Somehow, the discussion didn't make her real and I'd only thought of her in some abstract sort of way. Her dramatically made-up eyes and thin smile felt like a Dali painting had come to life right off the walls. I expected her face to start melting at any second.

"I'm Martin." I held my hand out to her, automatically, silently thanking Dad for drilling manners into my head.

Tia's hand felt beyond dainty and right into brittle, as she shook mine. If Wendy turned on her AC, this puny girl would probably float around the apartment on the air current, she was so thin. Her lips turned down to a frown, as I studied her. She glanced down her own body and tight shirt that clung to her curves. "What?" she asked, looking back up at me with her smoky-gray eyes.

I shook my head and bit my lip, wishing I had a pack of antacids in my pocket. I could feel the acid monster beginning to stir in my gut.

Wendy snorted, walking out of the kitchen. "The guys will be here soon. Beer?"

"Yes, please and thank you." The tension in the room felt colder than the beer. It seemed odd that Wendy didn't look at me, but glared at Tia, as she handed the bottle over. If I didn't know better, I'd say Wendy was jealous, but I didn't know why. Wendy was prettier, curvier, and more vibrant than Tia, who seemed ready to fade into oblivion at any moment. If anyone should have been jealous, it should have been me, as the one lusting after Seth. Hopefully, not so blatantly that anyone would know.

I sipped the cool beer, wishing I knew how to handle situations like this. Interacting socially with people had never been my thing. It hadn't been Daltrey's either. I didn't want to think about him and what we'd never be anymore. I resigned myself to sitting silently at the table across from Tia, and waiting.

Eventually, Seth and Alec showed up with more alcohol and more people. It didn't take long for the apartment to fill up. Pop music blared from the stereo, making me want to barf. People covered the sofa and chairs, stood around, moved in and out from the balcony and kitchen areas; all laughing and talking loudly over what passed for music. Wendy, Alec and Seth introduced me to most of the people there, but after a few minutes, I drifted to a corner of the dining room, content to watch the circus. Why hadn't I brought a pack of antacids?

"Hey! There you are." Alec leaned against the wall beside me. His big brown eyes sparkled as he smiled with his whole face.

"Great, uh, party?" I stuttered. Great? I hated it. I didn't know these people and I didn't want to, either.

"Look, uh, Martin. I'm sorry I was such a dick last night," Alec said, smiling a little crookedly.

"Dick? No, uh..." I shook my head. "You were fine."

"Nah. I was a dick. Sorry. I was just tired from work and all and shouldn't have taken it out on you." He clapped his hand on my shoulder. I stared down at it then back up into his deep brown eyes, wondering what he was thinking. "So. I have something to make up for it, dude."

"What?"

He reached in his pocket, pulled out a scrap of paper and handed it to me. A phone number was scrawled across the blank surface. "Talked to Mum. I told you I'd come through. I'm good like that. So, that's him." Alec pointed at the paper.

"Him?"

"Uh-huh, Daltrey's number. Well, his office in New

York." He winked at me and ran his tongue across his bottom lip. I realized he'd been standing entirely too close to me and my heart rate ratcheted up a few notches.

"Thanks," I muttered with none of the sincerity or shock that raged through my body and swirled around in that empty Daltrey-shaped hole carved in my heart. The phone number sparked a light in that dark hole, a light I labeled *hope*. I let a smile curve my lips as I tucked the paper into my jeans pocket. "Really, thanks." This time I sounded a bit more thankful.

"No problem, dude. Let's get fucked up. Come on." He grabbed my arm and led me into the living room where four or five people crowded around the glass topped coffee table. They leaned over it and then stood up and others took their place. I stepped closer to see what was going on. Their faces reflected back at me from the glass like a distorted mirror. White powder scratched into little rows of lines stretched out over the table. "Hit one." Alec nudged my arm.

"Oh. No, I'm not into that." I'd never done any drugs stronger than a few hits off a joint, and that had only been once or twice back in college after hitting the gay bars and picking up one-night stands. The shit usually put me to sleep, so I didn't like smoking pot and I'd never had the nerve to do anything stronger.

Wendy slid a shot glass of brown liquor in my hand. That I would happily do, despite my fear of becoming an alcoholic like my mother. I lifted the glass to her and slammed it down. She smiled at me wickedly. Alec slid his arm over my shoulder. What the hell?

"Hey, that's cool, Martin. I have something else better anyway." He handed me a neon-blue pill with a peace sign etched on it.

"What's this?"

"X." His eyes were wide and darker than they'd been before. Had he already taken some? I glared at him. "You know? Mollies, the love drug? You'll like it. Makes you feel all warm and cuddly, not out of control at all."

Wendy nudged me from the other side. "It's all good,

Martin. Relax a bit, man," she chided me.

I slid the pill from Alec's hand. "Ecstasy?" Of course I'd heard of it, seen others use it, but I never had. I stared down at the blue tab in my hand.

Wendy snorted. "One fucking pill ain't gonna make you flip. Just fuckin' take it already." She slunk off, leaving her jab floating around my head.

I popped the pill in my mouth and grabbed Alec's beer to swallow it down with. I wanted them to like me more than I feared taking the pill.

Alec sniggered, as he handed the bottle over. "You're all right, man." He squeezed my shoulder tighter and I kind of liked it. It almost felt like I had a boyfriend. Only Alec was Wendy's boyfriend, not mine and I could never forget that, despite how heavy his warm arm felt around my shoulder.

The music changed and Wendy popped up in front of me, grabbing my arms. "This is my jam! Come on, dance with me!" She pulled me away from the security of her boyfriend's arms and out to the middle of the living room. Two big guys shoved the coffee table out of the way, making room for several girls to start dancing, including Wendy, who still had her hands on my arms.

I'd never danced like this. I didn't dance. At the gay clubs, guys would grind on each other. I did that. This was different. Completely. For starters, it was all girls. Wendy has singled me out as the only guy out there with them. Did the other guys think of me as a chick, since I was gay? Or could I just get away with more? I didn't know, but I felt good, my shoulders relaxed a little and I let Wendy shake me as I started moving, dancing with the girls. Wendy squealed and I found I kind of liked being friends.

Whether it was the drug, the alcohol, or Wendy's hospitality, the rest of the night was fun. Dancing, drinking, and laughing with all these people felt bizarre on one level, as an experience that I'd never had but probably should have long ago. Finally, I fit in with a group and unwound in a way I'd never really been able to before. Euphoria hung on my skin in a prickly but not unpleasant sensation that made the night just a little more intense, a little more real. I wanted more of this feeling.

After dancing with Wendy, Tia, and a few other girls for what felt like hours, I made my way to the restroom and relieved myself. As I stepped out of the bathroom, I ran into Alec, literally chest to chest.

"Hey, again," Alec purred, pushing me back against the wall with one hand on my chest and one on the wall beside my head.

"Alec?"

He leaned in and kissed me. Softy. Surprisingly. Wendy's face flashed through my mind and I didn't kiss him back, but my lips and my tongue wanted to. Fire raced down to my groin proving my dick wanted it, too.

"Wendy's cool with it," he said, as if reading my mind. "She can join us. The three of us." He nodded down the hallway to the bedrooms. I knew where they were because their floor plan mirrored my own apartment.

"I...I, uh, no. I don't..." I shoved Alec forward. I had to get out of there. My mind screamed this could not happen, but my body was practically melting into goo, fighting to make it real. "No!" I said more firmly, pushing past Alec and heading for the front door. I took the stairs down to my apartment, two at a time. The memory of Alec's soft lips on mine floating around my head like an accusation.

Alec had been so cold to me, yet here he was coming on to me, wanting me in his bed. With Wendy. It made my head spin. I'd never experienced anything like that. I could feel the icy rise of need -- need for them to like me, accept me.

Back in the safety of my own room, I pulled on my headphones and cranked up some Marilyn Manson, guaranteed to make me stop thinking or feeling and flung myself on to my unmade bed.

My cock was hard as a rock and I was pissed as hell. Why had I run away? I'd never be able to face them again. For the first time in my life I'd had the opportunity and ability to be one of the gang, to be popular. To be cool. What did I do about it? Ran away like the socially inept nerd that I was.

Chapter 4 - Calling Daltrey

I woke up late and rolled over, throwing my pillow on the floor. I didn't have a headache, but my brain still felt foggy. Nothing a good cup of coffee couldn't cure. I staggered into my kitchen to start up my pot, thankful that I had milk and sugar this time.

Running my fingers through my hair, I thought about the party and Alec kissing me. It had been nice. Alec made me feel wanted. Wendy had too. She danced with me even after Alec had put his arm around my shoulder and kept it there. I liked them and should have...should have what?

Shaking my head, I poured my coffee, adding the coveted milk and sugar, and sipped it, walking back into the dining room and sitting at the table. I opened my laptop and Daltrey's profile picture popped up on the screen, right where I'd left it. Daltrey.

His number was still in the pocket of my slept-in jeans. He had been everything to me. There wasn't really a decision to be made. I needed to rule my own life and do the things I wanted to do and to hell with anyone else. I picked up my cell and dialed the number.

A female voice answered on the third ring. "Daltrey

Boxbaum's office. How can I help you?" Girlfriend? No way. Daltrey was gay like me. Wasn't he?

"Uh... Yes. I'd like to speak with Daltrey." My voice shook with fear.

"Sorry, he's unavailable. Can I help you?" She sang back at me, lyrically.

"No, uh, it's personal." What was I going to say? I should have taken more time to think things out.

"I'm Jenny Heathers, his personal assistant. I may be able to help." Her voice sounded a little flatter this time, frustrated.

I let out a long breath that I hadn't realized I'd been holding. "Can you give him a message? Tell him I called?"

"Sure. Name?"

"Martin Hannan. H-a-n-n-a-n, Hannan." I spelled my name, maybe out of habit. Then gave her my cell number.

"Okay, Martin. I'll tell him. Have a great day."

Well, at least I didn't think she was his girlfriend. Maybe.

The rest of the day was spent getting ready for work the next day. I had three brand new suits, two Armani's and one Hugo Boss, hanging in my closet. I could wear one of the old ones on Thursday and Friday was casual, jeans. I loved that idea. Then I could get my suits dry-cleaned over the weekend. I had plenty, but Dad would want me to wear the new ones on my first few days. Always following Dad's rules, even when I didn't think it mattered.

By late that night, I still hadn't heard back from Daltrey, though I'd checked my cell nearly a thousand times. I put on some Royal Blood, wanting to hear something with moody attitude. After moping around for a while, I finally caved in and opened Facebook. Had the PA even given him the message yet? It was Sunday, after all.

I opened a message screen. Maybe he'd see the message on his Facebook before Monday. I should have thought of that sooner. The PA would probably screen his messages anyway, but I had to try. I kept it simple:

Hi Daltrey,
So lovely to see your success. I'd like to talk with you sometime to

catch up. -Martin

That didn't sound too desperate, only curious and interested. I hoped it would work. I clicked the button to send before I chickened out. That was all I could do without become a full-fledged stalker. I pushed my laptop away and rested my forehead on the table.

Why would Daltrey want to talk to me anyway? What did I really have to offer? Everything I had in my life was courtesy of my dad. I thought about just going to bed and getting this rotten day over with, but then I heard a tapping on my door.

I opened it to Wendy, standing there wearing jean cut-offs and a tank top, holding a bottle of Wild Turkey. She held the whiskey up with an inviting look on her face and a mischievous tilt to her smile. I opened the door wider and gestured for her to come in.

We drank a few shots, sitting there at my table before we ever said anything. I liked the burn in my throat and the warmth in my stomach. Finally, my glare dared her to speak up. "So..." she started. "I know Alec, uh, hit on you last night."

I bit my bottom lip, sucking it between my teeth.

"I just want to let you know, it's okay," she said, pouring another round. "I put him up to it. So, don't think like I didn't know or something. 'Kay?" She looked down at the table as she spoke, almost as if she were hiding something, but I had no idea what that could be.

"Why?" She put him up to it? What the hell?

She slammed the shot and immediately poured another. "Look, you know? Parties are, uh, they get crazy sometimes. I like you and with the drugs and alcohol and shit, it makes us, you know, loosen up. I thought you were feeling pretty good. Right?"

I couldn't contain the smile that crept over my face. "I felt pretty good."

"I just..." She shrugged and slammed back the shot. I joined her this time. "Ah... We just wanted more."

I slid my shot glass over to her for another. "I get that. I probably shouldn't have run away. It just, kind of freaked me out a little. I guess."

Wendy smiled and laughed, pouring another round. "So?" the pitch in her voice rose. "Would you? You know, with us? Alec and me?"

Would I want to be with them? "I've never, uh, I've never been with a woman, Wendy." I didn't want to give her the wrong idea. "I don't know if I could, but, uh, if I could, you know? It'd be with you, I'm sure."

She was in the middle of drinking when she burst out laughing, sending whiskey spewing out everywhere, which only got her laughing harder. I couldn't help but join in.

Chapter 5 - First Day of Work

Arriving for work ten minutes late on my first day was not a great way to get things started, but considering my hangover had my head pounding like Lars Ulrich on a crazy Metallica-binge, I felt lucky to be only ten minutes late. My eyes stung and I knew they were red, but I didn't want to lose any more time stopping at the drugstore for eye drops. I'd just suffer through the day and get my shit together the rest of the week.

To hell with Wendy, pushing her shots on me and Alec's sly kisses in the hallway. I needed to concentrate on my real life. Thankfully, I'd already been through the HR bullshit and tour, and knew exactly where I was going. I managed to get to my tiny office without having to engage with others. No more drinking on Sundays.

No sooner had I sat down at my desk and rested my head in my hands, arms propped up, elbows on the desk, than my boss, Grant Warring, walked in. "Hannan. You're late." No shit.

"Sorry, uh, was up too late. Still unpacking and getting settled." At least I had on my best suit and my hair was slicked back into a professional style, even if it made me look a little like a Ken doll.

He cut in quickly, interrupting. "Look. I know who your dad is but it really doesn't matter here. You don't get a pass just because your dad is some Silicone Valley high roller." He pointed at me. "You still have to earn your spot. Got it?"

I nodded. "Yes, sir." He wasn't that much older than me, maybe in his early thirties. I couldn't blame him for the attitude though. I'd been dropped into his team without so much as an interview. I'd met him during the HR orientation briefly, and he had been cold then, but he wasn't the guy that hired me.

"Good. You should be set up. Jody dropped the stats for your first project in your mailbox. Know how to get that?"

I nodded and sucked the corner of my lip in my mouth to keep myself from saying anything smart-assed.

"Good. Get to work." He tapped the doorjamb and walked off. I relaxed in my chair, but just for a moment. Jody walked in almost as soon as he'd left.

"Hey guy. You look like shit." I knew she was right, despite the expensive suit, I probably looked even worse than I felt.

Wendy had left before we killed the whole bottle, but I was still figuring out how many shots of Turkey it took to get to the center of the drunken-tootsie roll. "Thanks a lot. Feel like it too."

"Water," she said, peering at me over the top of her fashionable glasses. I didn't know her well, but thought we'd at least get along. She was Grant's personal assistant, but unlike Grant, she seemed sympathetic, and why not? She was closer to my age, hadn't had the job long, and was also gay. We'd gotten all of that out within the first few minutes of meeting each other. Jody was easy to talk to. "Seriously," she added.

"What? Water?" I had no idea what she was talking about.

"Of course, dumb ass. When you're drinking you get dehydrated. Causes hangovers. Drink water before you go to bed. Or pass out. And more when you get up." She nodded and walked out, leaving me staring after her. She wore dark slacks, a dark blue silk blouse, and smart shoes, probably Clarks. Before I could decide, she was back with a large, cold bottle of water.

"I think you're a lifesaver," I said and meant it.

She smiled sweetly. "No sweat. You don't strike me as the partying type."

"I'm not." Screwing off the lid, I took a long pull on the refreshing water and felt better almost immediately.

"Good. Get to work," she said, imitating the boss and making me laugh despite how crappy I felt. Jody was a lifesaver for sure. "Call me if you need anything," she added and then left me alone to figure everything out.

Lunch time snuck up on me before I realized it and my stomach growled, incessantly. I thought about taking Jody out, since she'd been so nice. I got up to find her when my cell phone rang. Daltrey's New York office number came up on the caller ID. I tapped the screen to answer it without even thinking. How could I think? All the blood in my body had just split into two factions, half rushing to my head causing a heated flush of white noise, and the other half rushing to my cock, making it plump. "H...Hello?"

"Hi, Mister Hannan. This is Jenny Heathers."

"Yes?" Why was she calling? Had something happened to Daltrey? Maybe he didn't want to talk to me.

"Daltrey would like to speak with you this evening. He will be available at six, your time."

"Yes?"

"If you'll be available, I want to make sure this is a good number for him to call."

"Yes, of course." My heart leaped into my throat, practically choking me, but I managed to get the words out. "Any time, whenever he wants to call. This number. I'll be here."

"Great." Her voice sounded professionally-fake like the marketing and promotion girls that used to come to the school campus trying to get students to buy anything from Red Bull energy drinks to the latest technology gadgets. "I'll let him know. You have a great day."

She clicked off before I could ask anything else. Like why

didn't he just call himself? Fuck! It was going to be a long afternoon and six o'clock would not get here fast enough. Watching the clock all afternoon was only going to slow it down. I forgot about asking Jody to lunch and just grabbed something quick, then tried to concentrate on work. Visions of Daltrey kept sneaking up on me though. I couldn't help wonder what his voice would sound like. Would I recognize it? What would we talk about?

    I cut out five minutes early and on the way home I stopped at the drugstore. I needed antacids, eye drops, and lube because I was pretty sure I was going to jack-off a lot after my six o'clock phone call.

Chapter 6 - Reconnecting

When the phone rang, I almost dropped it, fumbling the damn cell in my fingers and finally tapping the screen. "Hello? Daltrey?" My voice sounded desperate and full of longing and hope. Could he hear that?

"Yeah. Martin? Marty?" Daltrey had been the only person ever to call me Marty and get away with it.

"Dal? You sound, uh, different." Using our old nicknames felt surreal. Five years of longing collapsed into seconds. Images of our last moments together filled my head, bringing tears to my eyes again. My throat closed tight as I thought about how I stood in his driveway watching his mother's car pull away. He looked back once and pushed his dark brown hair out of his eyes. I'd never seen such heartbreaking sadness on one face and I never wanted to see that desperation etched on there again.

His soft laughter brought me back to the present. "Well, you know, uh, it's been, what, like five years?"

"Too long. I..." Could I tell him how much I've missed him? "You seem to be really doing great, Dal. I'm proud of you." I swallowed down the emotion threatening to overtake me. Surely, this didn't mean nearly as much to him as it did to me. He sounded confident, sure, and why shouldn't he?

"Thanks," he said, his voice soft, almost as high pitched as it used to be. Silence lingered for a moment, but before it could get awkward, he added, "So, um, like, what have you been up to? Five years? Wow!"

"I know. The usual. College. Programming degree."

"Like your dad?" He was the only one who understood my relationship with my father, the only one that had a clue.

"Of course." Without Daltrey there to help give me the strength I needed, I gave in easily to whatever Dad wanted. I didn't have to tell him that. "It's fine." My voice was flat, anything but fine.

"Marty. I..." His words hung in the distorted air between us. When he spoke again, I was sure it wasn't what he originally intended to say, and that hurt a little. We had always shared everything, but it had been too long and we didn't even know each other anymore. "It was really good to hear from you. I, uh, never thought I would. You know?"

It was my turn to laugh, but my chuckle sounded forced. "Well, I met someone that knew of you through his mother."

"Right, the Randall kid. I heard." He laughed again and this time it sounded like cotton candy to a starving tongue. "This is, like, cool, right? I'm glad."

"Me too. I'd like to—" I wanted to see him in person, to be able to touch his face, to hold him in my arms again, to push that stray hair out of his eyes, or just look at him. "I'd like to talk to you. More, I mean."

"I'd like that too."

Something eased in my chest. The panic I didn't realize I'd been so close to backed off. Daltrey wasn't going anywhere. We could talk and get to know each other again and play by our own rules for once. "I missed you, Dal." The words slipped out before I'd realized what I said, but they were quiet and I wasn't sure if he heard me.

"Ahh, Marty. I freakin' missed you, too. I'm so-o-o glad you called." He sounded glad, relieved even, but also hesitant. "Um, so, what was college like?"

After that we talked for hours. I told him about college and my parents and the black metal card my dad had slipped me after graduation and the crazy neighbors upstairs and my dick-boss at work. He'd heard of the company, Apex, and thought I'd made a good choice.

He told me about his art and how his mom took over the business side of things as soon as he started having success. She'd managed to get him with a great agent and he'd sold a lot of work overseas and now had a following in New York. He'd been in Boston over the weekend showing at a prominent gallery. He told me about his PA, Jenny, and how she'd squealed when he told her who I was. They were best friends.

Neither of us talked about relationships or who we might have been with. I didn't bring it up because I didn't want to know if he had a boyfriend or that he'd ever been with anyone but me, and I didn't want him to know about my few anonymous bathroom sex guys I'd let fuck me over the years. I wanted us to be clean, to have a fresh start. Maybe he wanted that too, because he didn't bring it up either.

Hours later, I knew I had to go. I really couldn't afford to be late for work again. We said our goodbyes with promises to talk again later in the week.

I hung up reluctantly, then fell into bed and cried. I let out all the emotions that had been building as we spoke. I cried for the two boys that had been separated at the height of their love and what we could have been, and I cried for all that I wasn't and probably would never live up to. I cried because Daltrey sounded lonely. I'd do anything to make him happy, keep him smiling like the golden memories I had of him. I cried because I probably couldn't do that. I cried until I finally fell asleep.

Chapter 7 - Hanging With Friends

The week went by slowly, but managed to stay one long blur at the same time. Each day filled itself with programming and appointments and meetings at work and a lot of nothing at home. I played Xbox games online and watched crappy television sitting on the floor and wondered why Daltrey hadn't called and wondered what he'd been doing. He never returned my message on Facebook. Nothing. I started wondering if I'd imagined the entire thing.

Friday afternoon, I left work fortified with the decision that I would call him instead of waiting for him to call me, just because I'd drive myself nuts if I didn't.

I went home and trudged up the stairs to my apartment and literally ran into Wendy coming down, almost knocking her on her ass.

"Hey, Martin," she greeted me cheerfully, regaining her balance quicker than me. "Wanna come up and have a drink with us later?" She steadied me with a hand on my shoulder.

"Uh, sure. Us who?" I didn't feel like a room full of people if they were having a party and started thinking of ways to beg off.

"Just us, well, Seth and Tia, too. That's all."

I nodded. "Oh, okay. When?"

"Ahh? About an hour," she answered, looking at her watch. I noticed she had freckles on her arm, covering her skin from wrist to elbow.

I smiled, glad to be invited and happy it was just a few people. "Sure. Want me to bring anything?"

"Just yourself!" she called and headed down the last flight of stairs, humming happily as if I hadn't collided with her.

There was no way that I was going to show up empty handed. I turned around and followed her down the stairs and headed out to the grocery store again. I'd pick up a bottle of something a little nicer than the cheap whiskey we'd been drinking and stop for a quick dinner on the way back.

An hour later, I was tapping at their door with a full belly and a bottle of Jack Daniels. I didn't know a lot about alcohol, but Wild Turkey and Canadian Mist both seemed a bit less than Jack Daniels, which was always behind my dad's bar so it had to be the good stuff, though surprisingly not the most expensive bottle on the shelf.

Wendy opened the door and squealed, pulling me inside the apartment. The lights had been turned down low and soft music played in the background, nothing I recognized. Alec and Seth sat on the couch in the living room and Tia sat on the floor between Seth's legs, leaning back against him. They each held tumbler glasses; the kind for drinks on the rocks, squat and wide. I held out the bottle of Jack and Alec's eyes went wide. "Hell yeah! Open that baby up. Love me some Jack."

Seth and Tia made sounds of agreement and Wendy took the bottle from me. She seemed to enjoy playing bartender and quickly had the bottle open and poured into their glasses, including a new one for me that she'd grabbed from the kitchen.

We sipped the booze, sitting around the living room with all its beige walls and plush tan carpet. I sat in the club chair and Wendy sat on the floor in front of Alec, just like Tia against Seth. The conversation was minimal and comfortable. I didn't know the people they talked about and wondered how long I would be the new guy. How long would it take for me to have my own shared memories and mutual friends? Were they my friends now? Did Wendy and Alec consider me more than a neighbor? Did I want that? Under the surface, deep down, I thought perhaps I liked being accepted into their group more than I liked them as people.

Not long after, Seth and Tia excused themselves since they both had to work the next day. I stood to follow them out, but Wendy grabbed my arm. "Can't you stay a little longer?"

"Okay, sure." I sat back down in the living room because that's what Wendy wanted.

"Hey," Alec said, looking down at his cell phone. "Tad will be here in about ten."

Wendy giggled. "That's great. You have to hang, Martin, for sure." She refilled our glasses and took the glasses Seth and Tia used back to the kitchen.

I didn't know who Tad was and the apprehension made my stomach tremble. Meeting new people made me nervous. I swallowed back bile and wondered if I should go back downstairs and get an antacid tablet before this guy arrived. I rubbed at my chest, trying to sooth the fire rolling through it.

"Martin. You'll like Tad, really. He's not staying long, but you'll dig him, for sure."

"Uh, okay."

Alec laughed. He always seemed to be laughing, but it wasn't joy, he was laughing at something or someone and in this case, it felt like me. Again. I scrunched up my face in aggravation, but I couldn't stay mad.

"You like music, right?" Alec asked cutting into my thoughts.

Duh. "Of course."

"You listen to that heavy stuff. I've heard your music this week. Like old school Megadeth and Theory like Seth. Right?" he asked, and took another sip of Jack.

I nodded, wanting him to continue.

"Well, Tad's the drummer for Surf Sons. They're small

time, local."

"Oh fuck! I know them. Seen them play." My fanboy came out unexpectedly. I barely contained myself and managed not to squeal, but I wanted to.

Surf Sons were hot in the local music scene and getting hotter and that was just their music. They were all young hot guys, any gay-boy's dream, with long scruffy hair and faces full of smirking attitude. I practically bounced in my seat until he finally knocked on their door. I thought I was going to come unglued and really didn't even give a shit that Alec was laughing at me again.

Tad walked in the apartment with a sexy bad-boy attitude swaying his hips with every step. His legs were encased in skintight jeans and his T-shirt was ripped up and beyond faded, showing glimpses of white-pink skin. I feared making a fool of myself by drooling all over him.

Wendy handed Tad a drink and nodded to me. "This is Martin. Our neighbor from downstairs."

"Hey man." His voice was smoky rough, as he jerked his head in greeting. I wished he'd stick his hand out for me to shake, but he was just too cool for that.

I wanted to be just as cool. "Yeah, hey." I was just happy my voice didn't crack.

Alec stood up and dug in his pocket and pulled out his wallet. He gave Tad money and Tad handed him a little plastic bag. "Smoke?" Tad asked.

"Sure, go on," Alec said gesturing to the balcony door.

Tad pulled out a pack of cigarettes and started lighting one up before he'd made it out the door. My eyes shifted from the sliding glass door leading outside, back to Alec standing in the living room opening a bag of pills.

He handed me one. They were blue with peace signs etched into them, just like the one I'd had at the party. I took it without hesitation this time, wanting to relax. My stomach felt tight, tied in a knot that would make any sailor envious. I washed it down with my drink.

Alec leaned closer to me. "Go on out," he whispered,

nodding to the sliding glass door.

I raised my eyebrow, questioning him.

"He's gay. He's a musician. Fuck. Go for it, Martin. Do I have to spell it out? Seriously?" His chuckle made me feel like the butt of the joke, but I followed directions and slid out to the balcony.

"Hey," I said. "I've seen your band play. You're pretty good."

Tad stared at me with dark, shifty eyes under bushy eyebrows. He blew smoke out of the side of his mouth. "So?"

I let his snide question hang in the air unanswered.

He stretched his pack of cigarettes out toward me in offering, but I shook him off.

"So, what?" he asked, pocketing his smokes. "I'm Tad Ferretti, rock drummer, but not a super star. So? You wanna blow me or something?"

I rolled my eyes. For being cool, for being hot and talented, he was acting like a dick. "Fuck you." I spat my words at him with a jerk of my head and turned to go back in.

"Hey, wait."

I turned and gave him a look that asked what the hell he wanted because I surely had nothing.

"I'm being a dick. I'm glad you like our music." He smiled, but it was a crooked one. He took another drag of his cigarette then flicked the butt off the balcony. "I'm just tired. It's been a long day and getting longer."

"S'all right. I guess." I felt a little pouty, but willing to forgive. He probably caught shit from fans all the time and I didn't want to be just another groupie.

He gestured to the door and I slid it open. Before I could step inside, Tad was against my back, the heat of his body pressing into mine and his breath sizzling down my neck. "Any friend of Alec's is a friend of mine."

I stepped into the house, my foot tripping on the track, making me feel even stupider. Fuck him. I no longer wanted to go down that route with him, anyway. First he gave me the cold shoulder, then he was a dickhead, then he wanted to make a pass? I sat back down, flinging myself into the chair and when Tad slunk to the floor in front of the coffee table, across from me. He no longer looked as attractive as when he'd first walked in the apartment.

For the next twenty minutes, I ignored him, sipping my Jack and listening to Wendy and Alec laugh at whatever story he was telling. Eventually, I noticed him looking at me and I dared to meet his eyes. He shoved his hair back, showing me sultry eyes lined in black kohl and another crooked smile. "Well, it was nice meeting you, Martin." His rough baritone practically purred.

I would have rather punched him in the face than shake his hand. My anger might have been irrational, but this guy rubbed me all kinds of wrong ways and I just didn't give a fuck who he was or how talented he played. He could stick his drumstick up his ass for all I cared.

"Sure," was all I offered him, despite the way my stomach roiled. I didn't want to like him, didn't want what he offered. My head felt lighter and my shoulders slumped, watching him stand up and watching Alec walk him out of the room, but I didn't bother getting up. Part of me wished things would have played out differently, but it didn't really matter.

Wendy smacked my leg. "What's up with you?"

"He was a dick."

She laughed. "Was one or has one?" She even wiggled her neatly plucked eyebrows at me.

"Whatever." I rolled my eyes. In a moment, we were both laughing.

Wendy laid back on the floor, her auburn hair spilling around her, and when her giggles subsided she said, "Alec thought you'd like him. You know?"

"Ahh... Why are you trying to set me up?" They were trying entirely too hard for my benefit.

Wendy sat up and flung her arm over my knee. "We like you."

I sighed. "So?"

Alec came back in the room and sat on the floor in front

of me. "Sorry," he said.

I wanted to run my fingers through his short cropped hair, wanted to comfort him. A wash of heat swarmed through my body and I felt my cock stirring as I watched Alec lick his lips. He moved in closer and knelt up beside me, touching my knee and pressing his chest into the side of my leg. The drugs and alcohol made me braver. "So, what? Are you like bi or something?"

"I'm sort of whatever. You know? I'm committed to Wendy, but I want to be an actor." He shrugged, as if that explained it all.

"What do you mean?" I leaned forward and put my glass on the coffee table, noticing it was empty, but not remembering that I'd drank it.

"What if I ever get a job playing a gay guy? I have to know what it's like to some extent. Right?" He leaned up, stretching over my thighs, pressing his lips against mine, his arms twining behind my neck. He kissed me hard, tongue and all. This time I kissed him back. I let him have my tongue, let him explore my mouth with his. He bit at my bottom lip sending little shocks through me that I felt in my groin. His excuse sounded lame, but with my body slowly starting to burn with an unseen fire, I didn't really care.

Wendy's hand crept up the inside of my thigh. I let my own hands travel down Alec's sides. Wendy's hand snuck under my shirt, pressing against my hot skin.

"Let's go in the bedroom," she said with a husky tone that did thrilling things to my balls, as if they knew pleasure was coming for them. I wondered at that briefly, since I'd never had any attraction at all to women in my life. It was probably the drugs and the feel of Alec's lips trailing down my neck. Maybe I could do this.

I let Alec pull me up out of the chair and I did what I was told and followed him into the bedroom. A small lamp set on a stand next to the queen-sized bed provided the only light. The walls were a deep reddish-toned purple, the ceiling a stark white reflected the light from the lamp, and the curtains were dark, maybe black. I thought I'd never seen black curtains before.

"You like?" Wendy asked as I looked around the room. There was a huge black and white framed photo of Alec, full body, nude but with his body turned at an angle that hid his private parts. On another wall, a huge bulletin board had cut outs from magazines and newspapers and snap shots—all of Alec. "Come on," Wendy whispered and pulled me to the bed. She yanked back the black and gold comforter, exposing cream colored sheets.

Alec pulled my shirt off and tossed it on the floor, then pulled his off and pushed me on the bed, back first. "You know you want this. You want me. It's just sex, just fun. Just go with it." He was right. Just sex. Totally hot. I could do this.

Then she crawled up beside me, still fully dressed and snuggled into my side. Alec slipped out of his jeans and crawled up the other side.

I wasn't sure which set of hands unzipped my jeans, but it was Alec's lips pressed against my throat, licking down my chest. His tongue flicked my nipple, making it pop up, brown and hard. I hissed and lifted my hips as Wendy pulled my jeans off.

Everywhere they touched me was on fire. Wendy's fingers dragged down my thighs leaving a trail of tingles. Alec's hands clasped my shoulders, then wandered into my hair at the back of my neck. My mouth was dry and I was sweating, so were they, their hot bodies pressed against either side of me. Hands stroking me, touching me. Tongues slithering over my shoulders. Hands on my thighs. Reflexively, I spread my legs. Wendy's giggles sounded like jewelry—silvery bangles clinging together. Fingers on my cock, tickling across my balls, meeting their earlier expectations.

Wendy rolled a condom down my cock and it clung tightly, but I could ignore the discomfort with Alec nibbling on my earlobe, his hot breath sending goose bumps down my spine. My tongue licked across salty flesh.

"I want to fuck you," Alec murmured.

Time seemed to flash ahead. I couldn't get enough skin on skin contact, no longer caring if it was Alec or Wendy as long as the caresses continued. I pulled one of them closer and my body writhed against sticky skin.

I lurched forward, dark spots in my memory. Alec's naked body leaned above my head, his arms against the wall above the short headboard. His cock pointing at my face, bumping softly against my lips. The purple mushroom head begged to be licked and touched. I stuck out my tongue, flat against the bottom of my mouth and Alec fed his cock inside. Grabbing his hips, I pulled him forward, wanting to take more, wanting him to fuck my mouth. I feared my chest might explode from the need to feel Alec's silky hardness in my mouth that was building and buzzing through me.

My body tingled like electricity pricked at every bit of my skin. The feeling rolled through me from my mouth where I was sucking Alec, down my spine and chest at every point where I touched someone else's body, and into my cock which felt harder than it had ever felt before.

Desperate fingers slid over me, coating me with more electric tingles and cold strokes as they kneaded my skin. Tight, wet heat slid over my cock and I heard Wendy moan. A part of me knew that she was riding me, fucking me. I didn't let myself focus on that or I'd end up losing that hard-on; even as fond of Wendy as I was, she was still the wrong sex. I'd let her play though as I sucked Alec, pulling him in and out of my mouth, concentrating on his little moans and pleas. I ran the palms of my hands down his thighs and then up his ass, stroking his flank as I bobbed on his cock.

My jaw started aching. I'd never given a blow job that lasted that long in my life. Convinced I was doing something wrong, I added my fingers beneath his balls, tickling him and rubbing that sensitive spot between his balls and his hole. I flicked my tongue against the head of his cock and he moaned again.

He appeared to be strung tight and ready, but he hadn't cum and neither had I. Wendy was another story altogether. I had no idea whether she'd had an orgasm or fifty, but she'd stopped riding me and just sat there beside us, watching and panting like she'd run a marathon. I hadn't been paying much attention to her, maybe she had.

Time surged again and I sat on the edge of the bed, bare feet on the floor. Wendy and Alec lay behind me. "Don't go," Wendy pleaded, softly. I had my jeans in my hands. I didn't know where my underwear disappeared to and I didn't care.

One second I was in love with the couple behind me and the next I had to get out of there. My dick jutted out like a divining rod searching for water, but my cock didn't seem to know what it wanted to find, besides relief.

The condom was gone, freeing the blood flow, yet I had no idea where it had gone to or who had pulled it off. I was just content it was gone and I didn't have to worry about it.

Sweat poured from my forehead and down my shoulders and back, but I shivered from the cold. I needed to be in my own bed. I needed a bottle of water. But more than anything else I needed to be the fuck away from Wendy and Alec.

I pulled my jeans up, stood and headed for the door without looking back.

The light in the stairwell practically blinded me, piercing into my head like hot pokers. My apartment, when I finally pushed the door open, felt like an oasis. I took a long drink of cold water without turning on any of the lights. Energy pulsed through my veins with each swallow, pushing me to do something, anything.

I paced the floor.

I pulled up my Spotify app and clicked on one of my favorite playlists. The pounding drums and synthesized tones of In This Moment's best song, *Adrenalize*, poured out of my speakers. After spending time fucking the upstairs neighbors, this was the perfect song. I jerked my head back and forth listening to the music, the hoarse voice singing about sex and music and getting high. It felt exactly like the trip I'd just been on. I was still so horny and rock hard, with no relief in sight, even if I went back upstairs.

I played the song three times before I crashed on the floor. The edges of the carpet dug into my over sensitized back, making my skin crawl.

The playlist rolled over to Royal Blood. I stared at the ceiling. I had never sweat so much in my life, yet I was strangely cold. Too cold. I forced myself up and into the bathroom for a shower.

The water sprayed over my head and shoulders in a wash of heat and wet, making me think of Wendy's female parts. They'd been on me. I was inside her. I grabbed the soap and lathered up my hands and rubbed my cock and balls, my chest and shoulders, soaping up every spot I could get my hands on, and then returning to my cock again. I had to get her off of me, the feel, the scent, none of it was appealing and I questioned my sanity for going along with it—playing that role.

I thought more about Alec and his cock as I soaped up my cock one more time. My jaw still ached. How long had I been blowing him? It felt like ages and no time at all.

I stroked myself, recalling images of Alec and thoughts of other times and other men. My imagination flitted all over the place with images of sex. It felt good, so good, but I wasn't even close to getting there. I flicked my nipples and yanked on my balls, trying to push myself to the edge, but nothing was helping. My head felt light and my limbs heavy.

I rinsed off and went to bed.

Laying there examining my ceiling, I wondered two things. First, how could I be so damned tired and unable to sleep at the same time. Second, why had I gone along with Alec and Wendy and their little orgy scene? What the hell was wrong with me? I'd been so intent on figuring out how to get Daltrey back in my life, and then this. Once I was in their apartment, I hadn't shed a second thought of Daltrey. Was that the type of person I was? It wasn't who I wanted to be. What would Daltrey think about what I'd done?

What had I done, though? It was meaningless sex. It hadn't even been great. None of us had gotten off, really, at least not while I was there. I still hadn't.

A hollow feeling crept over me like a dark shadow that wanted to eat my soul. My body ached like I had the flu, the earlier energy that coursed through me was long gone. I closed my eyes, wishing for the bliss of sleep to take me and get rid of the empty feeling in my chest.

The next day, I woke unsurprisingly late, considering the hours and hours I lay awake the night before. The apartment was too quiet, but it was the kind of quiet even music wouldn't kill. I got dressed and grabbed my phone, intending to just get the hell out of there, when I noticed the message. Daltrey had texted me.

Hey, Wuz up?

Simple, curious. A start. I wanted to call him, but guilt burrowed into my heart like a rodent making a nest. I slid my cell in my pocket and headed out the door, determined to outrun this horrible day.

Chapter 8 - Relationships are Hard Work

The sun was shining on my face, a typical spring day in L.A. In a month, it would be too hot to run around in jeans. I lived on the Northeast side of town where there were plenty of parks and walkways, close enough to work that I didn't have to face the infamous traffic.

The park near my apartment was green and lush. I'd found a path through thick trees about a block away that led to the grounds where people walked and jogged along the pathways.

I squinted into the sun as I walked and it made me want the beach. I thought of planning a trip with Wendy and Alec down to Malibu or Long Beach, but then I pulled out my phone and looked at that message from Daltrey. It felt like a betrayal to do anything with my neighbors, but I wanted to be a part of their group so badly, it made my chest ache.

Plopping down on a bench, I decided I'd better answer and get it over with or I'd be making a run to the drugstore for more antacids. I bit my bottom lip and cringed a little, then tapped my phone screen to reply.

Walk n park. U?

Daltrey's response came back quickly, as if he'd been waiting for it, making me cringe. Why had I made him wait so long for such a simple answer? I didn't want to play games, but I didn't know what I was doing, either.

Hey! Painting. Call u later?

Did he want to talk to me or was this a blow-off for making him wait? I sucked in a deep breath, wishing I could inhale the sunshine and make my insides feel as cozy as my face and shoulders. My guts were ice cold.

Of course - anytime.

I typed the reply quickly and stuffed my phone back in my pocket. I knew I was overreacting, but I didn't want to see the rejection that I deserved.

##

I'd been home nearly an hour when Wendy knocked on the door, bringing Starbucks as some kind of peace offering. I took the hot drink and chin-jerked her inside.

"Let's talk," she said, sitting down at my kitchen table. I turned off my music, so we didn't have to talk over it. Wendy took a minute to let her eyes take in my bare bones apartment. "Heard of curtains?" she asked with an eye-roll.

I deserved that. Throw blankets were tacked over my dining room window and I still hadn't bought any furniture. "I'll just hire a decorator in a few weeks." I'd put it on Dad's Darth Vader black card and then feel guilty about it for a year, but he'd never question the purchase. I wondered what that said about our relationship.

"I can do it." Wendy's eyebrows arched up. "Really, why pay a decorator? Just pay for all the stuff and I'll get it and put it up. I'll even paint. I did our place and helped Tia with her apartment. No big."

"Maybe." I didn't commit to her because I didn't want to be sucked in to the relationship any further than I already was, so I sipped my coffee and let Wendy decide what she needed to say.

Finally, she set her own drink on the table and crossed her arms over her chest. "I'm your friend, Martin, whether you like it or not." She raised one eyebrow. "It's my job as your friend to tell you when you're fucking up."

"Fucking up?" I'd done what they wanted. There was sex and now instead of just an awkward silence between neighbors, she was in my space, accusing me of something, though I had no idea what. Being accepted into their group was harder than I'd ever thought it would be.

"Seriously, Martin. You're holding back. You're not putting in the effort. I get it, but, uh, you can't just go through the fucking motions without caring, without feelings."

"What are you talking about?"

"You know what I mean," she huffed. "Did you even call the number Alec gave you?" She rolled her eyes and picked up her coffee again, using it to gesture to everything that was apparently wrong with me. "Alec got that number for you. As a favor because he likes you. And you just ignore it. Is that how you usually pay back favors?"

"Wendy." I rubbed my forehead. "I don't—"

"Yes, you do!"

Did I owe her an explanation? Were we in a relationship because we fucked? I didn't know how to do any of this. "I called him. We're talking. There's, you know, five years apart, for Christ's sake!"

The answer didn't make her any happier, apparently. Her face squinted into a scowl. "You could have told me. I thought we were friends. Fuck, Martin. When were you going to tell me?"

Had I cheated on her, on them? What exactly did she expect? I did not want to deal with the drama that just seemed to ooze out of her every pore. The thought of being sucked even deeper into a relationship involving her, maybe fucking her again, made my stomach turn, yet I didn't think I could stop it. "What do you want from me?"

She stood up and stormed out without a word. I wasn't even sure what I'd done, but maybe her being pissed at me wouldn't be so bad. Maybe I wouldn't be expected to participate in any more bedroom high jinx, if that was the price I had to pay to be a part of their lives.

Leaning back in my chair, I sipped my coffee. The guilt-worms churned in my gut and I knew I couldn't finish the damned drink. I headed to the bathroom for another antacid.

The worst part of the conversation was that she was right. I couldn't even argue. I hadn't put anything into our friendship or whatever it was. I really hadn't invested in anything with Daltrey either. Maybe I just didn't know how to give what they expected. I didn't know what Daltrey needed or even what kind of relationship we could possibly have with him living in New York.

I turned my music back on and scrolled through Facebook, stopping on Daltrey's page. Staring at his picture, I wondered how long it would be until he called.

Chapter 9 - Fire Drills and Reflections

The Apex office building represented a work of modern sleekness. Everything was new including the layout. Break rooms occupied the center of each floor, with temporary hoteling cubicles spreading outward from the lounge-like area. Along the outsides of the cubicles were small glassed-in offices, some were permanently occupied like mine, but some were for everyone's use. Some were just small quiet spaces for meeting with people on a one on one basis. Along the far walls, conference rooms of various sizes stretched out with glass doors and floor to ceiling windows that offered unprecedented views of L.A. The skyline in the distance felt dramatic and important. Long tables took up the center of each conference room and all had the technical hookups a meeting could need or want: phones, flat screen, overhead speakers, comfy chairs that rocked back, white board walls, and again the spectacular views, at least from the fourteenth floor where I worked.

The view didn't help me get through the Monday morning status meeting, but my coffee helped. The best part of the break rooms happened to be free coffee.

I sipped my drink and listened to my teammates go on

about their projects. As the newest member, I didn't have anything yet to report. I also got stuck with all the shit work that left me spending the rest of my morning staring at unfamiliar code. The longer I stared at it, the less sense it made, which probably had more to do with me thinking about Daltrey and our phone call the night before than anything the code actually meant.

The conversation with Daltrey had felt more relaxed than before, easier. Listening to him talk about his art and what he'd accomplished had made it easier. I was proud of him. He seemed comfortable with himself in a way I couldn't understand, but it calmed me, and afterward I'd slept better than I had since moving in to my apartment, or maybe even longer. Despite being rested, my computer code and wandering thoughts still made for a long morning, and then alarms sounded.

Loud, blaring, and demanding, the signal to leave the building rang in my head long after it had stopped, and sent all of us to the stairwell to make our way down fourteen flights of stairs. The farther I descended, the more people crowded into the hall. My hands gripped the banisters hard enough to turn my knuckles white and I tried to focus my gaze to the center of the stairs where there were less people crowding in on me. My chest tightened feeling like some carpenter had just hammered nails between my pectoral muscles and my lungs felt as if they were breathing water. Gray cement walls stretched up and away, making me a little dizzy and I feared I'd pass out any minute as my heart rate continued to race.

It was bad enough that I'd probably stumble over my own feet and crash down over thirty or forty people in front of me, but now I might actually faint. I gripped the banister tighter, hoping it would keep me upright.

The line of people in front of me moved down two or three stairs at a time, then stopped again. It would take all day to get out of the building at this rate. Even though I logically knew I'd only been trapped in that stairwell a few minutes, it felt like it had been hours.

I could smell the sweaty excitement wafting off of the people around me, only making me more nervous. I wanted to jam my hands in my pockets to keep them from shaking, but I couldn't let go of the fucking handrail. My breath exhaled heavy and burning, like my chest was full of hot coals.

Others around me talked in hushed tones about how messed up the fire drill would make their day or speculating whether it was really a drill. Thoughts of a real fire didn't help the sweat beading up on my brow.

I reassured myself that if I hadn't passed out yet, I probably wouldn't. I wanted to wipe my forehead, but couldn't even dream of getting sweat stains on my Armani. Wouldn't my dad love to lecture me on that accomplishment?

I had no one to share my distress with. I didn't know anyone around. The few people I knew had disappeared, unconcerned with my whereabouts. Where were my co-workers and how had I ended up pressed in against strangers? I leaned against the wall in the crowded stairwell, waiting for the ceiling to cave in and wondering what would happen if I did pass out?

The chit chat around me had me feeling left out and isolated. No one paid any attention to me, the nervous sweaty guy that might or might not faint in the middle of the stairwell. My whole life felt like that; being stuck in this stairwell alone among strangers was just a reflection of the rest of my life. Was this how it was always going to be? I knew I should stop feeling sorry for myself and just get down the fucking stairs, but my soul ached.

I took a deep, long breath. My dad would not be happy with me right now. The only thing my dad had ever said about me being gay was that it didn't matter to him as long as I didn't appear weak. He said keep it under wraps so the competition couldn't use it against me, but his advice had left me unable to deal with a relationship of any kind. I couldn't look like less of a man. I couldn't let him down. Yet, I had isolated myself and I had no support. Keeping up appearances for his sake had left me vulnerable when it mattered most.

I made sure my exterior appeared calm, serene, just like my dad had taught me, yet underneath something started boiling, surging. A weird energy wanted to break loose and explode to the surface. I wanted to feel it, the anger, the passion, but I pushed it down, poured cold water into the inferno because I could never let it up. It was too dangerous and I was too afraid.

On the main floor, the people rushed out the glass doors of the building and swam out across the street and down the sidewalk to the garage. As I followed them, I turned and glanced over my shoulder. I saw a reflection of myself in the windows. The distorted image had a hard face, set and determined in my Armani suit, or was that look fear?

Later on the sidewalks, my work crew was still nowhere around. Anxiety kept me from seeking them out. What if they didn't want to talk to me or be seen with me? If they had, they wouldn't have left me. So far, I hadn't really connected with any of the other programmers. It felt like High School all over again. Only this time, I didn't have Daltrey to make it better, to hug me and ease my pain. Why was it so hard to be a part of a group?

I didn't know why I was bothered. Certainly, I was not some inept coward. No, I was just awkward, a little. How had Wendy and Alec not understood my problems relating to others socially? I had no experience. Why had I gone along with what they'd wanted? Was I afraid I would look feeble if I turned them down? They'd never invite me back? When it really counted, were they going to be there for me, or ditch me like my co-workers had done? None of this was getting me any closer to living my own life the way I wanted to live it.

Chapter 10 - More Parties

The week went by slowly in a never ending haze of computer code during the day, avoiding my upstairs neighbors when I got home, eating crappy take-out, and spending an hour or two on the phone with Daltrey. Those long conversations kept me going. Daltrey was rapidly becoming a warm comfort in my life now, so much like it had been all those years ago, and I didn't want to give that up for anything. Yet, it also felt like I didn't really have him. Daltrey was still just a fantasy and the reality was Wendy and Alec. I wanted to be a part of their inner circle, but I had pushed myself right back out as soon as I had one foot in the door.

On Friday, I opened a can of beef soup and dumped it in a bowl, then slung it in the microwave. It smelled homey and warm like my thoughts of Daltrey, but eating it was appallingly lacking like the rest of my life. If I hadn't been so hungry, I would have dumped it. After choking down the crap, I settled onto my bed and called Daltrey again, hoping I wouldn't end up like my crappy soup that had let me down, only seemingly comforting while moments later it was just crap. I wanted to be something to him, not just unfulfilling soup.

He picked up on the third ring, sounding distracted. "Hey,

Marty."

"What's up? You busy?" Noises in the background bothered me. What was he doing?

He sighed softly in that manner he had that made my heart flutter around like a little puppy, begging for attention. "I'm, uh, just finishing. Just a minute." It sounded like he put the phone down. My soul lurched. Was he with someone else? I strained my ears listening to what was going on.

After a moment or two, he picked the phone back up, sounding more like himself. "Sorry, Marty." He laughed softly. It was those gentle moments that had me obsessing over him and thinking about him all day long and dreaming about him at night. "I was in the middle of painting. Just finished, though."

"Ugh! Great timing, huh?"

"It's all good. What're you doin'?" he asked, cheerfully, as if he'd been waiting for me to call all day.

"God, nothing. Really, my day sucked. This is the best part of it." I couldn't help smiling and wondering if he could hear that in my voice.

More of that soft laughter, not teasing, just happy or content, danced through the phone. "For real. Besides the painting I just finished, I haven't really done anything today. Ha! Except, like, think about you."

He thought about me? Sure he did, but what exactly had he been thinking? "I thought about you, too. All day." My voice was so soft, I wasn't sure he'd heard me.

"Marty?"

"Don't. Let's just... What are you doing this weekend?" I didn't want the conversation to get deep. I just wanted to enjoy him for the moment. With him living in New York, that was all I could have any way.

The line was silent for a moment. "Uh, nothing? You?" That sounded very much like guilt.

Why didn't he want to tell me what was going on? I didn't have a right to ask him, but I wanted to push it, wanted to demand all of his attention. My chest tightened and I rubbed the ball of my hand against it, letting my eyebrows attack my nose in a painful grimace.

"Marty?" he asked softly.

I was about to dig into it, beg him to tell me why he sounded so guilty, but then my ceiling started pounding over my head. I walked out to my bare living room and it was even louder.

"What's that?" Daltrey asked.

"Fucking neighbors. Sounds like they're having another party."

"Oh? Why aren't you going?" I'd told him we were friends and that we'd had a little spat. "Haven't you straightened that out yet?"

"Uh, no." That was more of the same reason for the argument in the first place. Wendy was right and I had nothing to give them, and if I did have something, did I want to give it?

"So, go upstairs."

"Dal, I wasn't invited. For good reason." I sat in the middle of my floor, cross-legged, and leaned back on my arm that wasn't holding the phone. The ceiling rattled and I could hear muffled laughter. I wanted to go up and join the fun, to be a part of something instead of lingering on the outside.

"You should just, like, get a bottle of booze and knock on the door. If they turn you away, you can always complain about the noise. You know?" His tone was light, teasing, but I didn't want to hear it. Dealing with this issue was not on my weekend agenda.

"I don't know, Dal. I just feel like I already blew it with them."

"Um, really, you sound like you're whining. I'm sure your neighbors have some cheese and crackers to go with it," he laughed out.

"Nice, you're a riot, Dal."

He cleared his throat and contained his laughter. "Seriously, Marty. It's important for you to have friends, for real. It's a hella better way to spend your evening anyway, than sitting around talking to me. So, um, I tell you what. I'm going to be busy all day tomorrow—"

61

"Doing what?" I interrupted him. We were back to his guilty plans.

"Something. It's a surprise, sort of, for you. And me, I guess. For us. I'll call you, like Sunday afternoon and tell you about it. Until then go get some booze and make up with your friends, Marty. You can totally do that."

"A surprise? For me?"

"Marty!"

"I love it when you call me that. I miss you, Dal."

"I know, right! Ha! Now, go have fun, and Marty?"

"Yes?"

"Don't like freakin' drunk dial me at one in the morning. You know that's three, my time."

I laughed then. Daltrey always knew how to bring me out of myself and lighten things up. He made me feel better, even now. I really had missed that in my life. "Thanks, Dal. Talk to you Sunday."

"'Kay!"

I took his advice and headed down to the closest liquor store, relieved that I didn't have to use Dad's Vader-card any more. I'd received my first pay check and could shop without repercussions at the more convenient package store instead of trekking across town to the big grocery store where I'd been going. I picked up another bottle of Jack, since they'd liked it so much the last time, and made my way back to the apartment.

I changed into my best hip-hugging Seven jeans that I had sucked up my embarrassment enough to actually shop in the girl's section for. I wiggled them on over my tight Joe-Boxers with the lower waist band and pulled on a clean T-shirt in an aqua blue, knowing the color would highlight my eyes. I wasn't entirely sure why that was important. Daltrey wanted me to go make friends and have fun, not get laid, and highlighting my eyes and ass was the norm for trying to get laid. I shook it off. There was nothing wrong with wanting to look good and not getting laid. I grabbed my keys and the Jack and headed upstairs.

The music was still pumping with a pounding base and synthesized melodies when I knocked on the door. A tall, skinny girl wearing a skin tight T-shirt and a denim skirt, short enough to show off most of her lean thighs answered the door. Her brown hair was darker underneath with golden highlights. She looked up at me with big brown eyes, lined in way too much make up, which immediately made me assume she must be a friend of Tia's and her cheerleading-type world. Smiling, I handed her the Jack. "Well, all right!" she said, nodding me into the apartment. "Alec!" she called over the music, heading toward the kitchen with her newly acquired booze-prize.

Alec jogged up, seeing the bottle first, then his brown eyes latched on to me and he smiled. "This is Joy," he introduced me to the girl who promptly disappeared with the Jack, but not before I noticed how similar her eyes were to Alec's.

"Sister?" I asked, loudly, leaning closer.

He nodded fiercely and grabbed my shoulder, pulling me in for a hug that told me he wasn't angry, he forgave me, even though I hadn't really said sorry.

It didn't take long for Wendy to show up with Tia in tow and give me a questioning glare. I held my arms out, offering myself to her scrutiny, but still not really apologizing. She could take it however she wanted. After a second or two, thinking she would throw me out, she grabbed me and dragged me out to the dance floor, also known as the living room.

The music shifted into something I liked better. It still had a good strong beat, but more guitars, less electro-dance and more just good old rock and roll. Then I recognized it as some old Van Halen song as soon as David Lee Roth's voice hooted out. It was their version of *Dancing in the Streets*. Wendy and Tia rocked up against me, arms in the air and I let go and just enjoyed it, shaking my hips and gyrating around them, not thinking of anything else but letting the music move me. Then, I tripped.

The floor met my face, and after a moment of making sure I was okay, Wendy and Tia were on the floor beside me, laughing their asses off. I couldn't help laughing too. I hadn't even started drinking yet. A hand stretched out in front of me, and I looked up a long tan, muscular arm to the broad shoulders and shaggy blond hair of Seth. My heart thrummed a little harder, as I let him pull me up off my ass.

"Come on, Martin. Let's chill a little and let these women have the floor." I hadn't noticed him in the apartment, let alone on the dance floor. I followed him out onto the balcony with a shy smile, admitting to myself that I liked being involved with these people.

Out on the balcony, I rested my ass against the railing and watched him, enjoying his handsome face with high cheekbones and nonchalant attitude that curled his lip up on one side. He pulled out a joint and lit it up, taking a long toke, then handed it out to me. I took it and inhaled a little, holding the smoke in and passing it back. When I couldn't hold it in any longer, I exhaled a soft puff of smoke. Seth took another hit and stretched his arm out, offering it to me again. I shook my head. "That shit usually puts me out like a light."

"You just need to build up a little tolerance, man." He shook the joint, encouragingly and I took it. "A bit of this will help, too." He pulled a little vial out of the front pocket of his jeans and tapped out something along the knuckle of his index finger. He leaned forward offering me his hand like he had the joint.

I held the joint out to my side and leaned forward, eyeing the white powder suspiciously. "It's just coke, Martin. Just a quick little bump, not even a full line or anything, man. It'll keep you up, chilled with the pot."

I had no idea what he was talking about, but when he slid his coke-laced finger under my nose, I snorted it in, doing what he expected of me. It tingled in my nose a little and I imagined it dusting over my brain like snow falling over an open field, but otherwise, it didn't feel like much. I took another hit off the joint and passed it back.

"How do you have money for this shit?" I asked, curious since I didn't think Seth did much besides surf and model every now and then.

"It's the modeling. Kind of an unspoken, unwritten policy that models get whatever coke we want. I had a job today, so I got some. Keeps the models going, keeps us thin and working. You know? If we don't work, the studios don't make anything either." He shrugged like it was nothing.

"That's more than a little messed up, Seth."

"Eh. No big. I don't ever do a lot. Mostly share it with friends, man." He winked at me, did his own hit and put the vile back in his pocket.

I felt pretty good, braver than ever, and I wanted Seth to keep talking to me, involving me in his world. I took a breath and asked, "So, what? Are you going to get into acting like Alec?"

"Alec?" he scoffed. "He hasn't got a role yet, dude. Acting, though? Nah. I like where I'm at. I make enough to not have to worry about shit and still have time to do whatever, fuck around, you know? Hit the waves when I want."

"Sure." I wasn't sure I understood his perspective at all, but I didn't want to think too deeply on it, either.

"What do you do, Martin? Desk job or something, right?"

"Yes, I'm a programmer."

"Oh, like Microsoft? That where you work?" It occurred to me that Seth spent a lot of his fucking around time killing brain cells. Something I really couldn't afford to do. I had nothing in common with him. At all.

"No, not them. I work for Apex."

He raised a perfect honey-colored eyebrow. "Apex?"

"They're no Microsoft and the work's boring, but they're into everything. A big company and their LGBT friendly."

"What's that?"

"You know, gay. They support the gay and the alternative lifestyle community."

"Oh, right. That's cool." Seth nodded, agreeing with himself and took another hit off the joint before snuffing it out on the bottom of his Vans. His easy acceptance of me felt good and made my estimation of him rise. Maybe he was more than just some surfer-dude.

"Guess we should get back." He nodded over his shoulder to indicate the party that still raged inside.

I headed to the door, opened it and promptly tripped over the fucking track. Again. Before I could even think about being embarrassed, Seth's warm hands wrapped around my waist, lifting me up. Solid and comforting, I wanted his arms around me more. His touch had my cock waking up and pushing against my tight jeans a little painfully, but not unpleasantly. Before I could think about it, his hands were gone. He'd wrapped them around Tia instead. Oh right, girlfriend. I looked away only to catch Wendy watching me. I smiled and shrugged, feeling the heat of a blush cross my face.

People crammed into the small space and I pushed my way through them, choking back my embarrassment. I really needed a drink so I headed for the kitchen.

As I passed the dining room, I noticed several guys sitting around the table. Tad Ferretti and his whole damn band sat around doing shots and hanging out. Tad looked up at me with his cocky half smile. "Martin," he said with a knowing look.

"Hi, Tad." I pointed to the kitchen. "Gotta get a drink," I said as an excuse to not continue the conversation because, he was not someone I really wanted to talk to. Their music was cool, but he'd left an unpleasant taste in my mouth that desperately needed to be washed away, preferably with some Jack.

In the kitchen, Alec's sister was sitting on the counter with some guy between her legs. They were wrapped around him and I was pretty damn sure at least one of his hands was up her skirt. I shook that thought out of my head and grabbed the bottle of Jack sitting on the counter across from her. I found a rocks glass and poured it half full. They hadn't noticed me at all. Oddly, the hetero-pseudo sex on the kitchen counter did nothing to change the hardness of my own cock.

The music changed again as I made my way back to the living room. Band of Skulls was jamming on the stereo and I was sure that was a huge improvement. The melody of the guitar riffs sang in my veins as I watched people bob around in the living room, bodies pushed against each other, pulsing to the beat.

I slid down to my knees in front of the coffee table that had been pushed up against the couch. Tia was snorting a line of coke. She straightened up and handed me the red straw she'd been using. "Go for it, baby," she said with a wink.

Feeling really good, I figured it couldn't hurt to feel a little better. I sat my glass on the table and leaned forward with the straw, hovering over the white line of powder. I started snorting and opened my eyes. I could see the image of myself staring back, red straw in hand, double images of the lines of drug in the glass of the table. I pulled away only having snorted a little bit of the line. No way was I going to be able to keep going if I had to watch myself do it.

The little bit I had done left me feeling pretty happy, making me forget why I didn't want to do the shit in the first place. The music was flowing, people were having a good time, everything was just fine, and I fit, everything fit like a puzzle snapping together.

I tossed the rest of my drink back, loving the burn it made down my throat. Wendy caught my eye and nodded for me to join her in the center of the living room. I stood up and pressed my chest against hers and let my hips catch the beat, not bad for such a klutz like myself. She pressed into me, rhythmically. I didn't love it, but it wasn't bad, and the friction pulsing against my groin had my erection nice and firm and pushing against Wendy. If she noticed, she didn't say, just kept dancing, grinding.

A warm body leaned against my backside, and I could feel someone else's cock pushing into my ass making my body boil and lightning pulse at my balls. I assumed it was Alec, but when I looked up, I saw Alec on the other side of the room, watching us. His face was a cross between a happy smile and a scowl as if he couldn't quite make up his mind about what he saw. Did he like it or not? And who the fuck was grinding his cock against my ass? For a half a second, I didn't turn around hoping it was Seth. My muddled brain really did know better and eventually won the war, forcing me to turn and face Tad's half-smile that said so much more than I wanted to hear.

I pulled away from him which shoved my body up against Wendy. She opened her eyes and looked over my shoulder. Then she kissed me, sweeping her lips across mine. Her tongue teased at the edge of my mouth, but I pressed my lips together. I didn't want to kiss her. Then Alec was there, adding his lips to the kiss. I opened, letting Alec take my mouth, his tongue fucking into it, as Wendy kissed down my neck. Someone's hand was gripping my ass, a hand went up my shirt, flicking a nipple. It felt wonderful and safe. This was Alec and Wendy. Tad had been shoved aside, making me ecstatic and secure and amiable.

I let them pull and push me down the hall. More kisses landed along my neck. My shirt was pulled off, over my head. The music faded with the click of a door shutting, then more kisses trailed along my collarbone and a tongue lathed at my nipples. They'd never been particularly sensitive before, but now they were like battery terminals, charging me up.

In moments, we were naked on the bed, writhing together, unable to touch enough skin. "I want to fuck you, Martin," Alec whispered in my ear, licking around the shell of it. "Please, baby."

"Mmm," was all I managed before Alec pushed me up over the top of Wendy, between her spread legs.

"Condoms?" she asked.

Alec's big warm hands were on my cock, stroking it, and rolling a condom over it. His fingers flicked against my balls. "I want to watch you in her while I fuck you, Martin." My pulse pounded in my ears and my cock twitched, liking his breathy voice in my ear so much that I'd do anything he asked.

I practically purred my yes. His hands, up and down my back rubbing along my spine and my sides, had me wiggling and ready. "Do you know what to do?" I asked him.

"No. Not really," Alec said kissing and licking along my hip. He nibbled at the bone, making me squirm.

"Lube? You got lube?"

Alec leaned away and was back in a second with a bottle. I leaned down pressing my chest to Wendy's breast and sticking my ass up. "Fingers first. You gotta stretch it. Unlike girls, it won't do it by itself," I said into Wendy's neck, kissing her too soft skin. She smelled clean like soap and salty sweat that reminded me of the beach. She squirmed beneath me and buried her fingers in my hair.

A cool sticky finger slid into my hole. It'd been way too long, making me afraid I'd come before we ever got this started. "Hurry," Wendy whispered, but I shushed her. I needed Alec to take his time.

He added a second finger and I felt the high intense burn of stretch and moaned. "I like that," Alec said quickly adding another finger. "I'm getting the hang of this." It felt incredible and I pushed back against his hand, needing to feel him fucking me. "More?" he asked.

"No. I'm ready. Just go slow."

"M'kay." I felt the absence of his fingers immediately, but his cock was pushing in before I could miss them much. He shoved, forcing his cut head through the first ring of muscles, making me squeak with the force. "You okay? Martin?" He sounded panicky, moving one hand from the grip on my hips to press gently at the small of my back.

"Uh, sure... Just...wait a sec. Give me a sec." The three of us froze, unmoving. I wondered if this was what they'd been thinking when they'd beckoned me into their bed. This part was never really sexy, but you had to work through it. Wendy blew a piece of hair out of her face. I chuckled, deep in my throat, secretly enjoying her annoyance. "Okay. Go. But slow."

Alec's cock pushed in slowly but steadily like a pro and I bared down against him. When I felt his legs and balls push against me, he stopped. The hair on his legs rubbed against mine deliciously. I breathed out long and slow, letting my body adjust. Unable to contain myself longer, I huffed, "Go, move."

Alec took me at my word taking two long strokes, then he found his rhythm, and I did what they wanted and pushed my cock into Wendy's wet heat. The friction against my cock felt euphoric. Alec set the pace and both Wendy and I groaned as he pushed me into her, over and over. I closed my eyes and just fucked along with him, loving how it felt on my cock like a wet glove wrapped up tight.

I wanted it to go on forever, not giving a damn that it was a woman under me. Her fingers skated up my ribs and her nails flicked at my nipples while Alec's hands grabbed at my hips again, using them for leverage as he fucked. He leaned in and I could feel his hot breath against the back of my neck. I closed my eyes, concentrating on Alec's in and out.

For a while the pleasure of being fucked from both sides at once seemed like it would really never stop, until Alec started making sexy huffing noises and his rhythm faltered. I knew he was coming, and then it happened, he stroked hard and fast right across that certain spot that made me crazy. I groaned as my balls tingled and I felt it building in the small of my back and I was coming too. "Wendy?" I asked, unsure if she'd gotten her own orgasm. I just didn't have the experience, but I wanted it to be good for her.

"Fuck, you're so thick, Martin," she groaned, eyes closed, like a cat rolling blissfully in a pile of catnip.

"I guess that was okay for you?" I asked, still unsure.

"Fu-uck, yeah," she cooed and Alec laughed, so I let it go.

"Like a boss," Alec added.

We pulled out and cleaned up, tossing both condoms then laying tangled together in the bed, unable to sleep, but unwilling to move. Eventually, Alec got up and kicked everyone else out of the apartment and turned off the music before coming back to bed, but I barely registered it. My face was pressed into Wendy's back, her silky hair falling over my face. I liked cuddling with her more than the sex, but with Alec in my ass and my eyes closed, I didn't seem to have a problem proving that guys really will fuck just about anything.

Alec pushed his chest against my back and his thighs pressed against the back of my legs. His hand threaded through my hair that needed cutting, but I couldn't bring myself to do it. He played with it a moment before softly saying, "You should let Wendy cut it."

"Mmm. I kind of want to grow it out."

"You need to trim the ends or it won't grow," Wendy added with a yawn.

"Okay. Maybe."

We snuggled in together, content and ready to sleep. Just before I drifted off, I thought about Daltrey. This really couldn't have been what he'd intended when he told me to make up with Wendy, but he didn't know about this either. What was this exactly anyway? Could I just accept them and be with them and keep Daltrey as a friend? Was that my reality?

"I'm glad you came tonight," Wendy said with a giggle at her unintended innuendo.

"Um...right. I'm sorry. About before I mean."

Alec shushed us both then. "Go the fuck to sleep," he said and in his arms, snuggled up to Wendy, I slept pretty well.

Chapter 11 - Sunday Surprises

The rest of my weekend was spent avoiding Alec and Wendy. Again. Saturday morning, I crawled out of bed and took the walk of shame down the stairs. I didn't even stop at my apartment, but headed outside and down the street to get some good coffee. Part of me wanted to get some for Wendy and Alec too, but a bigger part of me wanted to hide from them. What had I done?

I really wanted to blame it on the drugs, but really, that was my own damn fault too. Nobody was forcing the coke up my nose. I wasn't so stoned that I didn't know what I was doing anyway. It had just felt so good to be touched, kissed, held loved. Though, I didn't really think it was love, but was it close enough?

Watching my reflection in the storefront windows as I walked by, had me wondering who I really was. I walked with my shoulders slumped, wearing rumpled clothes and a look of defeat on my face. Who did I want to be?

I barricaded myself in my apartment, only going out when my growling stomach demanded I find food. A freezer pizza and a six-pack of beer seemed a viable solution, so I picked them up from the store and went home again.

Still no sign of Alec or Wendy. No phone calls or texts from Daltrey either, not that I deserved to hear from him. How was I going to tell him what happened? What had happened? I'd thought it was just casual sex the first time, but Wendy hadn't been happy with me blowing them off afterward, and here I was doing it again. Relationships were too hard, took too much energy to keep it going.

I went to bed early, pulling the covers over my head and wishing I could run away from myself.

I slept until late Sunday morning when a pounding on my door got me up. I pulled on a pair of khaki shorts and opened the door. A hot, familiar looking guy with straight bleached blond hair falling all in his face stood there with his mouth open. "Uh, looking for Alec?"

I groaned a little and pointed at the stairs. "Upstairs, dude."

"Thanks, man," he said and turned away, but then he stopped and looked at me again. "Hey! Aren't you that guy Tad's all worked up about?"

I definitely knew the guy. He was in Tad's band. Guitarist, maybe? "Uh? What? Worked up?"

"Seriously." He pushed his hair back out of his eyes. "From the party Friday night."

"Oh. I mean, um, I know Tad, but didn't think he was worked up over me. Or anything, really." I lifted my eyebrow, thinking that was the truth. I'd never seen extreme emotion out of Tad one way or another. The guy was too cool and maybe that was what I didn't like about him.

The guy rolled his eyes. They were an unnatural shade of blue, almost neon. He had to have contacts in, but they were striking against the bleached hair and sharp cheekbones. He rolled his tongue across plump lips and fiddle with the hoop pierced through it. "Oh, well, I'd say he's worked up. Maybe he just wants what he can't have, but he's totally into you."

"Too bad," I said and shut the door. It wasn't particularly nice, but I didn't give a shit if he thought I was rude. Fuck Tad for being into me now. He'd blown his chance. And why the hell couldn't I be that assertive about anything else in my life?

Still, it felt a little exciting knowing he wanted me. I rolled my eyes at myself and went to start the coffee and then get a shower. Daltrey had promised to call and I couldn't wait to talk to him. It seemed like it'd been ages, not just one day.

By the time Daltrey called, I was at the park, wearing my khaki shorts and Aviator sunglasses and walking around aimlessly in the sunshine and trying to calm my acidy stomach that insisted on boiling over like a super-active volcano. I'd popped five antacids already and was just about to give in and call when the phone rang. "Dal! Hey!"

"Hey, Marty. Missed you." His happy voice made me glow like the sun. Distracted, I tripped over my own feet, stupid deck shoes, and fell into a bench.

I grunted. "Missed you too."

"You okay?"

"Sure, yes. Just, sitting down. At the park. What's up?" I didn't want to tell him what a freakin' klutz I was.

"So, like, I've been, um, working some stuff out and I've booked a show in L.A."

"What?" I gasped. L.A.? He was coming to L.A.? My heart stopped beating.

I heard his soft chuckle, sounding like he had his mouth covered. "That's what I've been working on and, uh, like, I had to get a lot of shit lined up yesterday and two of the paintings I've been working on, and like, I had to get those finished, so just busy, you know?" he rambled on, nervously. "Is that okay? Um, do you like want to see me? When I'm out there?"

"Fuck yes! Of course. When? When will you be here?" I stood up, barely able to contain myself. I wanted to jump up and down.

"Uh, two weeks. So, not this week, but the next Thursday."

"You did this for me?" I cringed at how awe-struck I sounded.

"Yes, of course. For you and me. Um, I want to see you, too. You know?" His soft voice calmed me. Why hadn't I even considered traveling out to see him? Well, if this went well, I would.

"Dal! This is so cool. I'm...I don't know what to say."

He really started laughing then. "Just say you'll see me. We can, uh, hang out, or whatever. You know?"

"I'll ask for Thursday and Friday off when I go in tomorrow."

"Okay. I forget you have to ask off. Funny."

"What's funny, Dal?"

"Just that I always kind of like had you pictured two ways. Um, I guess I'm trying to reconcile it. Just, I thought you would maybe follow your dad's footsteps or you'd do like something totally off the wall, like become a pro-skateboarder or something."

I laughed hard. "You must be kidding. Oh my God!"

Daltrey was laughing harder than me.

"No way," I said, "you remember when I broke my arm? The first time I ever got on that stupid thing. Slid it under my bed and never got on it again."

"It's probably still there," Daltrey said amidst another bout of laughter. I'd do or say anything to keep him laughing like that.

"Maybe."

"You don't know?" he asked.

"Haven't been home in a while. I guess."

No more laughing. "Well. See? At least you weren't afraid to try new things."

I hated that fucking skateboard. "Huh, never saw it that way." It didn't make a difference how I saw it.

"Oh?" Daltrey fished for more.

I didn't know what to tell him. "Still followed my Dad. Did what I was told."

"Well, um, what did you want to do? If you could like do something else? What would it be? Seriously?"

I swallowed hard, considering telling the truth or changing the subject, but this was Daltrey and if anyone would understand, he would, even if it hurt. "I don't know. Well, for a while, I thought about, uh, becoming a firefighter, but I'm too small."

Daltrey gasped, "Martin!" His low voice sounded wondrous...and sexy.

"Right. I never got over that, Dal. What your dad did." He'd changed our lives. Changed my life, wrecked it completely.

"I guess I haven't either, really. I'm just glad I was at your house when it happened."

I took in a deep breath. We'd never discussed this and I really needed him to know how I felt about it. "That fire was the worst thing to ever happen to me." Overwhelmed, I ran my free hand over my face, holding back tears.

"To you? My mom uprooted my entire life, Martin." He sounded angry, his voice rising an octave. I hadn't heard him sound like that in so long, not since we were kids fighting over stupid shit that never really mattered. This mattered.

"But, I lost you. I lost you, Dal. If your dad hadn't set that fire? Daltrey?" I listened to his heavy breathing for a minute. "Would we have stayed together?" my voice cracked, full of the sadness and longing I'd carried around in my chest for the past five years.

"I don't know, Marty. Who knows? But..."

I panted out desperately, "What? But what?"

"We can't change the last five years. We can only change the next."

"I'm glad I called you," I said. "Glad we're reconnecting."

"Me too."

The tightness in my chest eased a little like tectonic plates shifting. Seeing him again, I never thought it would really happen, even after we'd started talking on the phone. I walked home, floating on a cloud of possibility.

As I stepped into the stairwell, I could hear voices above me. Wendy and Alec were talking to another of our neighbors. It sounded like the guy was complaining about the noise. Alec kept saying they had shut the party down early, but neighbor-guy was still grumbling.

"We'll invite you to the next one if you want," Wendy finally said, shutting the guy up. He lived on my floor, just down the hall. I'd only seen him a few times since I'd moved in. He stomped passed me without another word. Alec started laughing at his retreat, his brown eyes laughing too. It was as if the whole world existed for Alec's entertainment, and his amusement was often twisted and derogatory.

"Hey guys," I said softly.

Wendy smirked. "Hey stranger."

"Want coffee or something?" I nodded toward my apartment to invite them.

"Sure," Wendy answered for them both and followed me.

I started the pot and called out from the kitchen. "Uh, I've got some news." I had to tell them about Daltrey. I didn't know what they'd think, but they needed to know that much. "So, uh, I was talking with Daltrey today, earlier today."

"Just spit it out, Martin," Alec sneered.

"He's coming to see me. In two weeks. He'll be here in two weeks. He has a show."

Alec crossed his arms over his chest and glanced around everywhere but at me.

Wendy's eyes grew wide. "What's this mean?" she asked, suspiciously.

"I don't know. I'd like you to see his show, though, maybe meet him. Just—"

"Just what?" Alec asked, accusingly.

"I don't want him to know we're anything more than friends." I did it. I spit the words out that had been haunting me all weekend. Score one for me!

Wendy made a strange noise in the back of her throat. "Are we anything more than friends, Martin?"

I didn't answer. I didn't know the answer. I poured three cups of coffee and brought two into the dining room, setting them on the table and went back in the kitchen for the third. Alec got up and walked out. Was he jealous or just mad at the situation or mad I didn't want to admit we'd slept together?

"What? Wendy? I'm trying." She had to see that. This was

the most effort I'd put into any relationship of any kind since... well, since Daltrey.

She picked up one of the cups and sipped on it. I'd fixed it how I knew she liked it, just a little milk and a ton of sugar. Okay, so maybe we were in a relationship, but we'd never talked about any of it.

She sat the cup on the table and looked up at me with hurt eyes lined in sparkling green shadow and her auburn hair falling around slim shoulders. "Do you think we just take anyone into our bed?" She put her hands over her face. "I thought you understood," she muttered into her palms.

"I don't know what the fuck I'm doing. But, I'm trying. You know what Daltrey means to me."

"What do we mean to you?"

I sat down hard in the chair beside her. "I don't know," I said softly. I wanted her to tell me how I should feel. "What do you think I should—?"

"I thought you'd figured it out before you showed up at the party," she snapped at me.

I shook my head. "I'm just trying and I want—"

"What? What exactly do you want, Martin?" She glared at me, her eyes hard and her lips pursed together. "It's okay. You're just a good fuck, Martin. Whatever." She slapped the table and then bolted out the door.

I was torn. I wanted to make them happy. They didn't really ask me for anything, but it was still too much. I needed them to understand my feelings for Daltrey, but I probably hadn't made it really clear. Now things were back to being fucked up with them and I hadn't even freaked out about having sex with a woman this time. Maybe I'd stopped thinking about Wendy as a woman. She was an extension of Alec and I liked Alec. Maybe too much. Still, I didn't know them or understand them. I'd been dismissed from their lives easily, perhaps I wasn't even really a good fuck. Surely I was nothing to them and never could be more.

I slid my cup away from me. My guts felt like ice and I shivered. I needed a hot shower, needed to wash away this bullshit and just relax.

The water was hot on my back, scalding my neck and massaging me into a more sedate mood. I washed my body, gliding over the muscles, noting how flat my stomach was, despite not having worked out in few weeks.

I wondered what Daltrey's stomach would look like, and his cock. It'd been five years, and I didn't remember, except his cock was cut like mine and Alec's. I'd been with a few guys that hadn't been, but of course they were just one-night stands, so I never thought about it further.

I soaped up, stroking my cock, slicking fingers over the head. It rose to attention thinking about cocks, thinking about Daltrey. His profile picture didn't do justice to his dark blue eyes and I wondered if they'd still be that dark. What would have changed over the years? Would his lips still like the feel of my cock?

I thought about him sucking me off as I stroked. I rubbed my thumb over the slit at the top of my cockhead for a moment, then I stroked harder, faster, twisting a little as I worked it, imagining Daltrey on his knees in front of me as I leaned one arm against the cold tile and fucked into my other hand, rolling my hips.

I thought about what it had been like to touch Daltrey, to suck him and I wanted to fuck him desperately. I closed my eyes and pictured my cock fucking into his tight hole and I squeezed my cock harder. I shifted and leaned my shoulders against the wall so I could use my other hand to pull on my sack. That familiar feeling started building up quickly, and in a moment I shot white streams of cum all over the shower curtain. Daltrey's name slipped from my lips as I came.

Chapter 12 - Dates and Dinners

Monday morning demanded I sit through more status meetings and lunch was just a quick sandwich from the cafeteria. I spent the early afternoon looking at code, until my cell phone rang. The caller ID said "Wendy." I instantly went into worry-mode. Wendy never called me, especially during work hours, so it was either an emergency or serious drama, neither of which I was ready for, but I answered the call anyway. "Hey!"

"Hey Martin." She sounded bored.

"Uh, hey. What's going on? Everything okay?"

"Yeah, fine. Just, uh, wondering..." Still sounding bored. I could even picture her eyes rolling.

"What?" I didn't mean to sound short, but I didn't need her crap at work, and she was starting to irritate me. More than usual.

"Well, we're having Tia and Seth over for dinner tonight. It's a celebration, 'cause Alec got a commercial. So, can you come? It's kind of a couple's thing, so can you like bring someone?"

"Like a date?"

"Yes a date. Can you?" Her nonchalant attitude

disappeared.

A date. I didn't have anyone to bring. None of my work colleagues needed to be exposed to Wendy and Alec and they knew all my other friends. They were my other friends. "I...I, uh, I don't think so."

"Jesus, Martin. What is with you? Can't you just do this one thing?" Now, she was pissed.

"Look Wendy. I don't think I can get anyone with this short of notice. I'll try, but seriously? Why is it so important I bring someone?"

"We're trying to make things work, Martin. I get it, but can't you just bring a date and we'll try to work this shit out, 'cause we like you and Alec wants you to come." She sounded like my dad. She wasn't asking me; she was ordering me. "You have to understand. It's all about Alec. And... Fuck! It will just be easier for me if you bring someone. That way I can focus on Alec."

Instinctively, I swallowed the urge to fight about it. It meant something to Alec. He'd finally got a real acting job and he wanted me there. They wanted me in their lives and that made me feel important. They probably didn't understand what a loner I had always been or how important it was for me to be included in their little party. I took a deep breath and let it out. "Okay. You're right, Wendy. I'll see what I can do." The promise fell off my lips with little thought.

"Great. See you tonight." She hung up the phone and I slid down in my chair, digging my hand through my hair. How the hell was I going to get a date?

##

At six, I drug my sorry ass up the stairs. Alone.

I asked a few people, but no one could or would make it. I'd even called someone I knew from college, but he swore he had plans and I couldn't argue that. We had never been close after all, so why would he drop his own plans for me? This thing had been last minute and I wasn't on good enough terms with anyone to do a last minute date. Hell, I had never really dated before anyway. Fuck Wendy for insisting I bring someone.

To make up for it, I dressed nice in dark slacks and a silky, black button up shirt. I bought a nice bottle of wine on my way home from work. They would just have to deal with it. Besides, it would be me feeling like the outsider, not her or any of them.

Alec opened the door with a smile and a quick hug. "Martin. I'm glad you came. No date?"

"No. Sorry, I couldn't get anyone with short notice."

Wendy's huffing came from over Alec's shoulder. "Oh, whatever, Martin. I knew you wouldn't bring anyone."

"Damn, Wendy. It's not like I didn't try. Shit. Give a guy notice next time."

She rolled her eyes and snagged the bottle of wine from my hands without another word, but her lips were pursed together so hard it smeared her lip gloss up over her top lip. My cringe couldn't be suppressed, as Alec nodded me inside.

Tia and Seth sat side by side on the couch, both dressed up. Tia wore a short skirt that fluffed around the tops of her thighs and had a tight bodice that pushed what little breasts she had up and out. Seth dressed like we'd been in the same closet, dark slacks, a deep blue button up and Ralph Lauren loafers. He didn't notice the similarity or anything else, as his eyes were focused on Tia's breasts. She smiled softly when I came in, "Hey Martin."

"Tia. Seth. Good to see you." I sat in the club chair, waiting for directions from Wendy and hoping the night wouldn't be too long and awkward.

My hopes were dashed as I heard Wendy and Alec arguing in the kitchen. My eyes drifted to the carpet between my feet encased in my Kenneth Cole loafers. Hearing my name being thrown around, I flinched and bit my lip.

Seth whispered a few curse words under his breath. Nice.

Alec's voice rose from the kitchen. "It's just dinner! Jeez, just our friends. Come on, Wendy!"

"Fuck you, Alec. This is important. Important to you!" Wendy screeched her answer.

Alec didn't give her time to add anything to her rant. "You're just being a drama-queen. Who cares that he didn't bring anyone? I didn't want some stranger here anyway. Fuck! At least he showed up, right?" he spat out.

Silence cut through the apartment feeling more dangerous than all of the yelling.

We waited. My sense of failure hung over the room like a tangible thing that put frowns across all our faces as if Seth and Tia carried the burden along with me. "I'm sorry, guys," I said, barely loud enough to be heard. Tia had the decency to look compassionate, but didn't say anything. Seth muttered something about needing a joint, then Tia smacked his leg and he pouted a little, not meeting my eyes.

Wendy finally came out and put a bowl of salad on the table. "Hey, come eat, guys!" she called, happy again, as if nothing had happened. We joined her at the table, and Alec came out of the kitchen with more food. Wendy poured wine. She'd opened the bottle I brought, so I took it as a good sign.

Soon, we were laughing and eating, as if my lack of a dinner companion had never been an issue. It felt too much like being at home with my parents. I couldn't tell if Wendy acted more like my dad or my mom. Dad was quick to make sure I knew he was disappointed in me and Mom chose to ignore everything and pretend we were just a peachy-keen perfect family, but she couldn't remember a fucking thing the next day. Alcohol made it easy to ignore the problems, apparently. Maybe I needed a lesson from Mom.

With that thought, I took a long gulp of the red blend I'd brought. The oaky scent lingered after the sip. It seemed a pity that with five people, we only got one round. "I should have bought two bottles," I said.

"Indeed," Tia agreed. "It's so bold you can practically chew it, Martin."

Wendy smirked a little then served up the pasta. The room fell into a quiet murmur, the only noises, that of our chewing and appreciating the food while we dug in, until the girls started chatting again. It didn't take us long to finish off the garlic bread and salad that accompanied the meal. Sated, the teasing began. It felt comfortable and fun to joke around with friends; something I rarely had in my life. It felt good to laugh.

Alec pulled out a bag of weed and dropped it on the table. "Bring that bong in here," he called out to Wendy who was putting dishes in the kitchen. In a moment, he was loading the little metal cup that jutted out from the purple-tinted glass pipe. "Now this is celebrating!"

I'd never used such a contraption, though it wasn't like I hadn't seen them before. I watched the others hit it and didn't hesitate when it passed to me. After a few rounds, the laughter in the small apartment increased and we were all saying stupid things and laughing as if it were the most hysterical thing we'd ever heard.

At some point, Wendy brought out a plate of brownies that were devoured in seconds between more bouts of hilarity. Tia smeared the gooey chocolate across Seth's face in an attempt to feed him that seemed a little like the wedding cake ritual and had all of us laughing again, until she fell out of her chair. That didn't even stop the laughter entirely, just made us move into the living room where Tia sat on the floor for safety reasons, between Seth's legs, as he sat on the couch and played with her hair. Wendy and Alec sat on the couch, cuddled up beside them, and I took the chair again. Eventually, the conversation lulled as we all sat in our own pot-hazed introspection.

An hour could have passed, maybe two, or just a few minutes. I had no idea. We were quiet and that rough yet pleasant feeling that laughing too hard left in my chest lingered and settled into something feeling a lot like contentment. Could I live my life like this? Always being the third or even fifth wheel, the odd man out, was that enough for me?

I thought about Daltrey again and wondered if we had a chance to be something more to each other. Lonely waves of doubt started darkening my mood by the time Seth stood up and announced they were leaving.

Tia had pretty much fallen asleep leaning against his leg, and drooled shamelessly down his slacks. Seth had to practically carry her out of the apartment and down to their car. I couldn't help ask if she was going to be okay.

"Huh! This is normal, dude," Seth answered, but I didn't miss Wendy's eyebrow arch up. That look bothered me and I looked hard at Tia's body curled up in Seth's arms. Tia had lost weight and she didn't have hardly an extra pound to spare. Her cheek bones stood out on her gaunt face, making a knot of worry curl in my stomach.

"You sure?" I asked, wanting him to reassure me so I could go back to that bubble of contentment where everything had been just fine.

Seth gave me an odd look. "It's cool. See ya later, man!" With that, he was gone.

Wendy and Alec stretched out on the couch. Alec smiled, seductively, his lip curling up on one side. "Want to join us?" he said, practically purring the words out and looking very much like a cat that was about to pounce on something, raising his eyebrows to reveal a twinkling in his eyes that seemed dangerous. The attractiveness of being wrapped up with him on that couch was undeniable. The doubt came from Wendy. She hadn't said anything. She didn't roll over, didn't issue her own invitation.

"Maybe I should just, uh, go. Downstairs."

Slowly, with purpose, Wendy sat up, the expression on her face moving through emotions I couldn't name and finally settling on resignation. Her lips pressed together in a deep red line, as if she'd been chewing on them or kissing someone hard. "Come on," she said with an exasperated sigh and a nudge of her head toward the hallway that lead back to the bedroom.

If I were looking for reassurance from her, that didn't quite give it. "Uh, I don't—"

"Fuck that!" Alec snorted. "This is my celebration. So,

knock it the fuck off!" I didn't know which of us he was directing his angry words at, maybe both of us. "Come on." He got up and walked down the hallway without looking back, as if he just took it for granted that we'd follow, but I still wasn't sure.

Wendy stood up and held her hand out to me. Her perfect manicure shimmered in the low lighting. "Truce," she said quietly. One word, but it meant so much more than that. She would do anything for Alec. Maybe she'd wanted me at some point, but if Alec didn't want me there, I wouldn't have even been invited. I wanted Alec and had to accept that Wendy was a part of that package. I'd have to deal with that.

How had I been sucked into this crazy mess? I didn't want Wendy, but I didn't want to come between them either. Could I really just join them, be a part of this? My cock wasn't starting to perk up, even at the thought of fucking Alec, but this was my opportunity to get my hands on his smoking hot body, and all I could think of was whether I could get it up and keep it up enough to satisfy Wendy. No matter how I pretended she was just an extension of Alec, I knew it wasn't true.

I cleared my throat and let Wendy pull me up out of the chair. "I, uh, I'm all for a truce. You know I like you guys. But..." I gazed longingly at the front door.

"It's important to Alec."

"I get that, but, I'm gay, Wendy. I..." The words that didn't come out of my mouth centered on not wanting to hurt her, but not wanting to fuck her either.

She shook her head and examined the floor. "Give me a minute," she finally said, heading down the hallway, not waiting for me tell her no again.

I tucked my thumb into the back pocket of my dress slacks. And waited, obediently.

Voices mumbling softly floated from the hall, but I couldn't tell what they were saying. The front door again held my interest. Why couldn't I just leave? Did being a part of their circle mean that much to me?

Before I could answer, Wendy came down the hall. "Here," she said, once again stretching her hand out to me, placating. But this time she offered drugs rather than her tolerance.

Taking the little blue pill, I glared at her.

"Fuck, Martin, just take it. It will help and you know it."

I did know it. The little pill would make me forget Wendy was in the room with us in any meaningful way. What I couldn't figure out was if that made me feel like I was using her or if they were using me. I wanted to give the pill back, knowing how good it would make me feel and also knowing how shitty I would feel the next day.

"Just. God, Martin. Give me something here!"

Wendy's eyes seemed more sincere now. Regardless of how we felt about each other, she loved Alec; that much I knew. I could respect that at least.

"You don't even like me, Wendy."

She huffed, "I do. Or I did. I get the gay thing, Martin. I don't really care how you feel about me. This is all Alec. He wants you and I'll do anything for him. So, accept this as my sacrifice and relax and let it happen."

I understood where she was coming from and I wanted Alec. I wanted to be accepted by them. I wanted things I'd never had. I also knew this would not be good for getting things started with Daltrey. Yet, he still seemed like a pipedream, something that would never be real. Alec and Wendy were real and in my face.

She stared at me with lowered brows, demanding that I do something. I didn't know what to do. I didn't know how to stand on my own. I only knew how to do what I was told. Wendy had taken over for my father, telling me what to do and how to do it, not giving a shit about my feelings.

Popping the pill in my mouth, I reluctantly followed her back to the bedroom, wondering if I was trading in my chance at happiness for a sure thing, even if it wasn't what I really wanted or needed.

Chapter 13 - Work Sucks

My date with Daltrey was coming up fast yet still too far away. I knew I shouldn't be fucking with Alec and Wendy if I wanted to get something started with him. Guilt followed me through the day.

I took a long swig of Gatorade, hoping it would make me feel better, knowing it wouldn't really make me feel better about myself, regardless of the physical healing it may offer. I was still chugging when my boss walked in and sat down in the chair facing my desk.

"Hi," I squeaked out, putting the bottle back on the desk.

Grant eyed me up and down, assessing and finally coming to some decision. "Look. Apex is a progressive company. We go beyond just liberal. You know what I mean?"

"Yes, sir." That was the reason I chose this organization. They were LGBT friendly, but they went beyond just accepting. They did a lot for the community. We all knew this, no one had to say it.

"I also get that you're young. First time out, really on your own." He ran his hands through his slightly graying hair, salt and pepper just at the sides. "And really? I don't care what you do on your own time. I don't care what you look like. Hell! I don't give a shit if you come in here in these expensive suites or faded jeans and flip flops."

Unsure where he was going, I glanced down my front, assessing myself. I wore the gray Armani with a light blue shirt and my gray Calvin Klein flannel tie with the white plaid stripes. My favorite Kenneth Cole loafers stretched out unseen under my desk. My dad would flip his lid if I had flip flops on at work. I didn't shop from his closet, but damned close. Regardless, I had no idea what that had to do with anything and maybe that was his point. "Okay..." I mumbled.

"What I care about is the work you do. That you put in enough quality time to get quality results. So, if your eyes are bloodshot every day? Fine." He tossed a hand in the air.

"They're not—" I started to protest, but then shut up when he glared at me, knowing as well as I did that it was bullshit. My eyes were almost always red, if not the drugs it was lack of sleep straining them. I had purposely avoided mirrors this morning getting ready, and rubbed my hand across my scruff because I didn't even shave that morning. Who knew what my blond hair looked like, especially since it had started growing out?

"Martin. You were hired for your talent. So, here's the thing. You've had enough time with everyone else's work. It's time for you to justify yourself. I have a project coming up. Think about who you want on your team."

"My team, sir?"

Grant nodded. "Yes. You'll get started next week, so you need to figure out who's on your team."

"How many? On my team? How many people do I get?" My focus totally shifted. I didn't care what I did for a living, but I had to admit I was getting bored and whether I pulled off a successful project or fell on my face, at least it would be more interesting, something different.

"Two or three, depending on who you want."

I opened my mouth to roll off my choices, but he held up a hand to stop me.

"Think about it. I won't have the final details until next

week. You have time off coming up. Use it to think about all this." He waved his arm around, taking in the paper work on my desk.

A little spark of something like a tiny sparrow flittered in my chest. Was it happiness or just hope? Either way, I really wanted to talk to someone, anyone. I needed to share the news. Why couldn't I just call Daltrey? I should, but that guilt swimming through my heart held me back, tainted my good news with my own stupidity, grounding that optimistic bird.

I thought about moving. Maybe the apartment complex could move me to a unit farther away. I let my forehead thunk down on the edge of my desk. Running away wouldn't solve my problems, but damned if I knew what would.

Chapter 14 - First Dates Again

When Thursday afternoon finally arrived I felt like a total mess. Nerves had my stomach ready to erupt like a volcano, swirling in toxic lava. We'd been talking, but seeing Daltrey face to face would be something totally different and unreal to a point that my imagination tumbled thousands of variations of our meeting through my head. What would we say? How would it feel?

I wanted to pick him up from the airport, dying for that romantic homecoming scene but he said it wouldn't be worth it. He would have an entourage there getting in the way and we would barely be able to say hello before he was whisked away. He had responsibilities for this visit; that was the price he'd pay to make it happen. He texted me when his plane touched down though, and then I waited until it was finally time to drive over and meet him at his hotel.

I hated driving into the heart of L.A., but of course the gallery showing Daltrey's work was just off of Santa Monica Boulevard and his hotel needed to be close. At least it gave me a great opportunity to take him to one of my favorite restaurants, a trendy little place in that same general area. I hadn't eaten there in a long time and thought he would enjoy it. Popping in my iPod, I played some Starset, wanting to use the dramatic power of the music to get to a better mindset on the drive over.

Traffic sucked, but I managed to get to his hotel early anyway. Daltrey texted me his room number and soon enough I stood in front of the door, hesitating to knock, knees trembling. "Now or never," I whispered to myself, searching for courage and really still not understanding why I was so afraid. Either the chemistry between us was still there or it wasn't. From our phone conversations, I was betting we still had it, but maybe that was why I was so nervous. If we still had something there, what the hell were we going to do with it?

Finally, my knuckles rapped on the door. It only took a second for him to open it and he was really there. I stared a moment into his super-dark blue eyes with their thick lashes and his pouty mouth and stark cheeks and jaw and I was back in high school again.

A smile spread across his face, showing white teeth. His back straight, he held himself proudly, as if he'd been waiting for that moment forever. I reached out for him without thinking and smiled as Daltrey stepped into my arms.

Holding him felt like home. I sighed and ran my fingers through his dark brown hair that he'd grown long enough to get a good handful of. When he pulled away from me, we looked at each other for a long slow minute. Daltrey was still long and lanky but he'd filled out nicely and his arms were thick muscles, hard round and cut, stretching out of his short sleeved polo. He had a splattering of freckles on his cheeks but not nearly as prominent as they'd been in high school.

I smiled, genuinely for the first time in a long time. "You look good."

"You too," he said softly, letting his gaze drift over me boldly, his smile turning smug as he checked me out. His voice was that same higher pitch I remembered that didn't come across quite as sexy over the phone as it did in person.

"I almost can't believe this," I said with awe. Life had a funny way of twisting things around. No matter what had happened before, right now I was standing in front of Daltrey Boxbaum, touching his arms, wanting to pull him to me again.

He blew his bangs out of his face. "Let's go eat!" He seemed eager to get going with his wide eyes. Maybe that would be a good thing. We turned to go and I tripped over my own feet. Daltrey grabbed me, holding me up, steadying me with a laugh. "Some things never change," he said with a giggle and an eye roll.

I laughed with him. Despite my embarrassment, I would go through any number of blushes to hear him giggle like that, sounding like joy and inspiration, easy and relaxing. I think it set us both at ease. "God, I'm still pretty klutzy."

Daltrey jutted his chin out. "I know, right!" His words weren't making fun of me, just lightening the mood and perhaps remembering our past. I'd always been that way, after all. Klutzy didn't begin to describe it accurately.

We managed to get to the restaurant without any more blunders and thankfully in one piece. The waiter showed us to a table and we ordered wine right off the bat and glanced at each other over the plastic covered menus.

"So, um, like what's good here?" he asked, casually. Those dark lashes fluttering, as his eyes bounced back and forth from the menu to me. He touched the top of his head and his eyes rolled up as if wondering what he looked like. His smile was still shy.

My mouth cracked into my own smile at his nervousness. "Everything, really. I've had almost everything at one time or another. My favorite is the salmon. You want an appetizer to start with?"

Daltrey had his lower lip sucked between his teeth when I glanced back to him. Our gazes caught again and heated up a new kind of fire in my gut, but this one led to my groin and I wanted nothing more than to stoke that fire by kissing those juicy lips.

He hummed and his foot tapped out a staccato under the table. "No. Um, let's just get to the meal." His gaze held a new heat I hadn't seen earlier, telling me he wanted to get somewhere private.

"I want to enjoy this," I said, trying to convey the need to wait. "All of it. So, get what you want. We have time for whatever we want." I arched an eyebrow, questioning whether he understood what I meant.

"All right." He put his menu down. "I know. Me too, but when you look at me like that." He closed his eyes and the tip of his tongue flashed across that plump bottom lip. His hands clutched at the menu.

A strange noise gurgled from the back of my throat, feeling very much like a growl. "I want you. I've always wanted you. That...I don't think that will ever change."

I couldn't help remembering those nights in my bedroom back home when he'd slept over. Holding him, touching him, every part of him. There wasn't one spot on his body that hadn't been touched by my hand and tongue. Going back to that type of relationship, especially after having him in my arms again and sitting at that table staring at him? Yes, I definitely wanted that again. I wanted more than that, maybe more than he could give me. "I've really fucking missed you in my life, Dal."

His smile was sweet, serene. "Let's get the goat-cheese flat bread and the salmon, and more wine. Okay?"

I ordered when the waiter came back around. We enjoyed our meal and talked of things past and what our lives had become. I told him about my potential project, feeling relieved to finally share that with him. "I'm excited. It should be great doing something different."

"Wow! That sounds awesome, Marty. So, um, what kind of program is it?" he asked with a bubbly excitement that danced under my skin and sent my heart racing better than any drug I could get from Wendy and her friends.

My shoulders lifted in a shrug. "I don't know. Most likely some add-on for a proprietary software some company has been using for the past ten years and they'd rather change it than upgrade or buy something altogether new. No one likes change and sometimes they do whatever they can to do as little of it as possible."

"Um, really, sounds like a short term fix that would only put things off." He rolled his eyes again, as if trying to add more drama or importance to his words. Why did I find that so adorable? I could have just ate him up in that moment. Daltrey's words were insightful, despite his sarcastic expressions, and I couldn't help think he was amazing.

"That's pretty much it, Dal."

Throughout our meal, I watched him eat little bites of salmon and wash it down with sips of wine. I'd ordered a Riesling to go with the Salmon, thinking Daltrey would appreciate a slightly sweeter choice, plus it would go well with the yogurt sauce. His Adam's apple bobbed as he swallowed, making me want to kiss and suck at his neck.

"What?" he asked, licking at his lips. Again. "Did I get some on me or something?" he asked with another jut of his chin.

"I'm enjoying you as much as the food."

He took another sip of wine. "Good. So, uh, let's get dessert, Marty." His words were decadent and teasing. I thought he was taking what I'd said earlier literally.

I would have bought him anything in that moment, even if it had meant using my dad's black card. "Fine, yes. Get what you want, Dal-baby," I said with other unspoken words lingering on my tongue.

We picked out a soufflé and ordered one with two spoons. Feeding each other bites instead of feeding ourselves, led to sparks flying between us, until Daltrey put his spoon down. "I'm about done with this. I mean, um, I don't assume or expect, and we've already..." He shrugged and rolled those dark eyes, using his entire face to make his point. "You said it earlier anyway, Marty. I want you."

I lifted my arm, signaling the waiter for our check.

##

I parked the car and we headed toward the hotel. Daltrey

stopped and looked around. "Damn. I can't believe how nice this is. Back home, we'd be wearing our jackets for sure right now."

"Is it cold there? In New York?"

"For real cold. This is nice, Marty. I forgot how nice it is out here. It's…been a long time since I've been here."

I took his hand and laced our fingers together. "Oh? You haven't been back since?"

"No." He stepped closer to me, still holding my hand. "I should have. It's…you know? It's difficult." He gulped as if trying to swallow down all the years since he had left.

"I know." I pulled him into my arms and held him tight. The way we left off the last time we'd seen each other hadn't given us any closure. We were in love and it just ended because of his parents. I still loved him and I knew it in my soul. "It's okay. No pressure. Let's just go up to your room. We can talk."

Daltrey led me up to his room. Inside it was a standard issue Holiday Inn with beige Berber carpeting with a cushy pile, a large window with gauzy curtains on the inside and thick blackout curtains that matched the bedspreads on the outside.

His room had two queen sized beds with black headboards mounted to the wall and generic art work hanging over each bed. It was odd that both pictures were identical. A black chest of drawers had a television sitting on top of it across from the beds and on the other side of it a black desk with an office chair waited. Daltrey had already set up his laptop there. He sat on the edge of the first bed and I stood there staring at him.

"If you don't kiss me soon, I'm going to go freakin' nuts," he huffed.

I didn't need any more encouragement. Rushing to his side, I pulled him close as I sat on the bed, wrapping my arms around him. He smelled like coconut and exotic fruits like papayas and kiwi. Our lips slid together with a gasp, but after the initial shock, it felt as if I'd never stopped kissing him. This was my Daltrey, finally back where he belonged in my arms.

He kissed me back and I felt the passion and need in

every swipe of his tongue. We undressed slowly, kissing and touching and reconnecting until Daltrey stood there in front of me in nothing but his sexy briefs. They were small, green shorts with a neon yellow waist band that had huge *2(X)ist* lettering across the front, so different than my plain black Emporio Armani cotton. I reached out and tucked my thumbs under that elastic band, slowly pulling them down his long thighs to expose that last piece of him I'd been waiting so long for. I wrapped my hand around his cock and his hands reached for my hips.

He looked and felt the same, his cock long and slim, pink fading to a more purple head. He pulled my briefs down below my knees and I kicked out of them leaving us standing naked and vulnerable together.

I pushed him back on the bed, leaning over him and bracing myself with my hands on the mattress on either side of his head. I stared down into his eyes, so dark I could barely tell the difference between the color and the black centers. I wasn't a big guy, and though he had filled out, grown up nicely, Daltrey was still smaller than me. I found I craved how that felt, his slight body beneath me. His heat trapped under mine sent a thrill through me. "Daltrey..." His name was a breath that I felt I'd been holding for five years.

"Marty. We know each other. We love each other. This is love, whatever the circumstances," he whispered as if he was afraid saying it louder would make it less true. "Let's just, like, leave it. Leave it there. Right? Just make this about love. We can figure the rest out later."

I nodded once, quick and sharp, then leaned forward and kissed him, putting all of that love that had been held back for years into it.

I pulled back to look at him again. I just needed to see his face. Needed to touch his skin, I slid my fingers down his ribs, watching goose bumps spring up where I'd touched him.

He shivered. "Um, there's lube. There." He pointed to the little side table. "In the drawer."

Leaning over, I opened the drawer to get a condom and

lube where it lay amidst the Gideon Bible, a long plastic card describing all the things to do on the strip, and a notebook outlining hotel policy and room service menu items. With a good squirt of the lube, I slid my greasy fingers down across his balls, along the silky flesh behind them and then circled around his hole.

His little moan shot right to my own balls, pulling them up tight and making my cock twitch. Wanting him was so different than any other sex. This was my Daltrey.

My fingertip slid around the edge of his hole, making him arch up. When I slid the tip in, he pushed against it and made that moaning noise again and his eyes rolled back in his head. I watched his face as I moved my finger in and pulled back.

Daltrey rocked his hips down against my hand. "More," he begged softly. His little noises had to be the most erotic thing I'd ever heard in my life. I couldn't remember him making them before, when we were young. Back then I'd been a lot more interested in how he was making me feel and chasing my own orgasms. Not that I'd been a greedy lover, just that we were both so young and inexperienced. We were each other's firsts. Five years later, I cared more about making it good for him; it felt like everything, those sexy noises slipping from his mouth. I almost didn't care whether I got off or not, except that I wanted him so frantically. I forced myself to take my time prepping him, though. How could I ever forgive myself if I hurt him?

I pumped and stretched my fingers, adding a second and a third until he was begging again. "Fuck me, baby. I need you now. Now!" His voice rose even higher than his natural pitch, whipping me into a frenzy.

The condom rolled over my dick and I squirted on another blob of lube, slowly stroking Daltrey's long, slim cock as I pushed mine against his hole. Daltrey breathed heavily and chanted, "Now, now..." with an urgent rock of his hips, and I couldn't hold back. I pushed in and rocked out, slowly going in farther and farther until I was fully inside him.

"Dal..." I leaned over him, pushing his legs up and staring

into his half-lidded eyes.

"I know, right?" he gasped, and then, "move...move now...Marty, please."

I didn't need any more encouragement as I started pumping into him, listening for his moans and groans and the emotions, lust and need, flashing across his radiant face, shiny and flushed. He looked elfish with precise features and overly-thick eye lashes. I could see the little sprinkle of freckles across his slim nose. I pushed forward and kissed his soft lips. He seemed so young, though I knew he was my own age.

He reached between us, grabbing his cock and started stroking, making me want something different. I pulled out and watched his eyes fly open. Before he could question me, I pushed him over on his knees. "Hands on the headboard," I ordered and he obeyed without protest. I slid back inside him from behind and pulled him back on me until he was squatting and half sitting down on my cock. I could easily grab him and stroke him with every thrust of my hips, and he met me with a downward lunge with every up stroke.

He started making a high pitched hum that seemed to come from deep in his throat. The rhythm picked up with both of us grunting in time and little hisses accentuating the beat.

Touching him felt the same as I remembered. His hot skin beneath my palms, under my tongue, felt the same as it ever had. His cock, always thinner but longer than my own, seemed like an old friend in my grasp. Until those moments, making love to him, thrusting into his tight hole, grasping his hip as I pulled him to me, I had forgotten how much I needed him. Daltrey had always given himself to me, completely, freely and I never fully appreciated it, never appreciated it enough.

"Now, God, Martin!" he screamed out, his voice several octaves higher and his cum shooting over my fingers.

"Agh! Dal!" I called out, as he squeezed down on my cock while he came, sending me over the edge with him. "You feel like home, Dal-baby." Reluctantly, I pulled out, removing the condom. It ended up on the floor beside the bed and Daltrey ended up on his side, in my arms where he belonged. I snuggled into his hair, loving the tropical scent. I didn't remember that smell or how perfect he felt in my arms, or the strange feeling in my chest that made me want to protect him from the outside world. I kissed and nuzzled the back of his neck and marveled in the salty sweat teasing my tongue. "I love you, Dal-baby."

"I love you too," he answered, as I stroked my fingers through his short hair. "I always have, Marty. Never stopped." He sounded sleepy and possibly even more adorable than before. I kissed down his neck to the curve of his shoulder, licking the spot where they met. This was the same spot where the brain meets the heart. That spot was where I wanted to be with him: always in his heart and in his mind.

##

Wet-hot sensation pulled at me and I opened my eyes. For a moment I didn't know where I was, except maybe heaven. I looked down to see Daltrey bringing my cock to life with his mouth and tongue. "Mmm...Dal..." I sighed.

He pulled up and looked at me. "You taste like condom," he laughed and rolled his eyes. I had to chuckle with him, as I pulled him up to me. I loved the sound of his laugh. Hell, I loved everything about him. He may have been smaller than me but his personality was bigger than life, as it always had been. That infectious energy breathed a new life in me, as if something in me had been dead these past five years and with Daltrey in my arms again, it had finally come alive.

He stretched out beside me, and we faced each other, hard cocks rubbing together in their own erotic dance. Daltrey grabbed the lube off the side table where I'd left it and soon his sticky-lubed hand slid over our cocks. My hand joined his in grasping our dicks, providing more friction and we fucked into our combined hands together until we both came hard against each other just like we used to do when we were teenagers. It was a glorious release.

"Let's totally get room service," Daltrey said with a sigh,

laying back against the mattress.

##

We snuggled in bed until room service knocked on the door with our food. Daltrey jumped up and slipped into a pair of sweatpants to open the door. The food smelled great, making my stomach growl and we both tore into the omelets we'd ordered.

"Mmm...fucking cheesy," Daltrey moaned around a huge bite. I even found him talking with his mouth full sexy as hell.

"I live off freezer food and take out. This is a real treat for sure."

Daltrey rolled his eyes. "I know, right! Sometimes Mom will bring something better over, but, like McDonald's is on my freakin' payroll."

I chuckled a little at that. I wanted to ask him about his mom, but I needed to keep things light between us. "My neighbors cook sometimes."

"That Alec guy?" he asked, shoveling in another forkful of eggs. "The Randall kid?"

"Uh, yep. His girlfriend, Wendy, cooks. I mentioned them, right?"

"Yeah, sure, said you hang with them, upstairs. They like to party."

I reached over and pushed stray hair out of his eyes, needing to see their deep blue depths. He remembered everything I said and that made something strange clutch at my heart. I wanted him more now than ever.

The atmosphere felt heavier; so much for keeping it light. I knew he felt it too when he popped out of his chair and dashed to his laptop. "Let's listen to some tunes," he said breathlessly.

Electronic noise came out of his speakers. "What's that?"

"Uh...Kasabian..." he answered, as if everyone should know that. Club music.

I groaned, "Tell me you don't listen to this...stuff."

"Of course! You can dance to it. Better than the shit you listen to. Like, I bet you still play that gothic metal shit. Right?"

"I like other stuff. Theory of A Deadman, Stone Sour, Manchester Orchestra, you know?"

"This is better," he said and tucked his chin in, giving me a sexy look. Then he started dancing. He moved his hips to the beat, twirled around and dropped down, bending his knees, touching the floor and shaking his ass as he rose up again. His arms worked like choreographed moves, making him look serious and way too sexy. He pointed at me and laughed. "Respect the music."

"You know what I respect? My cock. Up that tight ass." I grabbed him, pushing him down on the bed and yanking those low slung sweat pants off his ass. My lips traveled across his skin, finding that spot where his neck met his chest. "God, I want you."

Daltrey laughed again and in that moment, I would do absolutely anything to hear that sweet bell-like sound every day of my life.

The music changed, more electronic noise, but the words were all about clubbing and touching and giving someone what they needed. It felt oddly appropriate. "I could get used to this," I said, touching him, letting my hands wander down his legs across his ass.

"Yes... Marty, fuck, touch me," Daltrey huffed, panting. His hands slid down my back. "Now. I want you inside me now."

The lube bottle lay on its side on the nightstand where we'd left it. I grabbed it and shook it, dropping a blob in my hand and wiggling my fingers through it. It took only seconds for two of my fingers to find their way to his hole.

Daltrey moved with the music, pushing himself against my hand, fucking my fingers, and making me want him desperately. He had to be the sexiest thing I had ever seen in my life. This beat all the memories of our time together as teens, hands down. And there had been many nights spent with him in my bed back then. My mother had been too drunk to notice what we were up to. If she suspected anything, she'd never voiced it to me. Still, this was better. I didn't have to think about parents or rules or anything—just Daltrey.

"Baby..." he purred out, and I knew what he wanted. I wanted it to.

"I've got you, Dal," I said, pushing against the back of his thighs to spread his legs more. After rolling down a condom, I leaned over him and pushed the head of my cock against that tight ring of muscle. I wanted to see him come apart. I lost myself in his eyes as I pushed in. His face looked ecstatic, eyes half-lidded and his tongue sneaking out to lick his sexy lips.

He pushed his bangs back with one hand and smiled shyly. "I want to see you, too." No one got me like he did.

I kissed him and he opened his mouth for me. His tongue darted in, sliding against mine. He tasted like cheesy eggs and coffee. It was something else I could get used to.

Pulling away from the kiss, I looked down at him, as he closed his eyes. "Open your eyes, Dal-baby."

Slowly, his dark eyes stared up at me, begging for more. His mouth was open, slightly. "Shut up and fuck me," he groaned.

I couldn't help chuckle at that, making Daltrey's smile spread across his face, lighting up his features as sure as if I'd held a spotlight on him. "You got it, Dal-baby."

I started pumping my hips, taking small strokes and pumping farther in with each one. Daltrey started making those sexy, high pitched moans, and I thought I was going to lose it right there. I needed to slow down, make it good for both of us.

"Faster, more!" Daltrey groaned out, making slow and easy impossible.

I thrust my hips, changing angles until I saw his expression change from turned on to total ecstasy. Knowing I'd finally scraped over his prostate, I kept that angle and pounded against it, harder and faster in time with his cries.

I could see he was on the edge when he looked up at me with begging eyes. My hand slid over his cock, tightening around him, he called out my name as he came, spurting all over his chest and my hand. I followed right behind him, surprised that he actually got there first, but totally happy that he had.

The condom ended up on the floor where the first one had and I snuggled into the bed, not caring about the rest of the mess. Daltrey pulled the blanket over us and we entwined ourselves, arms and legs tangling together. The electronic pulses of the music no longer fit the mood, as we were sated and loving. "I should turn the music off," he said softly.

"No. Don't. Don't move. I don't care about the music." I pulled him closer and held him tighter. Daltrey snuggled against my chest. His hands slid down my back to cup one ass cheek. I couldn't get enough of how his skin rubbed against mine, chest to chest, and the friction of the hair on our legs as they danced together. My arms around him wished for an eternity there. I buried my nose in his hair, against his neck. Perfection.

After a few minutes, he asked me to go to his show, as if I wouldn't. "I can get extra tickets, too. You can bring the Randall kid and his girlfriend."

"No, uh, that's okay. I'll be there, but..." I let my words hang in the air. How could I tell him that I didn't want those two worlds colliding? Alec and Wendy needed to stay in their own hemisphere, far away where they could never taint what I had with Daltrey.

"That's okay," he said, his voice sad. He rolled away from me.

"Daltrey?" I asked, grabbing for him. I needed to pull him close again. We needed to be touching. "What's wrong?"

"You don't want me to meet your friends. I..." He put his hands over his face.

I thought I was going to lose it, seeing him like that, and this time not in a good way. I grabbed his shoulders and yanked him back against me. "No. I don't. They aren't good enough for you." I breathed the words into his ear and against the skin of his neck.

"Marty?"

"I mean it. They aren't. I want you to myself. They just don't matter."

"How can you say that? I mean, like, how can they not be great? He got my number for you. Um, I'm so grateful. You know?"

I bit back a growl. There was no way he was going to understand my relationship with them. "Dal-baby. I'm grateful too, but they aren't important right now. You? You're everything. Don't you know that?" I couldn't explain myself and everything was going to come out wrong. "I love you, but I'm scared and I don't really know what I'm doing. I just know I want you. However much I can get. And, and I don't want them, my friends, interfering with that or invading what little time we have together."

Daltrey pushed up and leaned over me, staring down into my eyes. "It's okay. I don't have any answers right now either." He blew out a long breath. "Just come to my show, okay?"

I nodded. "Of course." I pulled him back down on me and we lay there quietly as the sun peeked in between the curtains and made its way across the floor. The music still blared out its urgent up-beat message, urging everyone to dance with their hands in the air. I'd been transported to a different world and I knew I was becoming a different person with the heat of Daltrey's body pushed against me. This man just did it for me in every way.

Eventually, the sticky got to me and my body begged to move. Daltrey's breathing was deep and steady and I didn't want to wake him, but I had to get up. I carefully slid out from under his arm and made my way to the bathroom, shutting the door behind me.

The tiled room was cool after the heat of the bed, and large for a hotel bathroom. The counter, sink and mirror were in the enclosed room with the toilet and shower. I decided I needed to use both.

After a quick piss, I turned to the sink and looked into the mirror. The bright florescent light lit my image. I was amazed at what I saw in my reflection. Happy. I was happy for the first time since... I couldn't even remember ever being this happy, even back in those teen years when I'd had him with me every day. Suddenly, I didn't recognize my own face. Someone else with eyes that had seen too much peered back out at me from the mirror, making me shutter.

I grabbed a quick shower and made my way back to the main room. Daltrey was sitting up with his legs crossed, Indian-style in bed with the sheets wrapped around his knees and a sketchbook on top of them. His hand and fingers working furiously at the image he worked on. "Can I see?" I hadn't seen his artwork, aside from what was posted on line, in ages.

A blush crept over his face and he pulled the book to his chest. "It's not done."

"Please?"

He looked down at what he'd drawn, considering the image and whether he wanted to share it. Finally, he gave a curt nod and extended it out to me.

The graphite pencil markings were crude through most of the figure, but he'd started adding detail to the face—my face. He used to draw me all the time and it had never bothered me. This? It was new in a bizarre way. Maybe it had been too long since we'd had this, but it felt like I was a different person and the drawing wasn't of me at all.

"You don't like it? I, um, like, I told you it wasn't done." He pulled at the hair that had been sliding over his eyes.

"I like it. I just haven't... It feels odd."

"Been a long time? I never stopped drawing you." He looked down and that blush rushed across his cheeks again. "Never stopped loving you." He spoke so softly, I almost hadn't heard his words.

I set the pad down and crawled across the bed, wrapping my arms around him. "Daltrey. I've never stopped loving you either. Not for a second." The electricity between us burst forward. Our lips smashed against each other's, kicking that need up even higher. "I could do this forever," I spoke into his open mouth and followed the words with my tongue.

Chapter 15 - Faces

All the way home, the sun was blasting into my eyes and warming my face. Despite my dark shades, I still had to squint a bit as I drove north through the traffic, but it didn't irritate me like it normally did. Something about today's warmth was pleasing, uplifting. My soul felt freer.

I walked into the building and up the stairs, ready to jump in the shower and get cleaned up before meeting Daltrey for his show. I was looking forward to seeing his work and him. His legs and arms were more muscular and well defined than before, though still not bulky. I couldn't stop thinking about him and his hot ass that curved into his slim waist. I didn't know if it was so much that Daltrey was my type, or that because it was Daltrey I liked everything about him. I caught myself licking my lips as I stepped out of the stairwell at my floor.

"Hey! Martin, hey!" Wendy called, just before the door shut behind me. Against my better judgment, I turned and opened it back up, letting Wendy step out behind me. "Hey. Didn't expect to see you. Aren't you supposed to be with the art-dude this weekend? Hm? The high school sweetie?" she asked with a roll of her eyes. Her eye rolls were nasty and sarcastic, nothing like Daltrey's fun, playful ones. I didn't like Wendy's at all. All the lighthearted feel-goods I'd had left-over from my time with Daltrey disappeared faced with her negativity.

"I'm getting ready to go back. His art show is tonight, so I need to look nice."

"Ohmygod! Let me help you." Her tone completely changed in just that instant and she sounded eager to be supportive of me for once. It reminded me of the first day we met when she'd helped me unpack the kitchen. I figured there was a niceness there somewhere underneath all her selfish jealousy. I didn't think I'd ever get used to her mood swings, though, and wondered how Alec dealt with it.

She followed me down the dark hall and I let her into my apartment. "Sure, I guess. I'm not sure what I'm going to wear or anything."

"M'kay. Get in the shower and I'll pick out some clothes. Then I'll do your hair. It needs a little help."

I didn't pay much attention to her planning, lured into submission by the thought of a hot shower. I jumped in and let the hot water wash over me, trying not to think about Daltrey. The last thing I was going to do was jack off while Wendy was in my room, going through my things. I could almost feel my soul twisting and writhing at the thought of Wendy being in my home.

She was still flipping through my shirts when I stepped into the room with a towel tied around my waist. She had dark jeans and a pair of dark blue Hugo Boss briefs, the bikini cut, tossed on the bed. They were one of my favorite pairs with the label name printed in white across the black band. My dad had turned me into a clothes whore.

"Fuck! I love your closet, Martin," Wendy teased, playfully, then turned to look over her shoulder at me. "Hey, I've seen you naked. Don't sweat it, man." A corner of her lip turned up in a sneer.

She had seen me naked a few times, but that was completely different and mostly dark. In my well lit bedroom with Alec nowhere around, I didn't like her seeing me naked one tiny bit. I felt my poor dick shriveling up at the thought as if my shower had been a cold one. It was finally my turn to do the eye-roll thing. "So?"

I grabbed the underwear, sliding them up my legs under the towel. My jeans came next and only then did I toss the towel on the floor.

Wendy snorted. "Come on. I got ideas for your hair. How much time you got?"

"Enough."

I followed her into the kitchen. She dragged a chair around the counter to the center of the floor. "Sit here. I'll be back. I gotta get my stuff."

It didn't take bravery to let Wendy do my hair. The other guys around our group that let her cut their hair all looked hot, hotter than me with my dark blond, overgrown Ken doll style.

She didn't knock, just thundered back in like she always did, and started attacking my hair with comb and scissors. I didn't move, afraid she'd fuck it up if I did.

"Okay," she said brushing the clippings off my shoulders. "I didn't cut much, just styled. Wait till you see. Here, first..." She grabbed a long skinny bottle she'd brought with her and sprayed mouse in her palm. I never used that stuff, just gel. She rubbed it between her hands and then grabbed at my hair with it, pulling, yanking and shaking it around. "Come on. Go look." She shoved me toward the bathroom.

Some hot stranger gazed at me from my mirror. The lighter sun-kissed tones of my hair were gone, clipped off, leaving rich darker blond locks that were styled in a messy wave. I looked younger, more decadent.

"Okay. Get your shirt on now. I'm not done with you."

I didn't have a lot of casual clothes. Most of what I'd worn in college had been destroyed or thrown out, but I had a few things left and Wendy managed to find one of my favorites. The T-shirt was a very dark navy, almost black, reminding me of Daltrey's eyes. The top part of the shirt was solid across the chest, but the rest was a strange almost stripped, slightly diagonal pattern of that same dark navy and gray. I didn't remember who the designer was, it'd been so long since I'd worn it.

"That's gonna look great under this." Wendy shoved my Armani suit jacket at me. "Wear those Converse high tops with it."

I nodded.

"First, come here. Sit." She shoved me down on the end of the bed. "Look up."

I tilted my head up and she put her hands on my face, pulling at my eyes and then drawing on them with a pencil. "Don't blink."

"What the fuck?"

"This is gonna look so fucking hot!" She finished and shoved at me again. "Go look."

One more trip to the mirror and this time, it really was something surreal: a stranger wearing my face, so not me. The hair, the eyes popping out so blue like a cloudless sky, made my features more striking. It was so much easier to see my mother's features echoed in my own like this. My cheek bones were delicate, lips full, but my jaw was strong. The eyeliner was light, natural. It didn't look bad at all.

Wendy had made me look good for Daltrey. I hadn't expected that. Maybe her friendship was worth more than I'd thought, if she actually cared how my date went.

"You could probably use some mascara, too. But this passes," she said, leaning against the door jamb. Her little smile seemed sincere.

"Uh, thanks. I look good?" I wondered why she was being this nice when she had been so nasty about it before. Maybe she just liked fucking with my hair. Or my head. I wanted to trust her, though.

She smiled, one of the rare ones that I hadn't seen in a while. "You really are pretty hot, Martin." She hugged me and pushed me toward the door. "Get out of here and go see your man."

I hoped he'd like the change as well.

##

The area surrounding the gallery was packed and I had to park about a block away on a side street and walk over. It was amazing to see so many people there wanting to see Daltrey's art. I knew he was talented, but to see others taking such an enthusiastic interest warmed my heart. He deserved the attention.

The gallery was just off the main drag through town, a few blocks away from the hotel where Daltrey was staying. The front of the building was a wall of glass with greenery growing up around and between the panes, making the facade look like something I would expect to see in Paris. Not that I'd ever been to Paris.

Daltrey found me quickly, running over and bouncing up and down. "Martin! Ohmygod! You look...ah, fabulous. This is unreal. I'm so excited." I expected him to start clapping his hands, but he tucked this fingers into the back of his tight blue jeans. The dark red golf shirt he wore complimented his dark hair and eyes. He wore a black fedora hat and a pair of strange looking shoes, some kind of brown and tan oxfords. The look was casual but somehow stylish and certainly worked for him.

"You look good, too. This place is packed."

He jumped into my arms then, literally. His feet even came off the ground for a second as I hugged him, holding him up. "Yes! I can't believe it." He actually squealed.

I held him tight and kissed his lips quickly when he turned his head up to me.

"Damn, Marty. Your friend's mother had a lot to do with this and, um..." He rolled his eyes and his smile lit up the room brighter than the huge chandelier hanging over our heads. "Like, the LGBT community spread the word, too."

"You deserve it." I kissed his cheek, rubbing my thumb over the other one before finally releasing him, but he didn't move away. Instead, he grabbed my hand and bounced up and down in place.

"Marty! I have to show you...like everything." His voice was breathy and excited and I felt my own excitement build seeing him that way.

He pulled me through the gallery floor, beneath the chandelier. I tilted my head to view the magnificent structure as we passed. The light reflecting through the crystal shined magnificently, sending light throughout the main floor. Daltrey pulled me to a set of stairs on the far side that turned almost ninety degrees before hitting the second floor mezzanine that overlooked the ground floor and gave me an even better view of the chandelier. It dripped toward the second floor like sculpted ice, catching reflections of the room in each crystal shard. Although it had caught my attention, I wasn't there to gawk at the lighting.

Daltrey pulled me through a crowd of people into a hallway with canvases of varying sizes hanging on the walls. I could see at the far end, the hall opened into a larger room that had been sectioned off and had even more art. Daltrey stopped short, pointing to one of the first paintings. "I like this one," he said. "I was inspired by a simple walk through Central Park. See the light streaming through the leaves?"

The piece was layered with greens and yellows and sparks of gold and silver, inviting me to reach out and touch it to feel the texture, rough in some places and smooth as ice in others. "I like it."

Daltrey giggled and pulled me away, leading me farther into the hall. "Oh! These!" He pointed out a series of framed sketches of body parts: arms, legs, eyes, noses, and belly buttons. The parts were aligned in different ways in each sketch, but all resembled each other. "A friend of mine modeled for these. She was very patient."

He yanked me farther down the hall and then across to the opposite wall. "And I want to show you this one. I want to show you all of it." He was bouncing again, the backs of his heels going up and down. I couldn't help but smile.

Then I looked at the canvas on the wall. "How big is this?" It seemed to encompass the entire wall. I had to step back to take it all in.

"Thirty-six, forty-eight. Is that all you have to ask?" The corners of his mouth turned down in disappointment, even that was adorable.

"No." I looked again at the art.

The painting was of me.

"My God! Daltrey!" I knew my mouth was hanging open, but I couldn't seem to care. The painting was incredible. It wasn't me as a teenager, really. It seemed more recent, but when had he ever had time to paint it? The dark and light colors entwined together in an almost abstract way. I had to focus to see the face, the blond hair falling over blue eyes. It couldn't be anyone else but me. In fact, it reminded me of my profile picture from Facebook. "How did you do this?"

"Like it?" His eyes begged me to say yes.

"My God! I love it. But...when?"

Daltrey's bell-like laughter echoed through the hall, over the heads of the other people crowded in the room. "That weekend. You know? When we didn't talk for a few days, remember?" He rolled his eyes again in that happy way that made me want to kiss his entire face. He'd painted me before, and I knew he'd spent many hours sketching me, but this was unlike any of that. The painting was in another league altogether. It was warmth and passion and hope.

"I love it, Dal-baby," I whispered, pulling him close to me and nuzzling his ear, making him giggle.

Around us, the crowds started noticing us, noticing me. I overheard comments of "that's him" and "just like the painting" and "how romantic." The last floored me. Romantic? But, it was. Daltrey painting and displaying me and his feelings for me in such a public way was the most romantic thing...ever.

"No one has ever..." I said, staring at him, as if he were the art and not the artist. To me he was.

He shoved my shoulder. "Come on. There's more."

There were several other paintings of me in various sizes and modes and even a series of sketches, but none of them were as fabulous as the first and he had so much other work that was better where I wasn't the subject. He led me through it all, explaining his inspiration and what he'd been thinking. I loved his excitement and happiness at sharing it with me.

Then I stopped short in front of his center piece. It was probably three times larger than that first painting of me. It was beautiful. It was sunshine and laughter.

"It's called, *Sunsplatter*," he explained. "See?" He pointed to various parts of the canvas. Streaks of gold, yellow, white, silver in varying shades danced together across the entire canvas. On top of it all tiny metallic splotches were scattered, almost like someone splashed a mirror with a toothbrush. The effect was amazing. "I saw the light coming in my window and splattering across my wall. It's brick. Um, the wall in my loft. Anyway, I liked it, but I didn't want the wall. Just the light."

"I get it. I love it. I'm buying this."

Daltrey gasped. "What? Um, no. It's really..."

I pulled him close to me again. "I have to have it." My nose found that spot on his neck that it always seemed to go to.

"Where would you put it?" he asked, shoving me away.

"My folks have a huge cabin out in Colorado. This would be perfect there, actually. My folks will love it, too."

He stared down at his feet. "Um, I don't know."

"Don't know what? Daltrey, I mean it. It's spectacular and if I don't buy it, it'll go to some stuffy museum and I'll never get to see it. I want it and I'm getting it."

His face flushed, making me want to take him right there in the gallery in front of everyone.

Daltrey grabbed my arm and pulled me through the gallery, his head scanning the crowds as we walked back to the center, parting the crowd along the way. "There," he called out pointing to someone across the way. "Mrs. Randall," he called again, as we closed in on a tall, slim woman with elegant golden brown hair piled on her head in some intricate style.

She turned around and I could immediately see Alec in her face. He took after her greatly with the soft brown eyes and the same long sleek nose. Her cheeks, chin, and jaw were softer, rounder, but similarly shaped. If she had many wrinkles around her eyes, she hid them well under her perfect make-up. "Daltrey, dear." The love of drama dripped from every drawn out syllable. "Everything is going so well. You've made such an impression tonight. We'll need you to do some autographs in a bit."

"Yes, of course. Uh, this is my friend, Martin."

The woman immediately scanned me, head to toe, but her judgment had already been made. "Alec's friend?" she asked with one manicured eyebrow lifted slightly.

I could see Daltrey watching us. He couldn't help but notice the strange energy flowing between us and I couldn't help wonder exactly what Alec had told her about me. "Yes, it was very nice of you to help me out with Daltrey's number. I hadn't seen him in years." The polished charm of my upbringing came out of my mouth like a river bursting from a dam. "Thank you, Mrs. Randall."

That eyebrow stayed cocked and was joined by a smirk. "Well. Alec's friends aren't normally—How do you know him?"

"I live downstairs from him." I wanted to deny my friendship with him, as she didn't seem to think highly of her son and his acquaintances.

Daltrey cleared his throat. "You know, this is Martin Hannan. As in the son of Steven Hannan. You know? THE Steven Hannan." My savior raised his own eyebrow at her. "He's a hot-shot programmer at Apex. He's buying *Sunsplatter*."

Her painted red lips made a big "O" before that eyebrow dropped like a penny in a fountain. I knew she saw dollar signs. My father's name was no joke, especially in L.A. Normally, I hated being associated with it, but I knew it bought me something with this woman and I'd allow that for Daltrey. Putting me in a better light with him was fine by me.

It was Daltrey's description of me as some hot-shot that had me stunned, though. I had never thought of myself that way. My job didn't ever define me, though my father and his reputation often did. The latter was a legacy I could never live up to and the former a way to pay the bills and make my father proud. I had the job because I was always trying to live up to that legacy whether I thought I would ever succeed or not.

To hear Daltrey come out and toot my horn for me flipped the equation on me. I wasn't merely a product of good genes, but had something to offer the world. My boss had recently given me a new assignment. Surely, that was based on something besides Steven Hannan. More importantly, Daltrey saw that in me. I think my chest puffed out at the thought.

"Well...let me introduce you to Vickie, darling. She can help you arrange the purchase." Suddenly, I was a darling and not Alec's scum-buddy. Interesting.

I let her lead me away. Daltrey waived. "I'll be downstairs, signing autographs. 'Kay?"

"Sure, I'll catch up to you in a few minutes," I answered, following after Alec's mother, and looking back at him as he shifted his weight from foot to foot.

Alec's mom stopped near a door in the very back of the second floor display. She turned to me and lifted that eyebrow again. "You have me wondering just how well you know my son, Mr. Hannan."

"Not very. You know? They're always throwing parties and passing me in the stairwell." I shrugged my shoulders, hoping the movement would shrug off my association with Alec and Wendy as well because this woman made me feel low that I even knew them, let alone hung out with them. I could only assume she knew nothing of what her son got up to in the bedroom.

"Well...*Sunsplatter* is very expensive." Her face was frozen like an elegant ice sculpture. Her eyes held a dare.

I had no choice. I let the smirk slip over my lips as I pulled out my wallet. I held out the black card and watched her eyes go wide. She knew damn well what that little metal card was. "I got it, Mrs. Randall," I said.

With a curt nod, she opened the door and called for Vicki, the girl in charge of purchases. "It's Rosalyn, darling." I couldn't help feel victorious, even if my dad was going to kill me for buying the painting. I just didn't care. It would help Daltrey and I loved that painting instantly. Almost as much as I loved him.

##

I found my way to the autograph table where Daltrey was finishing up his social interaction time with his fans. I was still impressed with just how many people came to see him and his art. I hoped I wasn't the only one to make a purchase, but I had probably made the biggest single purchase.

I stood behind him, rubbing my palms down his shoulders. "Done yet?"

"Just a second," he sighed as he finished the last signature, smiling and thanking the guy. "I gotta get out of here and get these fucking shoes off."

I smiled and grabbed his hand, pulling him toward the exit. Outside I pushed him to sit on a brick retaining wall that ran along the side of the building and grabbed a foot. I untied his shoes and pulled them off. "Come on." We started walking toward my car. He hopped around a little and wiggled his toes.

"Damn you're cute," I told him, surprised the words had actually escaped.

Daltrey crinkled his nose and narrowed his eyes at me. "You think? Whatever. My fucking feet hurt." He was even cute when he was cussing mad. I kind of liked him dropping the f-bomb.

"Fuck! I'm in trouble." I grabbed him around his waist and lifted him off his feet, enjoying how he squealed and giggled. When I put him back down, I slung an arm around his shoulders and carried his shoes out to my car.

With Daltrey situated next to me, shoes in lap, I cranked my car up and the music immediately blared out of the speakers. Daltrey rolled his eyes with a sly smile and leaned over and turned the stereo off. "You always listen to that crap?"

"What?" The music was Marilyn Manson, so not the

worst thing I listened too. "It's good," I protested, which only gained me another eye roll. I chuckled, loving every minute of him, and quietly pulled out of the parking spot.

"Listen, Marty," Daltrey broke the pleasant silence we'd found. "I want to, like, you know, talk to you." He rolled his hand over.

"Sure, babe. What about?" My voice sounded so hopeful, yet my gut started immediately filling with acid, making me wonder if I had any antacids in the car, maybe in the glove compartment. It'd been a while since I needed them, but the tone of his voice when he said he wanted to talk made me want to throw up. I didn't think I wanted to hear what was coming.

"Okay. Don't, like, get mad. It's, um, just that, uh, Rosalyn, Mrs. Randall. She talks, like a lot." He added one of his famous, at least to me, eye rolls. "Talks about her kids too. Alec and his little sister."

"So?" I had some idea where he was going with the conversation and wanted it done, like ripping off the Band-Aid with one quick pull. It was going to sting, but then it could be over.

Daltrey sucked in a long breath. "She doesn't have very good things to say about him. Um, says he's troubled and a trouble maker and into, uh, things..."

"He has a girlfriend, and I'm not interested—"

"Calls the girlfriend a whore," he spit out interrupting me.

"Lots of mothers don't like their children's partners."

I pulled up to the hotel parking lot in silence and not knowing if the conversation was over, but hoping it was.

"Marty, it's just, you know, I'm concerned. Worried?" Why was that last bit a question? He was allowed to worry about me. He got out of the car and stood there holding his shoes until I came around. He looked up at me with those deep blue eyes sparkling in the crappy orange parking lot light.

"Maybe I could meet them." He licked his lips. "I need to know you're okay," he said so softly that I wasn't sure at first he'd said it. His head dropped, looking down at his socked feet.

"Dal-baby, I'm fine. Like I told her. We don't know each other well. They live in my building and they're nice. Mostly." I gave him half a shrug and half a smile. My words were true, mostly. "Well, they're kind of assholes, too. No one close enough to me that you'd need to meet them." There was no way I was going to taint Daltrey with Wendy and Alec, especially after that conversation.

"Okay. Um, let's go upstairs. Fucking feet." He hopped around the pebbles of the parking lot bothering his feet.

My stomach churned a little at the emotions rolling through me. I wondered how deep I could possibly love someone when I hated myself so much. Even though I had a new promising assignment, mostly I hated my boring job. I hated my friends, and even my family, but him? Daltrey? Him, I loved immensely.

In his room, I pushed him down on the bed and started working open his pants, my hard cock thinking talk-time was over, but I was wrong. "Marty. I don't want you stay over."

"What?" My dick deflated a little with the rejection. "You don't...want me?" I sucked my bottom lip between my teeth and bit down hard. No way was I going to cry, but I felt the burn in the back of my throat.

"No. Yes. I meant. Uh!" He threw his hands across his face. "I want you desperately. Always. It's just, like, um, I have to get up, like early. Early-early. To get to the airport and it's going to be hard. If you're here, it's going to be impossible."

"Right, so fucking hard," I said under my breath, meaning two different things at the same time. I palmed my cock, adjusting it to a better position as it came to life at the sight of the strip of skin he'd exposed where his shirt had ridden up.

"You know what I mean, Marty?"

I sighed. "I do, but I want you and I don't want to just, you know, leave you after."

"I know." His stare froze me in place. He didn't want to have sex again. He wanted me gone.

"Daltrey...don't do this. Please," I begged him. I wasn't above begging. "Does this have to do with what that woman said?"

Daltrey sat up, I could see the tears in his eyes in the low lighting. His pain punched me in the gut. I really needed an antacid and thought seriously about asking him if he had any, but his face was so sad, I couldn't say anything.

I rushed to him, kneeling on the floor and pulling him into my arms. "I don't want you to hurt, Dal-baby."

"There's not anything you can do." He ran his hands through my hair, destroying all the mousse Wendy had used. I pressed my face into his stomach with one cheek resting on his upper thigh and my arms wrapped tight around his waist. "I just want, like, I mean, I don't want, you know, this is just so fucking difficult. It's nothing to do with her. So, fucking hard, Marty. I can't even say it. I don't want to make it worse, but I just... I've been thinking and I don't think I can do this-this long distance thing. No tough good-byes. We'll talk and text, you know. It's going to be okay."

It was never going to be okay whether his lie was for me or for himself. None of that mattered. I knew the truth was that I wasn't enough for him and he deserved so much more. I couldn't ask him to wait for me and I wasn't ready to change anything in my life—didn't know how. I wanted to change, though. I wanted to give Daltrey what he needed, but didn't think I'd ever be able to live up to it. "It's all hard. All of it," I mumbled into the muscles of his stomach.

"Ahh...Marty. You make me want to stay here in L.A., but I can't. I have to go back to New York. More of you is just going to break my heart."

He pet me for a while and I never ever, ever wanted to move, but I had to. It was getting late and this was getting us nowhere. Reluctantly, I stood up and wiped my face. I hadn't even realized the tears had fallen, but he would know, they were all over his thigh and his stomach where my cum should have been instead. "Let me know when you get home. I worry too."

Daltrey nodded, looking very much like he couldn't possibly find his voice in a throat that barely held back a sob.

Since I felt the same way, I turned away from him, hoping he wouldn't cry too much after I left. By the time I got to my car, devastation flowed over me and sat on my chest and strangled my throat with hands like claws.

I glanced at my reflection in the rearview mirror as I got in the vehicle, expecting to see an actual monster attacking me, but it was just me. Although, I didn't think my image truly looked how I felt it should. The incongruence of vision and emotion left a wavering feeling in my chest, surreal and warped. Inside my heart, I was so different, but my reflection hadn't changed a bit. My eyes looked a little more haunted, maybe. It didn't seem fair that they were so blue, yet so lifeless. Daltrey stripped any happiness from them when he sent me away, but I couldn't blame him. I wouldn't want me either. I felt so guilty and there was nothing I could say to him. It didn't matter what Rosalyn Randall said to him. How could I argue? Most of her insinuations were probably true.

I wondered if he thought I'd tried to buy him with that damn painting. I just wanted it. That was a lie; I needed it like I needed my heart to beat in my chest. *Sunsplatter* represented something to me, our love in its purest form. It wasn't just a painting; it was Daltrey. The truth? I didn't want anyone else to see it. Maybe that was selfish, but I certainly wasn't trying to buy him. I fought back the urge to call or text to tell him just that, but I was being stupid and didn't really think Daltrey had thought that for a minute. He knew me and knew how I felt about him. The painting didn't matter to either of us. My doubts were just my own insecurity.

Pushing back my sobs and yanking on my pride, I stabbed my keys into the ignition and cranked up the car. I had to get the hell out of there before I did something really foolish like marching my stupid ass back up to his hotel room and banging on his door. Instead, I headed for the pharmacy on the corner and picked up antacids. I emptied nearly half the pack before I pulled into my apartment complex, eating them as if they'd ease the pain in my heart as well as my stomach.

Home at last, and yet I felt a million miles away from

home. My body and soul knew that Daltrey was home, not this cold, empty apartment. I missed him terribly, like a physical ache, as if someone had ripped something vital from my body. How was I going to live like that? With that frozen hole inside me?

I searched my kitchen for a bottle of Jack, I could have sworn I'd stashed there. Most likely, I'd already drank it all. I could go get more or go upstairs and see what chemicals Wendy and Alec could spare for me to numb the pain.

Falling back on my bed, I pulled my pillow over my head. How had my life become so gray and stormy and fucking miserable? Wasn't I the hot-shot programmer at Apex? Wasn't that what Daltrey had said? He did, but it wasn't true. At least the power and prestige and goodness I had associated with that title wasn't true. I wasn't any of those things. Hot-shot programmer might as well mean scum of the earth, alcoholic, drug addicted, sex addicted boy with no spine. Jelly fish. Ready to cave at the first sign of trouble. The only thing I wouldn't do would be running home to Daddy. That would be the worst. But then, I had. I bought *Sunsplatter* with Daddy's magic card.

What had Rosalyn Randall told Daltrey about Alec anyway? Did she know about the after party sex-fest? Did she tell Daltrey I was sleeping with Alec? And Wendy? Did she know? Did she suspect we were more than just neighbors? Is that what Daltrey had been trying to say? I didn't want him to know that about me. I wanted to be as golden as his painting.

I wasn't.

I was nowhere near good enough for him and I knew I had to either make myself better, or just let him go. I didn't know if I could do either.

Chapter 16 - Back to Normal

Monday morning's status meeting sludged by, heavy with what I needed to accomplish during the week, and my inability to care about it. I knew I should, but knowing you should and actually doing it weren't always anywhere close to the same thing. I wanted to go home and crawl back into my bed where I'd hid ever since leaving Daltrey at his hotel.

As soon as the meeting was over, I fled, heading straight to my office. I needed to meet with my team, but I didn't want to. I didn't want to stare at code all day either. I sat in my office with my face in my hands, feeling like my tie was going to choke me death. What a headline that would be—*Dior Homme Tie Chokes Hot-shot Apex Programmer to Death!*

A tap at my door, then it slid open and Jody popped her head in. "Hey, Martin."

"Hey, what's up?" I tried to put some excitement in my voice, but I couldn't really. The flatness reflected how I felt and I couldn't hide it.

She slid the door shut behind her and dropped into one of the two chairs facing my desk. She looked as sleek and polished as the rest of Apex. Her hair was back in a bun and she wore a gray pant suit with a dark red, silk blouse. Red high heels graced her feet giving her a completely polished look, full of confidence. "Grant wants something on this project. You need to tell him who's on the team and when you plan on meeting."

I grumbled under my breath, "When hell freezes over."

"Martin. Snap out of it. What the fuck is wrong with you?"

Jody was a firecracker, assertive. She said whatever she thought with no apologies. I admired her, and we'd become pretty good work-friends. She made things bearable and I trusted her. Did I trust her enough to spill my guts about my personal life? No. The person I could trust like that just didn't exist. "Sorry, I had a crappy weekend."

"What happened? Your boyfriend break up with you?" she asked lightly.

"Yes. Something like that." The smile dropped off her face with my admission. She must have thought that was the last thing I would say or admit to. "It doesn't matter. It's just that trying not to think about something is a sure way to only think about that thing you're trying not to think about. Right?"

"I need some coffee. Come on." She jerked her head to the door. "We're going out."

I followed Jody to the elevators and we rode down in silence. I could feel her eyes on me, taking me in, and scrutinizing my features. I knew what I looked like. Shit. I hadn't slept well, nor eaten much. I couldn't remember the last time I'd worked out. My shirt was starched and crisp and my tie perfectly knotted and quite fashionable, but underneath that facade my walls were quickly crumbling, and Jody's intense gaze threatened to expose the goo behind the wall.

She led me to the cafeteria and paid for our coffees. I wanted to go back to my office, but she made me sit with her at one of the small round tables set up in the middle of the seating area. Swallowing back the need to share how vulnerable and exposed it made me feel, I pulled out the chair and sat across from her.

"I'm sorry to hear about your breakup," she said softly,

with enough emphasis that I thought she meant it for a second. "But, you have to suck it up and get on with it. This is Apex, Martin."

"Can't you just be a friend? Shoulder to cry on?" I sipped my coffee, loving the heat and the bitter aftertaste.

"I am being a friend. A real friend. I'm not going to coddle you. Hell, I don't have that in me." She snorted and sipped her own coffee. Her gaze slowly wavered until she stared into my eyes. "Really. I'm trying to help and you seem to need to hear this. Get your shit together and do your job. Break down on your own time." Jody stood and patted my arm before walking off.

She'd left me there to wallow in my heartbreak and loneliness, and fuck her for being right. Leaning back, I sipped on my coffee and closed my eyes. I needed to leave all of that crap behind. I needed to fortify my walls and get on with my life, because with or without Daltrey, I had a job to do. My father wouldn't let anything or anyone stand in his way and he'd expect nothing less of me. Fuck him for being right, too.

I sucked in the longest, deepest breath of my life and stood up. I dumped my coffee in the garbage bin and exhaled loudly on the way out the door. Hoping to symbolically dump all my maudlin feelings there as well.

Back in my office, I got busy. I sent Grant my choices for my team and started outlining what we'd need to get done. Once I heard back from Grant, I set up our first team meeting for the next day. I felt like I'd accomplished something in the day for a moment, but by the end of the day, none of my team had accepted my invite on their calendars. None of them had called or emailed or instant messaged me to find out more details or tell me why they wouldn't be there.

I walked around the office to see if I could catch up with any of them but everyone seemed to be ignoring me, and none of my team were around. If they rejected my leadership on this project, it would fail. No doubt about it, and I knew they probably wanted me to fail, but success or failure on this one project meant little to me. They needed to understand they would only be hurting themselves. My goals were different. I just wanted to do something interesting. Success was only a means to an end. I had a safety cushion that they didn't have and his name was Steven Hannan.

I rubbed my hand over my face as I contemplated my father. I hated that I wouldn't hesitate to use him, despite wanting to stand on my own without him. I wanted my co-workers to like me for who I was and respect me for the work I did, not because of who my father happened to be. Yet, they didn't and my dad was still who he was and his name meant something in the computing world, like Gates and Jobs, Steven Hannan had made his name into an icon. Fuck my life, but I was going to use that name. My father wouldn't let this go and I wasn't going to either.

After I jotted down a few notes on how I wanted the meeting to go, I used the instant message system to ping all the members and let them know I expected them at the meeting even if they didn't accept the invite. Then I shut down my computer and vowed to hit the liquor store on my way home. I'd drown my rejection in a bottle of Jack Daniels rather than wander up to my neighbors. If that was the only thing I could do for Daltrey at the moment, then I'd do it.

##

Determined to just get through the night, I poured a glass of Jack and moved to my laptop to put some music on. Before I could select my tunes, someone knocked at my door. I couldn't help but cringe. It had to be Wendy and I didn't want to face her.

The knocking came again and I squared my shoulders, contemplating telling her to just fuck off. I pulled the door open and stared right into Alec's broody eyes. "Hey, Martin. Can I come in a minute?"

I opened the door and spread my arms wide, letting him in.

"Look, uh... My mom called me earlier today and I got the

impression that she might have fucked things up for you and the painter dude."

I shrugged.

"She told him how shitty I am. How shitty my life is." He drug his hands through his hair, tugging a little.

I shut the door and followed him inside. "Hey, it doesn't matter what she said. Daltrey lives in New York and I live here. That's an unbreachable canyon. The rest of it's just bullshit."

"Martin?" Alec asked, stepping into my personal space. Face to face, I could see the gold and green flecks marring the cocoa brown in his eyes. I could smell Doritos on his breath.

I put my hand on his shoulder, not sure if I wanted to push him away or pull him closer. "What do you want from me?" I whimpered.

He leaned in quick, crossing what little space had been between us, and pushed his lips against my own.

Immediately, I opened for him and he dove in as if we'd been lovers for real. His tongue slithered against mine, feeling rough and warm and sweet like Coke and tangy chips. I needed more of it and grabbed his face, pushing my tongue in his mouth to give back as good as I was getting.

Alec's hand slid down my back and his fingers into the top of my slacks. I could feel them begging for entrance. My cock plumped up like a blood pressure cuff in the doctor's office, a little more with each flick of his tongue. When his hand couldn't find its way into my pants, it dove into my hair. I lowered my hands to his waist and yanked him closer, humping against him.

He slid his hand down my back and cupped my ass. I wanted it, wanted to feel his body pressed to mine and when he reached around and grabbed my dick through my pants, I almost gave in. He rubbed his fingers along the length of my cock, then focused on the tip. My body shook. I thought I was going to cum in my pants right there.

His lips were plastered to mine the whole time he groped me. I wasn't going to be the first to break the kiss, but eventually, we pulled away from each other. Alec searched my face, his mouth slightly open and lips a bruising red from the kiss. "Damn, Martin," he sighed. "You are my exception to, like everything."

He leaned back in to kiss me, his hands still touching me everywhere, but I pulled away. I didn't want to be anyone's exception. I wanted to be their everything. "Alec?"

"You know Wendy doesn't care."

I knew she didn't care on the surface, but she had to on a deeper level. She was going along with what Alec wanted because she loved him. Or maybe because she thought she'd lose him if she didn't. None of that was my problem and I was damned tired of being pulled into the middle of it.

His fingers tried to shove farther into my pants and he tugged at my shirt with his other hand, pulling the tails out of my slacks. "Stop. Alec. Seriously." I gently shoved at his chest.

"I want you, Martin." He pulled closer with a groan and tried to kiss me again, but I turned my head. "Don't play hard to get, baby," he whispered in my ear, making me shiver from his breath on me.

"I'm not. Alec. I just don't think we should be doing this..."

"Come on."

"Without Wendy?"

He had his hand up my shirt and moved his searching fingers to the button on the front of my slacks. He was damned sexy and hard to resist. "Alec?"

Finally he stopped and looked at me. "Sorry. I'm such a shit. My mom was right. I just thought. I don't know. Maybe I could make you feel better."

"Thanks. You make me feel better. I'm just not..."

Alec nodded and leaned in toward me again. He smacked a kiss on me, half on my lips and half on the side of my mouth. I watched him back toward the door and part of me wanted to push him up against it and take what he'd been offering. The other part of me wanted to fall on the floor and cry.

I let him go.

Then I grabbed my Jack Daniels, slammed it back and

poured another.

Chapter 17 - Drunk Texting

A few lonely shots of Jack would have anyone doing stupid shit and I was certainly no exception. My fingers found the key pad of my phone and I sent Daltrey a text. *Miss you. Are you home?*

He hadn't let me know he'd made it safely back to New York and I was a little pissed at him for it, so the liquid courage I'd named Jack, had me feeling justified. When he didn't text me back, I sent another. *Dal - I need 2 hear from U.* After a few minutes, I added another. *I luv U. Don't shut me out. Pls.*

Every second that ticked by on the clock had my heart cracking open more and more. Tick. Break. Tick. Break.

I logged on to my laptop and opened Facebook, searching for his name and the little green dot that would say he was on, but he wasn't. I felt hollow. Maybe he hadn't made it back to New York. Maybe he was with someone else. Maybe he had someone like Alec to cheer him up.

In my half-drunk state, I couldn't stop the tears that had welled up in my eyes from dropping down my cheeks and making cold, wet trails that needed brushing away. My body ached for Daltrey to be there to wipe my tears, but that was just one more damned thing I had to do on my own. I headed to the bathroom to take a piss and wash my face and hope that Daltrey would answer my texts.

I poured myself another shot of Jack and started to trowel in new mortar on the broken wall around my heart. That slight bit of hope that I might be able to survive losing Daltrey came crashing down when my phone buzzed. He'd finally texted me back. I was thanking God, as I tapped the text open.

I'm home. Miss U 2. Been painting. Talk Later.

What the hell did that mean? Below my fuzzy alcohol soaked brain, I knew he'd been painting and that his art was how he dealt with things. I drank—Daltrey painted or sketched. The drinking part had me feeling guilty and I just needed more. *R we ok?* I texted him again.

I guess - need to define ok.

I wasn't anywhere close to being happy with his answer, but before I could text him back, my phone buzzed again. *Go 2 FB - txt is 2 hard.*

I flipped my laptop open and saw his message right away. *Martin, I do love you and care for you, but I'm in NY and I can't see how this is going to work.*

If I had to be honest with myself, I knew he was right and I knew that if I couldn't give him what he needed and couldn't make changes in my life that I needed to make, then it wouldn't work even if he were in LA. I wanted to tell him that, but I couldn't bring myself to do it. It was impossible enough just admitting it to myself.

I took another shot of Jack before I answered him. *I was invited to a party next weekend at Tia's.*

Staring at my screen, I searched desperately for the *Daltrey is typing* message. After a moment, it showed up and I could breathe again. Why had I told him about the party?

You should go.

That was the last thing I wanted Daltrey to say. I didn't want to go; I wanted to fly out to NY to be with him. *Don't want to, but probably will.*

Will Alec be there?

He probably already knew the answer to that. Alec was the ring leader of our little crowd, or rather Wendy was the leader and they were attached at the hip and mouth. Still, maybe I just wanted someone to reassure me that going to the party didn't mean I had to end up in bed with them. I felt trapped by their friendship and I didn't understand why it even meant so much to me.

Guess so. It's that crowd. Bonfire at Tia's folk's house. Should be ok. Rather be with you, though.

For a long minute, nothing. The tiny writing below the message assured me that he'd seen it, but he wasn't writing back. I couldn't push the panic back and finally typed another message. *Can we talk? Call me?? Please?*

I waited. Begging the phone to ring or for another message or even a text to pop up. What was he waiting for? Didn't he know I needed him? Or maybe that was the problem.

The Facebook message won. *Go to bed, Martin. Have a good week. Enjoy the party. We can talk next week. Call me Sunday afternoon. I have to paint now.*

He left me feeling like an asshole. I'd interrupted his life, his art. He'd made a sacrifice coming out to L.A., but really, it had benefited his career and he wouldn't have done it otherwise. Maybe. Or maybe I wasn't being very reasonable or fair. I felt like nothing more than a fling to him after that message and I didn't like it. Alec and Wendy made me feel that way all the time and now Daltrey, who I thought was so much more. More what? I didn't know the answer, but now I felt like shit again, because I knew better. I knew Daltrey really loved me and was hurting over this just as much as I was, but I was being selfish because I wanted more and Daltrey couldn't give me anything else, even if he wanted to. I knew the answers were not going to be found by hooking up with Wendy and Alec either, but I was afraid that's where I'd end up. I always did what I was told, followed directions. Why was I listening to Wendy when so much was at stake with Daltrey? Fuck. I felt like a fucking mess. I slammed back another shot of Jack.

I went to bed and passed out, fully dressed on top of the covers.

Chapter 18 - Bonfire Hearts

I made it through my work week. The meetings went better than planned. When my top rival realized I would let him do whatever he wanted, he stopped bucking the system. After a half hour of slinging testosterone and thumping our chests, we managed to really get into the project, setting up the work for the rest of the week. Even though I never felt truly connected to any of them, it had still been a bit of fun. It made the days go by easier, but my nights still sucked.

Daltrey had texted me a few times, but the content had been around easy topics. We chatted back and forth about the painting he had been working on. We chatted about the old days some. There were no declarations of love, no "I miss you" texts, and certainly no talk about being together or planning our futures. I couldn't see a future without Daltrey in it, but Daltrey didn't need to hear that and I couldn't bring myself to say it.

I'd just scratch my way through the darkness until I figured out what to do about it all, half knowing that there wasn't anything I could do, but not wanting to face that because living in the dark felt bleak. At my lowest times, I thought about the painting, *Sunsplatter*. Maybe I would fly out to Colorado when they installed it, because I needed to see it again. I would let my eyes feast on the light and love that was Daltrey.

When Saturday rolled around, I dressed for the party. I pulled on a pair of Levi's with no underwear and an American Eagle flannel over a plain gray T-shirt. I wore my Timberland boots as well, feeling like a fake lumberjack. My build wasn't big enough to be a mountain man; I'd never be accused of being a bear, but I wasn't a twink, either. I needed to get back to the gym, but there'd be time for that later. I pulled up Tia's address on my GPS app and headed out.

The sun was setting, sending streaks of pink and purple and soft orange across the sky by the time I pulled into Tia's driveway. The long road wound between palm trees then opened up to a huge paved area in front of a huge Greco-Roman style house; the real size of it obscured by large palms and other trees.

I parked my Saab next to a little red Miata. Several other cars were parked in the area, including a beat up Toyota Celica convertible with the top down and a gleaming Rolls-Royce. She was maroon and silver and came with the winged fairy hood ornament flying on the front and everything. I'd seen nice cars my entire life, but this one was pure elegance and style worthy of lusting over. I had to suppress a groan as I walked by and up to the huge door.

Potted loquat plants, budding with fruit, stretched out across the porch. The others weren't kidding when they said Tia came from money. I hadn't realized just what that meant until the car and the house. Hell, it wasn't a house; it was a mansion. It made what my dad lived in look like a tiny built-by-hand log cabin. I rang the doorbell before I could chicken out and run away with my tail tucked between my legs, because I knew I was out of my league.

The door opened as I was contemplating leaving and of course it had to be Tad Ferretti. "Hey, Martin," he called out, extending his hand for a shake. It seemed nice, but his eyes were hooded with lust. He looked sexy as hell in jeans, one of his band's T-shirts, and bare feet. Tad could have been my fantasy, but I knew what a conceited ass he could be.

"Hey, Tad. Good to see ya." I shook his hand and pulled away quickly, not wanting to give him any ideas.

Tad gave me a knowing smile before nodding me inside. "Everyone's back there in the kitchenette. We'll all go out to the fire in a bit."

I muttered a thank you and headed off in the direction he'd pointed out, glad that he didn't follow on my heels. It was bad enough that I felt his eyes boring into me, most likely checking out my ass, as I walked away.

The kitchenette area was more of a fancy dining room with a sidebar connected to a kitchen area by a swinging door. A few people I didn't know, but had more than likely seen at other parties, stood around whispering to each other about who knew what. I could hear voices in the kitchen. I put my hand on the swinging door and froze when I heard Wendy laugh, followed by Alec's tenor. "Hope he shows up. Hell, we haven't seen much of Martin lately. Kinda miss those sexy bedroom eyes."

More laughter when Wendy added, "He has a body that just won't stop. Gawd, his abs, to die. Hope he shows. Hell, hope we can get him in bed again."

"Mmm. I'd like a piece of that. Run my hands through his hair. I dig the blond. It's natural, isn't it?" I almost didn't recognize Tia's voice. I hadn't heard her speak a lot, but when she giggled, I knew for sure it was her.

They were all talking about me. Wanting sex with me. I shook my head, not sure I could believe what I heard.

"Oh yeah," Wendy said. "Natural. He's too fine. Too shy, though. Wish he'd just come out of that shell."

"I'll make him come!" Alec laughed.

I took a step back, it was just too much for me at the moment. I'd never thought inheriting my mother's looks -- the blond hair, blue eyes, well defined cheekbones -- would ever be a curse. My mom the cheerleader. She'd been perfect and ended up perfectly ruined. I wondered if I was inheriting more than her looks.

I heard one more comment from Alec as I turned away. "I'd like another shot at that fine ass for sure. Mm... I'd fuck him so—"

Shoving some kid out of the way, I made a direct line back to the front of the house. I thought I could hide in the bathroom, but I didn't know where it was. I passed Tad again, lingering with another member of his band and a few skinny girls. He looked up as I raced past him. I held up my phone, as if that were an answer to an unspoken question.

Once out on the front porch, I felt the heat in my cheeks and neck, and wondered if Tad had talked about me like that as well. I stared at my phone, wanting desperately to call Daltrey. I needed to be in his light again. Thinking about *Sunsplatter*, I dialed my father instead. He answered on the third ring. "Hannan."

"Hey, Dad. Uh, I need to tell you something."

"Sure. Haven't heard from you much, Martin. How is work going?"

Work. That's all that mattered to my father. "Work's good, dad. Listen. Uh, I bought something. A painting for the cabin. It's huge and it'll look perfect in the great room. I put it on your card, but I'll pay you back. Okay?"

"Don't worry about that, son. Art is a good investment. Who's the artist?" His voice sounded genuinely interested. He'd never been much on investing in art in the past. Stocks, bonds, blue chips, NASDAQ, not art. Maybe real estate, but other than their home and the cabin, they didn't have much of that either, as far as I knew.

"Right, so, remember my old friend in high school, Daltrey?" I had to wonder how much my father knew about us. He hadn't been around much and the issue of my sexuality never really came up. My dad's attitude was simply about not letting relationships get in the way of business.

"Boxbaum? Daltrey Boxbaum?" he asked.

"Yes, sir. That's him. You know he was always drawing and stuff when we were kids? He's pretty famous now, I guess."

"Well, that's fine, but..."

"But what?"

"You aren't still friends with him? He's just like his father, I'm sure. His dad was artsy-fartsy too. He was a graphic designer, you know? Until he had that breakdown and set their house on fire. Killed himself after that. No, Martin, you shouldn't be hanging out with his kind of people. It's one thing to support the arts, and hell, if he's a good up and coming artist, I can't fault the investment, but don't get too involved."

Killed himself? Why had my father not mentioned that before? Why hadn't Daltrey? We'd talked about the fire, but Daltrey never said anything.

And not be friends with Daltrey? That could never happen.

My dad was still talking, but I couldn't hear him. He just didn't know how sweet and caring Daltrey was, how perfect. Daltrey was the best thing to ever happen to me. My chest had a gaping hole torn out of it like my dad had just tossed in a hand grenade, yelled for cover, and watched as my world imploded. My stomach churned with acid burning up my soul. Without Daltrey, I had nothing but darkness to look forward to.

"Okay, gotta go, Dad. I'm at a party." I hung up without bothering to say a real goodbye or get one from him.

The night had set in, the loquats smelling delicious and fruity. Part of me wanted to enjoy the night sitting here on the front porch alone, but I knew Tad would tell the others I'd been there and they'd come looking. I made my way around the side and to the back of the house, following the path through Coral trees, more palms, and Silk Floss. The grounds were beautiful and the laughter dancing in the air made it seem like paradise, but the burning in my gut and the tight pain in my chest made it feel more like "Paradise Lost."

Knowing what they'd been saying, I dreaded facing Wendy, Alec, and Tia. Putting it off wouldn't help the situation any. I just needed to face it—face them.

The path led to an open area with a fire pit in the center. Citronella torches lined the outer circle. Lawn chairs and benches circled the fire and people lingered everywhere, talking and laughing. I sat on a bench and stared into the orange flames, watching them leap and dance and crackle along the logs. It looked like a dragon's lair in the center with the coals roiling white and orange.

An arm around my shoulder pulled my attention away from the fire. "Hey, man," Seth said, shaking me a little. "You all right?"

"Yep. Just watching the fire. Where's everyone?"

Seth handed me a joint and I took it reflexively, toking a little and passing it back with barely a thought. He shrugged, toked on the joint and passed it off to someone else, nonchalantly. "They're around." He shrugged. "Everyone will end up here at some point," he said, gesturing to the fire.

I flicked my tongue out, lingering over the dry taste of the pot on my lips. A cool breeze brushed the back of my neck, making me realize I'd started sweating. I stood up and pulled off my flannel and tied it around my waist before sitting back down. Another joint was passed to me, and I took a small toke out of politeness and passed it back. I didn't want to get too stoned and risk ending up with my face in the dirt, literally.

Seth sat beside me, bumping my shoulder every now and then, but otherwise, he was quiet. Before I could garner enough nerve to ask what was going on with him, Tia came skipping up to us and threw herself in my lap, straddling me. I would have much rather had Seth there, but he was bigger than me. Most guys were, except Daltrey.

Tia was a bundle of wiggle and giggle and then whispering in my ear. "I'm glad you're here, Martin. You know I really like you." This bold Tia was an interesting change of pace.

Remembering what she'd said in the kitchen along with her blatant flirting made me see her in a new light, and that light was more like a black light at a crime scene, exposing dirty, incriminating things you wouldn't normally want to see.

My hands at her hips pushed her gently, trying to dislodge

the petite brunette from my lap. I could feel her bones under my fingers and smell puke on her breath hidden beneath minty toothpaste. I wondered how no one had noticed this before. "You get anything to eat, Tia?" I asked, trying to be polite, but also suggesting she needed something in her stomach.

Smokey gray eyes grew wide, staring at me, as if she thought I'd just unleashed all of her secrets. "Yes, uh, sure, Martin. You hungry? 'Cause I'm not." She leaned in to whisper in my ear again, "Well, I'm hungry for you." She licked my ear.

I stood up, practically dropping her on the ground. Seth looked up and grabbed her, pulling her to his chest before she hit the dirt. "What?" he asked.

I shook my head and started to walk away.

"Fuck you, Martin. You can do it with them, but what? You think you're too good for us? Come on," Tia slurred her words, trying to grab my shoulder, but I pulled away.

It wasn't about being too good for her or them. It wasn't about having been with Wendy and Alec, or what they'd said about me. I knew what they thought, but I didn't want to be a plaything, not for her or Wendy or even Alec. This time I wasn't just going to do what I was told. "Nice party, Tia. See ya."

The walk back to my car was lonely and my cock had filled up against my will with thoughts of Alec and Seth and what it might be like with the three of us without the girls, as if that would ever happen. Why was I thinking about that anyway, when I only really wanted Daltrey?

Sitting behind the wheel, I flipped on my iPod that was docked there and flipped through until some Stone Sour came on. One of their more aggressive tunes blared through my speakers, suiting my mood. My head felt light, but not enough to stay parked at Tia's. I pulled out and drove home, jamming to my tunes, banging my head and ignoring my hard dick.

At home alone in the dark, I thought about Alec and Seth and even Tad. I knew I could have Tad if I wanted him, but I didn't. I wanted Daltrey. I remembered our night together in his hotel room. I thought about touching him, licking him. I wanted my tongue in his ear, like Tia had done to me earlier by the fire. If Daltrey had been there with me, the party would have been so different. Daltrey wouldn't have smoked any pot and that would have made me brave enough to say no, too. I would have had my lover wrapped up with me instead of Tia's skinny ass.

Daltrey could be everything I wanted, and I thought about pushing him back on the bed and sucking his dick into my mouth. I stroked my own cock, thinking about fucking up into Daltrey's tight hole. His body would be perfect with the heat of his skin pressed against my thighs and my chest. I thought about stroking him as I fucked up into him and pulled my cock faster and flicked a thumb across my nipple. Thinking about Daltrey and his perfect lips, his high pitched laugh, and the merriment on his face when he rolled his eyes at me. It was too much. I bit my teeth into my lip as I shot off. I came hard, but it was nothing like coming with Daltrey really there, yet it was good enough to let me get to sleep.

The next day I stalked around my empty apartment feeling guilty. I hadn't cheated on Daltrey. We didn't have a relationship and I hadn't done anything with Tia and Seth. I hadn't even wanted to, yet I still felt guilty, as if somehow I'd betrayed Daltrey. My brain insisted I was being ridiculous, but my heart was on a different level.

Finally, I picked up my phone to text him. *Can we talk?*

A few minutes later, my cell rang. I'd changed his tune to Puddle of Mudd's *Control*. I answered quickly, "Hey."

"Hey, Marty! What's going on?" His high pitched voice sounded excited.

"Just wanted to talk."

There was noise in the background, as if Daltrey were getting situated. "Sure. You went to that party last night?"

"I did. It sucked." I waited a minute for him to ask, but when he didn't, I just started rambling. "Alec and Wendy were talking about me. You know, my looks. I overheard them. Later on, Tia hit on me."

"Um, Marty? Don't they know you're gay?"

"Yes! I don't think they care, though. She did it right in front of her boyfriend. I don't know. Maybe it's a game to see if she can get the gay-boy interested. Fuck. I don't know."

Daltrey laughed. "Maybe she didn't really mean anything. You know? Like, um, she was just teasing."

"You don't know her." But, I really didn't know her either, and she was acting a lot different than she normally did. "Maybe she was doing X or something."

"Right?"

"Why didn't you ever tell me?" I asked, changing the subject, abruptly.

"Tell you what?"

"About your dad. I called my dad to tell him about *Sunsplatter*, and he said, he, uh, told me. About your dad, I mean."

Daltrey sighed heavily. "Marty. I just. I don't like to talk about it. Hell, I didn't really even know him. He was sick and... I-I try not to think about it. Like *trauma* doesn't even begin to cover that experience."

I flopped back on my bed and closed my eyes. "My dad said you take after him."

"My mom says that too."

"I'm sorry. For what it's worth."

"That means a lot, Marty."

We sat listening to the silence for a good long time. I wondered if I'd pushed him too far. "I...I miss you, Dal-baby," I finally broke the tension.

"I know, but...you know, like, we're not in a relationship, Marty. We can't be. We live on opposite coasts and seriously. It breaks my heart, Marty."

I rolled over onto my side, wishing I could see Daltrey's face, the little freckles scattered across his nose and his dark eyes. "Can we Skype?" I asked.

Daltrey groaned. Maybe I was pushing too hard. "You know? I felt jealous when you said that girl hit on you. It's wrong, like, on so-oo many levels." He drug his words out in long syllables. "It doesn't change anything though."

The silence that settled over us was not companionable. I could feel the tension as if it were a living thing. "Dal-baby. I know you're right, but I still feel, I've always felt for you. I...I want you."

"I know, baby." His voice was barely above a whisper. I imagined him lying on his bed, mirroring my own position, but I couldn't ask him about it. "Marty?"

"Huh?"

"I know you want more. Between us, I mean."

"Yes. I don't know how to make it happen, though. Fuck! I'm broken. I'm all kinds of fucked up. Maybe I'm not even capable of having what I want, of loving someone, but if I could, it would be you."

"I'm not sure what you're talking about," Daltrey said with a dramatic sigh. "I don't know, like anything, really. So, like, we need to just be friends, I guess. For now. That's for the best, right?" He sounded unsure of himself. That was so unlike him and I wondered what he really wanted or how we could ever go back to being just friends. We had stopped being *just* friends years ago.

"I don't know, either." I wanted him to encourage me to try for more. He didn't say anything. "What do you want me to do?" I finally asked.

"I can't tell you what to do Marty."

That was what made him different. Everyone told me what to do...my dad, my friends, my boss and co-workers, but never Daltrey. I would have to figure it out myself. "If I could do just one thing, Dal, what would you want that to be?"

"Marty." Just the one word, my name. He wasn't going to tell me. He'd never ask me for more.

"This shit is just so fucked up."

"Right?" His tone was light, but just for a moment. "Listen, I can't tell you what to do, and I can't make promises I can't keep. Um, you know? I don't want that from you either. Right now. Right now I don't want anyone but you, but how that looks long term? I just can't say right now. You know? And. And. Just..."

"I do know, Dal-baby. I know what you're saying. I don't have a right to ask you to wait for me or to not see anyone, but the thought of you being with someone else makes me want to rip my arm off and beat myself with it. Or beat whoever would dare be with you."

"That doesn't even make sense."

"I know. It just makes me crazy. I want to be with you and I don't know what to do."

"Okay." Another big sigh. My man could be so dramatic, and damned if I didn't love that about him, too. "So just think about this. 'Kay? I do love you and I do want more. This long distance thing, it hurts. So, just think about coming out here, to New York. Would you?"

It was everything I wanted to hear from him, but leaving everything behind in L.A. was terrifying. I wasn't sure I could do it, even for him. I would think about it, though I knew I wasn't good enough for him. I knew I was ruined and Daltrey should have more. All I could say was, "I will."

"I, um, have to go now. Call me later."

"Bye." We hung up. I wanted to call him back and tell him I loved him, but I didn't.

Chapter 19 - One Side Makes You Grow Taller

Work went so well that week. My co-workers were pitching in and coming up with creative solutions and we were almost ready to test our code, ahead of schedule. I kept repeating that in my head because it was the only thing in my life going well. Everything else sucked.

Daltrey hadn't called me, I was avoiding my neighbors, and the acid was creating a bigger and bigger hole in my stomach by the minute. I forced myself to hit the gym almost every night to avoid Alec and Wendy. While it helped my physique, it made me feel like a traitor. Didn't I owe my friends more than that? Probably, but I didn't have anything else to give them. Anything good inside of me had been sucked out like dirt being sucked out of a carpet with a vacuum cleaner.

Late Thursday night, I finally broke down and sent Daltrey a Facebook message and prayed he'd message me back. His green dot was there. A few minutes later, he replied. *Hey, Marty! Miss you!*

It had been so long since we talked that I had to jump right in and go straight for the jugular. I typed fast and hit enter before I could change my mind. *Dal - can we set up a time to call this weekend? Saturday? I miss you.*

I'm sure I sounded needy, but I was needy. I stared down the hands on my cheap wall clock that hung over my table, waiting. The three minutes felt like three hours until he replied. *You know it really is the time difference, Marty. I'm not ignoring you. It's just been hard to catch up with you.*

Hard to catch up? Time difference? I didn't get it. I was more than willing to do whatever it took to continue. I swallowed hard, knowing that wasn't entirely true. I hadn't let Daltrey see the darkness inside me and I hadn't told him the truth about Wendy and Alec. Those things were a hell of a lot more important than the time zones and waking up three hours early to catch a phone call.

I stood up, went into the bathroom and grabbed my giant-sized bottle of antacids without much thought about the bitterness crawling up my throat from the acid-factory in my stomach.

When I got back to my computer, Daltrey hadn't written anything else. I needed to talk to him though. I needed to tell him the truth and if I couldn't do it face to face, it at least needed to be over a real phone call. Even if it ruined things between us, I had to get this off my chest. Maybe it would end our friendship altogether, but I couldn't keep going, the guilt tearing me up, without talking to him. I typed, *Please let's talk on Saturday. Whenever you're free. Plz.*

Time ceased to have meaning as I stared at the message trail, waiting again.

Ok Marty. 1 pm your time. I'll call you.

Thank you. Good night. I added the last because I felt I should, but it wasn't what I wanted to say. That was becoming a pattern with me. If I thought on it, I figured that had been the case my entire life. From my first words as a baby until now, I'd never said what I really wanted to say. The closest I'd ever come was with Daltrey and I wanted that back.

I took another antacid and went to bed, wishing he was there with me warming my cold heart.

Saturday morning I was so keyed up I couldn't stand

myself. I woke earlier than I intended, ate cereal, went for a quick jog, came home and showered, and it still wasn't even noon. My stomach started churning out more acid, so I skipped lunch. Through my whole day, I couldn't stop thinking about Daltrey. I stalked around my apartment, wishing he were there, waiting desperately for him to call. I needed to occupy my mind or I would drive myself nuts.

Another glance around my apartment gave me something to do. I logged on to my laptop and started surfing the Internet for new furniture. I found a couch and matching club chair and purchased both, but I still had twenty minutes left before Daltrey's call.

I put on a pair of athletic shorts, tank top, and my Puma running shoes and headed out to the park. I didn't intend to run; I just wanted to be comfortable. The days were getting hotter and I wanted to be outside.

I walked around the park thinking about Daltrey and my life and where I wanted to go. I wanted to see *Sunsplatter* again. It would be breathtaking hanging in the cabin. Daltrey would love it and it would be fun to take him to Colorado. I daydreamed about planning a trip soon until I realized Daltrey hadn't called yet, and it was well after one. So, I called him.

The call went straight to voicemail. "Dal-baby. It's Marty. Uh, I'm waiting for your call. Uh, okay." I hung up, feeling inadequate. I knew I hadn't misunderstood the time.

I stopped at the pharmacy on my way home and picked up another pack of antacids. My world continued to spiral down a dark hole and I didn't know how to stop falling.

I walked into the front lobby of my apartment complex just as Wendy stepped out of the stairwell. "Martin! Hey." She sounded genuinely happy to see me, though I wanted to crawl in a hole and die. "Someone kill your cat?"

"Funny."

"I thought it was. Seriously, hey!" She grabbed my arm spinning me back to face her as I passed. "Martin. Listen. I don't know what's wrong and I know we haven't been, you know, best friends, but come on. Talk to me. Let me help."

"It's nothing." I faked a smile.

Wendy screwed up her face, making her nose wrinkle. "Fine. If you're okay, then come up to our party tonight."

"Tonight?" I wasn't ready for social interaction; I might never be ready again.

She grabbed both my arms and shook me a little. "If you don't come up, I'm going to send Alec and Seth down to drag you up. Don't put yourself through that humiliation."

My fake smile spread wider across my face. I could do this. Maybe I needed to go to her party. "Well, okay. I'll be there."

"You better." She let go and skipped out the front door. I watched her walk away until she was too far down the sidewalk to see from where I stood.

My life was nothing but an evil merry-go-round, like something out of a Stephen King novel, that I couldn't get off of. Every time my foot hit the ground, the bars bumped me back on. I had hoped Daltrey would help me keep my feet where they belonged, but I was wrong. He didn't want me. I couldn't blame him, either.

At nine, I finally made my way upstairs. I had pulled on a pair of Matinique pants that were gray and hugged my thighs and hips and clung down my legs. My T-shirt was a Tommy Hilfiger standard in a darker gray than my pants. It pulled tighter across my pecks than the last time I wore it, but that made me feel just a bit sexier and I needed that little boost. I pulled on a pair of black socks, deciding to skip shoes altogether. Just to go to their party, I didn't need them.

Their apartment was dark but they'd strung tiny white party lights along the ceiling around the living room. They had also brought in temporary wood flooring to dance on. The place looked festive and inviting.

Wendy and Tia buzzed around with trays of little hors d'oeuvres, fussing over the snack foods as if it were a fancy four course meal. The few guests lounging around barely noticed them. I found a beer and a dark corner and contented myself with watching, unwilling to commit to participation.

My throat burned with the need to escape, but I wasn't entirely sure what from. The party should have been the escape rather than warring with that need, yet it was difficult to let my guard down and relax. I tried though, and took a few deep breaths and another swig of my beer.

Tia leered at me and handed someone a cracker with something piled on top of it, but I didn't want to find out what it was or what she was thinking with her narrow-eyed gaze. She studiously ignored me, and I thought I could deal with that better than a frisky Tia. Even as she avoided me, she cast long looks across the room at me. I considered asking Seth to keep her away from me.

I didn't get the chance to voice my concerns, as the front door practically burst open and a crowd of people piled into the living room with a cacophony of laughter and shouting. And Tad Ferretti. He looked exceedingly hot in a pair of tight green leather-like pants that practically lived on his legs like his own skin and ended in a pair of golden ostrich boots. The T-shirt he wore looked soft, thin, and barely there. I couldn't help notice. I may have blown him off, but I had never denied my attraction to the man. His hair looked longer than the last time I saw him, sandy and covering the tops of his ears and spiked across the top in a sexy, carefree style.

The whole group laughed and carried on as if they were the party in and of themselves, and perhaps that wasn't far off the mark, because until they'd walked in, it had been sufficiently boring and quiet. The disruption had everyone's attention, including mine.

My mouth felt dry as I watched Tad cavort with the others, and I sucked down the last of my beer. I needed to make my way back to the kitchen for another, but that would mean crossing the living room where Tad's entourage had landed, claiming the space and everyone in it. It would be difficult to suck up enough nerve to make it happen, especially when Tad bent over some other guy that was reclining on the couch. It wasn't so much jealousy as just wanting to touch what Tad was offering someone else when I knew it could have been mine. Plus his ass in those dark green pants begged for attention that my cock was telling me it would be happy to dish out as it throbbed a bit in my slacks.

I swallowed hard just as Tad looked up from the guy and turned, catching my eye. His gaze heated under my scrutiny and for a moment his lips pulled tight. Then he smiled. His eyes sparkled above his white teeth, making him look every bit the rock star, and I couldn't deny wanting that, at least a taste.

He started walking toward me and I stepped forward to meet him half-way. Maybe the night would turn out better than I'd thought. I'd just started thinking that maybe Tad wouldn't be such an ass and we could fool around a bit. That's when my socked foot slid across the cherry finished, temporary dance floor Wendy had put down, and I started falling. I knew for sure I was going to bust my ass in front of Tad and God and everyone. My face heated in what had to be a blush to rival Wendy's fire engine lipstick. Before my ass hit the floor, though, Tad had his arms around my waist and shoulder, holding me up. He leaned closer, nuzzling under my ear. "Damn, you smell good."

"Thanks," I breathed the word out slowly, my heart pounding wanting to make its own escape.

Tad laughed a little, sounding pleased rather than spewing the sarcasm that normally oozed out from him. "Hey," he said, staring into my eyes. I liked this Tad much better than the one from our previous encounters and I wanted to stay there in his arms with him breathing alcohol and mint in my face and pressing the heat of his body against mine.

The longing only lasted a second. This wasn't Daltrey, but Tad. The same Tad that could be explosive as dynamite in a moment's notice or snarky and just downright mean the next.

I pulled away, flashed him a quick smile, trying not to be mean. "I need a beer." He let me go and I made it to the kitchen without another mishap. My hand shook when I grabbed another beer. I wondered how much of that had been the fall and how much was the fact that I'd enjoyed being wrapped up in Tad. Was I that starved for human touch and affection?

"Hey, Martin," his voice behind me made me jump. "Hey, I just wanted to apologize. I didn't mean to startle you."

"Apologize? For what?"

Tad's eyes were wide and his tongue darted across his lips. "Being a dick. I mean, you know, before. I've been shitty to you, but I was under a lot of stress and I didn't know you."

"You don't know me now." I cocked my head to the side, wondering where he was going with this conversation.

He chuckled a bit and I found I didn't mind the sound, though he was no Daltrey tangling up my insides with his uninhibited giggles.

"I know you a bit better and I like what I know," he said, raising one eyebrow. His sharp masculine face appealed to me, and I wanted to see that eyebrow raised again.

"Okay," I answered, still feeling like I was walking on that slick floor in my sock-feet in danger of sliding any second.

Tad sighed, as he reached in his pocket and pulled out something small. Surely, nothing but the tiniest of things could survive without being crushed by the tightness of that pocket. He held it out to me and I recognized the ecstasy tablet right away. "Here. My last one, but you seem like you could use it."

I took it and popped it in my mouth, swallowing it down with my fresh beer. I knew how it would make me feel and in that moment in the kitchen staring at my living, breathing wet dream, I didn't care. He seemed to want me and he was an unashamed gay man, so unlike Alec or worse, Seth. At least Alec admitted he wanted to fuck guys, Seth was so far in the closet he'd never see daylight. Although, it seemed Tia wanted to drag him out, even if it meant him kicking and screaming the entire way. To be fair, he hadn't said a damn word when Tia had hit on me at the bonfire. I didn't know what to make of him, truthfully. Tad, though, I knew exactly what to make of him and he wasn't three thousand miles away, nor was he turning his back on me. Quite the opposite.

"Hey," he said again. "Let's go out on the balcony and get some fresh air." His voice was soft, the crooning tones I loved on some of his ballads. I loved his screaming, screeching, rock extravagance from most of their songs, but the ballads were incomparable. I thought that maybe I could get him to sing for me.

Giving him a nod, we took our drinks out to the balcony, avoiding the dance floor. The evening was warm against my skin with just the softest of breezes playing in my hair. I closed my eyes, allowing the effects of the drug to wash over me slowly.

Heat on my face had me opening my eyes. Tad was right in front of me, standing so close I could lick his lips without moving any closer, so I did. One swipe of my tongue across the smooth skin of his lips, and he pushed forward, diving into my mouth with his tongue. His hot and juicy mouth demanded my compliance.

The kiss lingered on my tongue sending a tingling sensation across my face and down my neck to where Tad's hand clutched my shoulder. The sparks traveled from the pressure of his hand straight down my spine and into my balls. My brain stopped churning for the first time in a week, leaving me with only one thought. *More.*

I would like to think that in the back of my mind something would have warned me that I wasn't kissing Daltrey, but I doubt that's true. The sensations against my skin left me incapable of thinking about anything else.

I broke away from the kiss, smiling into Tad's confused eyes, but only long enough to set my beer on the little side table behind me. I needed Tad closer, skin on skin, touching me and making me tingle. I took Tad's beer from him, setting it on the table next to mine, and then grabbed his hands and shoved them up my shirt. One hand touched my bare skin sending sizzling streaks of warmth over me, while the other, cold from the beer, sent icy chills chasing the warmth. My hands went inside his shirt to hopefully give him the same sensations.

Tad moaned at my touch and yanked me closer, pressing his lips against mine again. His moan turned into my name as he pulled away from the kiss and slid his hands lower, letting a finger sneak along the waistband of my pants. "You want more? I'll make this so good for you, Martin." Tad bit my bottom lip, pulling it away from my mouth with his teeth.

"Yes," I breathed out, unable to coherently say anything else.

He shoved my shoulders, pushing me back and gave me a hard look. "You made me wait a long time for this." He laughed, but I wasn't sure if it was happy or frustrated.

Fearing his anger, I tried to explain. "I've wanted you, but you scare me."

That gave him a confident little smirk, as his eyes traveled up and down my body. The hungry look made my cock twitch, though I was pretty sure it couldn't possibly get any harder. He attacked my neck, releasing new sensations to march across my skin. I pressed my hips forward, pushing my hard-on into his crotch.

"We need somewhere more private. I want you naked."

"Me too," I agreed, but neither of us moved to leave. My hands groped Tad's body, sliding from the skin on his back to his ass through leather pants, and then a hand shoved through his hair. My body became one throbbing organ demanding Tad's touch and the more he touched, the more I felt, and the more I needed.

I figured Tad had given up on finding privacy when his fingers flicked the button of my pants open. He slid the tips of his fingers inside the elastic of my briefs. They caressed my hip and skidded around my skin to the small of my back, teasing and sparking like lightning. With a little tug, his hand went farther down my pants and cupped my ass cheek. My whole body trembled.

"Hey! What are you guys doing?" A feminine voice called out along with the shushing noise of the sliding glass door opening. Wendy leveled a suspicious gaze at us.

Tad started giggling. I fell forward into his arms, laughing myself. His hand came out of my pants and wrapped around my shoulders, hugging me, holding me. It felt right, like maybe

I belonged there. I nuzzled my nose into the crook of his neck, smelling sweat and the remnants of his spicy cologne on his bare skin. I couldn't help but think that this was what it was supposed to be like...being with a guy that just wanted the same thing I did -- to get through the night and not be alone.

"Come inside. They've got coke lined up, dudes."

Wendy left us still wrapped up together. I wanted to stay there and just feel this man, his arms around me, and maybe he'd even suck my cock. What was wrong with that? I wasn't asking for much, but Tad pulled out of the embrace, my request going unanswered. "Wait," I said, sounding too desperate even for my own ears.

"Hey, no," he answered. "Let's hit a line then go back to your place. When I have you naked, I don't want to be interrupted." It sounded like a good plan, but all good plans are meant for destruction.

I followed him in and let him lead me to the coffee table. I snorted a line up each side of my nose, no longer caring about the consequences. I could sleep it off the next day. My focus narrowed down to nothing more than getting Tad in my bed. Tad's focus, however, had expanded. He started making out with the guy he'd been laughing with earlier. The coke numbed my nose and my face and my emotions. I didn't feel jealous at all. In fact, I started remembering why I hadn't wanted to get anything started with Tad in the first place.

The kitchen and a promise of a cold beer called me away from the scene in the living room. I downed half the cold, frothy beverage in one go. I thought about going back to my place and getting off on fantasies of what could have been with Tad while I swigged down the second half of the beer. Feeling refreshed, I grabbed yet another beer and headed back to the rest of the party.

I talked and laughed with people, never fully sure of what I said. Some of the girls pulled me to dance in the living room, but my socks kept slipping on the hardwood floors. I hoped Tad would rescue me again, but he'd left the party with his other friend. If I had thought he'd changed, I was wrong, though I didn't much care. I was just glad it hadn't gone too far between us before I'd received that reminder.

Everything around me shined brightly. The music pumped loudly from the stereo and laughter rang out. I resigned myself to having fun and enjoying it.

I drank a few more beers, and I suspect I did another line of coke, maybe more than that. I couldn't walk straight into the kitchen. Needed another beer. Nothing else mattered. I laughed at myself, grasping the counter. The room spun to the left, jerked back to the right, and spun left again. I closed my eyes, but that made it worse.

"Martin? You okay?" A rough baritone asked. Alec or Seth? Or someone else? Had Tad come back?

I turned, wobbly, to see Alec's sandy hair and big brown eyes. "Maybe you should go home?"

"Wanna join me?" The words sounded slurred even to me, and I knew I was fucked up.

Alec laughed. "Come on."

"Nah, I'm goo-ood." I felt pretty mellow, despite the room moving at a slightly different angle than I was walking.

The night moved on. Sounds and voices and faces blurred. Time ceased to have a linear form. I went from drinking a beer in the kitchen to making out with someone on the couch, and I didn't know who, and then dancing again. My feet bare. I didn't know how or when I lost my socks. Tia danced seductively in front of me, but a hard cock ground into the crease of my ass behind me. Masculine hands danced down my shoulders. On bare skin. My shirt had left with my socks at some unknown point.

The world moved, leaving me in the kitchen holding another beer, panting hard, sweat dripping from my forehead. The floor did that jerk spin thing again.

Someone said Tia had been acting strange. What the hell was wrong with her? Wendy's screeching tones whined in my ears, but I didn't comprehend her words. I couldn't comprehend my own thoughts. I closed my eyes wondering where I'd be when I opened them again, yet I really didn't care.

The numbness I'd felt on my face earlier had spread into the rest of my body, infecting my soul. I spread my arms against a cool surface. Hot and cold blurred to insignificance. In that moment, as I lost my last connections to the universe, I wondered if I would just disappear. Could I sink into the floor and cease to exist as quickly as Tad's affections? As quickly as Daltrey's?

Chapter 20 - Death by Diamonds and Pearls

One ray of sunshine escaped through the blinds and attacked my face. *Fuck my life*! My head had a sledgehammer inside it, pounding on my brain and sending flashes of pain out to my temples. My stomach roiled, but that wasn't new. I swallowed back acid, tasting nasty funk in my mouth. I had to brush my teeth. As the rest of my body started catching up, I felt the heat of another against my feet and my ass.

I turned over, planting my nose in someone's back, between their shoulder blades. I ran my fingers over broad shoulders and down to a trim waist. The shaggy, sun-bleached blond hair had to be Seth's. I sat up, slowly, peering over his shoulder. His arms were curled around a petite girl with brown hair sticking up everywhere. *Fucking Tia!* Well, hopefully, he hadn't, at least not in my bed.

Without waking them, I made my way to the bathroom and fulfilled the promise to my mouth with not only a brushing, but a long rinse with mouthwash. I spit the blue liquid back into the sink with a gasp at the sharpness of the alcohol content. I'd had enough alcohol the previous night. In fact, the floor was still a bit wonky under my feet.

I'd managed to make it to the living room and sit down on the floor. My furniture would be here on Monday or Tuesday. Something to look forward to. I flipped open my laptop, wondering where my phone had gone. I opened my browser and clicked on Facebook out of habit, not really paying attention and thinking about coffee.

The little red square over the message icon informed me that I had a private message waiting. I held my breath as I clicked on it. Daltrey. I exhaled slowly, clicking on his profile pic that would open the message.

Marty! Sorry bout yesterday. I got held up. Call me whenever. Really - sorry.

Short and sweet and full of second chances, the message said everything I craved from him.

I needed to find my phone. Thinking it would probably be with my clothes, I tiptoed back into the bedroom. My pants had been dumped on the floor. Thankfully, just my pants. I still wore my briefs, though nothing else. I had no idea where my shirt and socks were, but my phone was in my pants pocket.

Seth stirred as I tried to leave quietly, but I bumped into the door and cursed. "Mm. Hey, Martin," he groaned and shuffled in the sheets. "Ugh. What? Fuck!" he screamed, catching my attention. I jerked around to see him push himself backwards out of the bed, practically stumbling over himself to get away from Tia.

My face puckered up, not understanding what Seth was doing. He started wailing, "Check her! Check her pulse, God damn it! Check her!"

I rushed to the bed and touched her shoulder, turning her over. Her skin was deathly cold. Her eyes closed, face slack. I grabbed her arm, checking for a pulse, but the sinking feeling crawling up my gut was more than acid this time. "I can't. I can't." There was no pulse. Tia's skin was gray and placid.

She was dead.

Seth sobbed hard and loud, tears and snot pouring from his face. I lifted my phone and pushed the buttons, 9-1-1. I didn't know how to comfort him. His grief felt like an elephant sitting on my bed between her body lying prone and his body crumpled on the floor.

I gave the dispatcher my address and the bitter information about Tia. They promised to have someone out quickly. I couldn't help read into her tone, morbidly; there was no rush—the girl was already dead.

Losing my detachment, I coughed and gagged and rushed to the bathroom. I dry heaved over the toilet, figuring I'd probably emptied my stomach the night before, by the taste I'd woken up with. It didn't keep me from gagging and spitting up bile and acid. It felt like my stomach lining had ripped away and pressed into my throat.

When I finally stopped, my hand shook so badly I could barely hold the phone, but I managed to dial Daltrey. He answered on the second ring. "Marty?"

"Oh God, Dal. Uh, shit. Things are bad here. I'm waiting for the cops to come."

"What? What the hell? Marty? Are you alright?"

"I am. For now. Someone died. A girl."

"OhmyGod! Did you know her?" He sounded surprised and disturbed. I wanted him to be worried about me, anything I could get. How selfish of me? Tia was dead.

"I knew her, yes. She died in my bed. She's there. In my bed." My voice shook along with my hand and the rest of my body. I was near collapse.

"What? I don't understand."

"I don't either. Wendy and Alec—"

"Alec?" he interrupted. "You should stay away from him. I thought you understood, Marty. His mom said he was bad news, trouble with a capital T."

"It wasn't Alec...or Wendy. Their friends Tia and Seth. Seth is a mess."

A banging on the door interrupted my conversation. "LAPD. Open the door."

"Hang on, Dal." I grabbed my slacks from the floor, tripping into them, as I raced to the door and flung it open.

Two officers came in, just as a wide-eyed Seth emerged from the hall wearing his jeans and a T-shirt he'd pulled from one of my drawers. "I think I need to go. I'll call you back." I hung up without saying anything else.

The officers came in and had both Seth and I leaning against my kitchen counter while they inspected the rest of my apartment. I had no idea what had happened the night before, didn't even remember leaving the party and certainly not with Seth and Tia. The cop would eventually start asking us questions, but relying on Seth to have the answers didn't settle my stomach at all. He could barely hold his head up and kept running his hands through his hair. His eyes darted around my kitchen as if looking for an escape.

Seth didn't say much and gave his work address as some surf shop down in Santa Monica. As paramedics came in with a gurney to take her body, they released Seth, telling him not to leave town. As he walked out the front door without looking back, I had a strange feeling I wouldn't ever see him again. Instead of calling out or asking him if he would be alright, I bit my lower lip and cringed, unable to do anything but watch the world continue to move around me. It was disconcerting to feel like that was my normal state. Sitting back and letting everyone else do their thing, only acting when others demanded it.

"Is this registered?" The cop that had been strolling through my apartment asked.

"What? Is what registered?"

"This gun. From under your bed."

"What?" I didn't have a gun under my bed. "I don't own a gun. What are you talking about?"

He held up a small, black handgun between gloved fingers. "Found it under the bed where the girl was. Assumed it was yours. You are the homeowner?"

"I rent the apartment, but I've never seen that before. It must be Seth's." I couldn't recall seeing Seth or anyone else with a firearm at the party or ever for that matter. "I have no idea, really."

Both police officers looked at each other as if sending telepathic messages or some unspoken cop-code between them. Then they leveled their steady gazes on me. The one holding the gun raised an eyebrow.

"Seriously," I said. I had nothing to hide.

The other officer must have decided my confused expression meant it would be a good time to start drilling me about what happened the night before. "How do you know the victim?"

"Victim?" That word felt like an accusation, but I'd done nothing wrong. My eyes grew wide at the thought. Surely, he didn't think I had anything to do with her death. Surely it had been accidental.

"The dead girl," he said, bluntly.

"Friend, uh, she was a friend."

"Uh-huh. And how did she end up in your bed?"

I sighed, wishing I had more coffee made and that the pounding in my head would just back off a bit. "Don't know," I answered truthfully.

"Hm. Don't know anything about the gun under your bed or the dead girl in it. That's convenient."

"Seth would probably know more, but you let him go."

"That was the other fellow? How would he know more?"

"He was her boyfriend." I couldn't understand why Seth had been set free without much questioning, yet I had a figurative spotlight glaring in my eyes.

"Were you attracted to her? Sleeping with her?"

I snorted. "Not even."

"Why's that? Pretty girl." The cop glared at me, looking all official in his dark blue uniform. He had no clue.

"I would more likely have been attracted to and slept with Seth, but that didn't happen either."

"Oh!" His eyes went wide as he figured it out, but then they narrowed again, probably using my sexuality as another reason to prosecute me. "So, how'd they both end up in your bed?" he smirked a little as he asked the question.

"Again. I don't know." I could see he didn't want that

answer, but I didn't have another one. "We'd been at a party upstairs. I got really drunk. I guess maybe they wanted to make sure I got home okay and then just crashed."

"That sounds like you don't know."

"I just said that. I was drunk." My tone rose an octave in volume as my anger festered beneath the surface and I could feel my nostrils flaring. This guy intentionally pushed my buttons, but I couldn't do anything about it. I took in a deep breath to calm myself.

The cop nodded and jotted something in his notebook before looking back up at me. "What's her name? The girl? Full name?"

"Tia Witherspoon."

"Tia Wi-Wi Witherspoon? *The* Tia Witherspoon?"

"Yep, I'm pretty sure she has a 'the' in front of her name." I could no longer reign in the sarcasm.

"Shit. I'd hate to be you right now."

I raised an eyebrow. "Why's that?"

"Her parents are going to eat you alive. You're probably going down for this, but off the record, I get it. You were with the wrong people at the wrong time. I have some advice for you though." He gestured at me with his pen.

"What's that?"

"You should know what you let in your apartment, whether that be things or people."

I grunted, assuming twenty questions was over and crossed my arms over my chest, staring down the coffee pot, longingly.

The officer turned to walk out of my kitchen, but did the typical stop and look back over his shoulder. "Don't go anywhere, Mr. Hannan."

I shook my head and watched the officer meet up with the other one in my living room and just minutes later, the paramedic team wheeled out Tia's covered body.

"Oh God. I've got to get a new bed," I said, softly, as my body started to shake all over.

The officer that had been questioning me turned. "What?

Why?"

Bile crawled up my throat as I started to panic. "I can't. I can't. Sleep there. I can't. The bed. I can't sleep on the bed." My brain was like a scared rabbit, running this way and that, trying desperately to think around the image of Tia lying dead, cold and lifeless, in my bed. I didn't know if I could even set foot in the room again, let alone sleep in the bed. I looked up at the officers, as if they'd have an answer for me. Weren't cops supposed to know the answers? "I have to get a new bed."

They shook their heads, but didn't comment. I followed them into the living room and once they left, and I sank to the floor, running my hands through the plush carpet. I needed to call the furniture shop and see if they could bring me a bed along with the couch.

I lost track of time, sitting there fixated on couches and beds, finally snapping out of my trance when my cell phone rang. I answered without looking, and felt a tiny spark of joy flip through my heart at Daltrey's concerned voice. "Marty? What's going on? Like, uh, you hadn't called me back."

"Hey, Dal. Sorry. Listen. They're gone and I'm, I'm... I don't know."

I heard his soft breath over the phone. "I'm sure you're in shock. This is, you know, a lot. To take in and deal with, I mean. I can't imagine."

"I don't know. I don't remember much, Daltrey. I went to their stupid party and honestly, I was pretty fucked up. I don't remember leaving the party. I sure as hell don't remember leaving with Tia and Seth. I'm pretty sure we were all fucked up."

"You know, Marty? That's not my scene. Partying, drugs. I'm sure there were drugs at the party. Alec has been in trouble for drugs before and so has Wendy."

"Is that fact, or just his mother's speculation?" I asked, not understanding why I'd defend those two, but it kind of pissed me off that Alec's mother was feeding Daltrey this crap. She should let him make up his own mind, rather than casting doubts on me, someone she didn't even know.

"I think it's a fact, but um, you know, it doesn't matter. I don't want anything to do with it. If you're going to fuck around with them, I don't want anything to do with you. Are you? Fucking them, I mean?" Daltrey's voice was soft, quiet, yet full of danger. Alec's mother had filled him in, assuredly guessing about the sex, but confident about the drugs. What did it matter? Tia died.

"She was acting strange, even before the party really got started, but yes, there were drugs. Coke, X, who knows what else," I confessed to that much.

"And the rest?"

I couldn't answer him. If he knew for sure I'd slept with them, he really wouldn't want me. Inside of me, something like anger shifted in my stomach and chest like a tangible thing, like a black hole sucking me in, a painful whirlpool ready to burst me apart. I wanted to lash out, scream, or punch something or someone. I'd spent my life doing what my parents wanted, and then I had blindly followed Wendy and Alec. I didn't need another set of parents. Why couldn't I get away from this? Stand on my own—do what I want—live my own life?

Finally, I cleared my throat. "Is that? Is this? Is this why you wouldn't sleep with me again or ask me to go to New York with you?"

Daltrey made a strange noise like he had strangled himself. I heard the tears in his voice when he spoke. "Something like that, yeah."

"Daltrey, I-I... You don't understand," my voice trailed off. I'd never be able to explain it to him. Just the day before I had thought I could make this right. I was wrong. He'd never understand; he deserved better.

"Look, Martin. Here's the deal. I do love you. So much. More than *you* understand. But, I can't watch you do this to yourself and I won't have it in my life. You have to figure out what the hell you want. You want to be a party boy? I guess if that's where you are in your life, so be it, but I'm not going to be a part of that. When you get passed it all, call me."

"Daltrey," I begged. I wanted to tell him that I didn't want to be involved with Wendy and Alec or drugs and alcohol, or any of it. I wanted him. Just him. But, he couldn't want me now and he'd never asked me for more.

A banging on the door stopped me from saying any of it. "Fuck, hang on."

A deep voice huffed, "LAPD." The cop banged on the door again before I could open it, when I did, the same officers were back. "Mr. Hannan, you're under arrest."

"Daltrey," I choked out. "Call my dad. They're arresting me."

Chapter 21 - Jailhouse Rock

Jail is just one big waiting room. You wait. That's all you do. Wait in the area that looks like a bus terminal, only the trip you're waiting on isn't one you want to take. When they finally call you up to the counter, you wonder why it looks like a bank. You half expect a teller to come out to ask you what they can do for you, but you get an angry officer that would rather be anywhere else than here booking the criminals into the system.

I answered a million questions, had photos taken, and it sure as hell wasn't like the prom. No one looks good in a mug shot because it's the walk of shame captured forever for anyone to see. They post it on the internet now also, so any one in the whole world can find it. Then an electronic scan of your hand takes all your prints at once. No ink. Those days are over, but this version sure isn't any less humiliating.

Then it was back to waiting. This time waiting meant standing around a room with cement walls and nowhere to sit until they finally called your name again, only to be told that you didn't qualify for bail and you'd have to see the judge.

They ushered me through another door and into a room with a long line of phones that looked like they'd been stolen from the 1980's. You could only make collect calls. Who the hell was I going to call? I didn't want anyone to know I'd been arrested and I especially didn't want my dad to know because no matter what I said, he'd find fault. I didn't kill that girl. I didn't do anything, but I still associated with *those* people. I was drunk, had drugs in my system, the same drugs that I knew were in Tia's system. It didn't really matter that Seth had been there or that it was his gun and his drugs. As far as my dad was concerned, I would be guilty. Guilty for hanging around the wrong people. Guilty for becoming involved in illicit things. I should have known better. No, my dad was the last person on earth I wanted to call. Yet, there wasn't anyone else to call. Plus, he probably already knew. Daltrey would have called him like I asked. Why had I asked him that? Hell, it didn't really matter.

I picked the phone up with a sigh and placed my collect call. My dad immediately started reaming me out, but I just couldn't listen to it. "Dad," I interrupted. "Listen, there's not much time before they cut me off. I need a lawyer. They didn't give me bail. I have to wait to see the judge. And. And I need a lawyer."

"Martin. Maybe you need to sit in jail. Maybe you need to figure out just why you're there."

"Are you going to get me a lawyer?"

Dad huffed. "We'll see." He hung up before we were cut off, leaving me staring at the handset.

What the hell? He'd done everything for me. He'd given me everything. Even shit I didn't want or ask for. The one time I actually needed something...we'll see? What the fuck? I hung up the receiver just a little harder than I had intended which garnered me the evil eye from the cop standing by the door with his arms crossed over his chest.

Then I had more waiting. I had to wait in the phone room until enough people finished their calls. Then I had to wait for them to issue me clothes. Boxer shorts and an orange jumpsuit and a pair of ankle socks. Then I had to wait while they watched me strip. Everything. Shoes, socks, pants, shirt, underwear. I stood there buck naked while strangers watched me dress in the jail clothes, as if the mug shot and phone call weren't humiliating enough.

Finally they gave me a piece of paper with my new address and walked me to my cell; my new home where I sat on the bed and waited some more. There was nothing else to do but sit there and wait until something happened. I was terrified to do anything else, terrified that if I called too much attention to myself I'd get beat up—or worse. No, I sat there numbly waiting, wondering if that's how I would spend the rest of my life.

How had it come to this? I cradled my head in my hands, elbows on knees and closed my eyes tight, wishing I could change something, anything. Wondering why I hadn't tried harder to change things when I had the chance. Why had I let Daltrey slip away with my head stuck in the sand, content to follow Wendy and Alec? Had I needed their attention that badly?

My chest was empty, a gaping hole where my heart used to be. As usual, my stomach churned with acid build up, but I didn't have access to any antacids. That made everything worse. How was I going to make it through even one day in a place like this?

My throat itched a little and my eyes burned, but I refused to cry. God help me if I was going to get labeled as the crybaby gay-boy in here. If there really was a backbone running from my head to my ass, this was the time to find it. I couldn't go on like before, doing what everyone else wanted.

That was over.

Everything was over. I'd lose my job, my apartment, any money I'd saved up because I sure as hell wasn't counting on my dad after all of this, after his, "We'll see."

I sat waiting in a tiny cement, gray room with barely enough room for two twin bunks and a crapper. I prayed I'd be out of there before I had to shit. I couldn't imagine going with so little privacy.

The door stayed open until they started calling for lights

out. I assumed some wandering must have been permitted, but why? I could sit here and wait with my heart pounding in my chest like a jackrabbit racing for cover inside while I appeared calm and cool on the outside.

I'd see the judge the next day, so one night, minimum. It had to be just one night. After that, the judge would see that I could do bail and dad would post it. I'd be home with my parents before dinner the next day. We'd get takeout and hope mom didn't pass out at the table. Just like old times. I almost thought it more comforting to stay in jail.

##

The next morning the entire jail got started way too early and I hadn't slept much at all, tossing and turning and worrying about my future and my past. Never in a million years would I have suspected I'd end up in in jail. Yet, I couldn't deny it. The cement walls and floors held the cold in, not allowing a second of warmth or comfort.

After a shitty breakfast of powdered eggs and cold, dry toast, the correction officers took me to a room with a monitor and microphone system in it sometime around nine that morning for First Appearance.

Someone off screen read the charges, three of them: involuntary manslaughter, possession of an illegal firearm, and possession of a concealed weapon. Possession? I'd never touched the gun. I plead not guilty and then the judge asked me if I had a lawyer or needed one appointed to me. Even without my father, I had the means to obtain a lawyer and said as much. Then the railroading began.

"The defendant has the means to travel and close relations in New York. We feel he is at risk and ask that bail be denied," the representative from the District Attorney's office demanded.

"What? No. My father is Steven Hannan. He's local. That's my tie and I'm not going anywhere."

"Mr. Hannan," the judge said. "The police report states

you don't have furniture in your apartment. That makes it very easy to just pack up and go."

"I'm sorry, bail is determined on apartment furnishings? That's strange," I said boldly, wondering how I had been reduced to defending my interior design choices.

"Keep arguing and I'll find you in contempt as well." With those last words, my two minutes of courtroom fame were over and the Corrections Officer, or CO, released me back into the main jail area. I'd thought to say my furniture would probably be arriving at my apartment while they had me tied up in court, but it was too late, and it didn't even fucking matter.

I'd been lucky to say anything at all. Getting a lawyer became the number one priority in my life. How had my father not done as I asked and let me face that judge alone? I needed help and he owed me that. Didn't he? I'd always done everything he wanted; I was the good boy. So where was he now?

I spent the rest of that morning, trying to figure out how I'd ended up in jail and what I could do about it. My paltry musings were eventually interrupted when they brought lunch. I ate the horrible food, scarfing every bit of it down without complaint, knowing I'd need it. Then I figured out where the phones were located and how to make a collect call. Turns out when facing harsh realities—like sitting in jail—I felt better making a plan and taking action. Not getting a lawyer was not an option.

"Dad, please," I begged when he answered. "I need a lawyer. This is all wrong. I didn't do anything."

"Martin, I don't know what you expect. You can't live your life so recklessly and not have consequences."

"Dad. Lecture me later. I don't have much time and unless you put money on the account, I won't be able to call you again." My fellow inmates informed me of that little boon. They'd been delighted to share any news with me that might crush my soul.

"We'll see, Martin."

"Dad, no. Please. I need more of an answer than that. I already got railroaded at the first appearance. They're not letting me bail out because I have no furniture, for Christ's sakes!"

"Where's your furniture? You had my card. Why haven't you bought furniture?"

"Dad, it's supposed to be delivered like today or tomorrow. It took me a while to decide what I wanted. I have bedroom furniture. Just not the living room."

"For crying-out-loud, Martin."

"Damn, Dad. I've never asked you for anything. You know that. Never. Please, just help me."

"Your mother—"

"What does she have to do with it?" I interrupted. I couldn't take the thought of my mother being in charge of whether they helped me. Half the time she didn't even know who she was.

"This has hit her hard, Martin."

"She's not the one in jail," I muttered.

"Your sarcasm isn't going to help you." My dad delivered all his lines on cue without emotion. The man was a robot. I had nothing left to say; I had pleaded my case. He would either help or not, but I still couldn't hang up the phone. I didn't want to cut the one tie that I had to the outside world.

"Sorry," I muttered. "This is hard, Dad. You have no idea."

"No, and I don't intend to find out."

I had no answer to that. I held the receiver tightly, listening to the steady breathing of my father. A minute later a beep sounded with a recorded message that we had two minutes left. "Martin," my dad said after the message. "I'll put more money on the phone account. You can call me later. Wait until after five. I should have news by then."

"Thanks Dad."

"Don't thank me yet." He hung up on that dramatic note that represented the one tiny ounce of emotion he had for me. To be fair, he had none for my mother either and she'd locked herself up in her drunken state, hiding from sobriety and the rest of the world, a long time ago.

Chapter 22 - Law Is a Foreign Language

Two days. Two whole stinking miserable days later. It took my father two days to get a lawyer to represent me. I suspected he waited to teach me a lesson, well bravo, lesson learned. Don't trust my father when I really needed him. It might have been harsh, but I couldn't stand being in jail. It made me feel insignificant, forgotten. The whole world boiled down to this orange and gray microcosm where Martin Hannan didn't have meaning.

Days and nights ran together only to be separated by the COs waking you up in the morning and calling, "Lights out," in the evening. Everything existing between these two events involved not paying too much attention to all the other men around me, but paying enough attention to know what was going on at all times. I left the others alone and prayed for the same from them. Any time someone looked at me, my heart threatened to escape my chest. What were they thinking? Do they know I'm gay? Were they planning to beat the crap out of me?

I lived in the cracks and crannies of my own mind, a devilish place to be. Anger and disbelief constantly warred with loneliness and longing for more. By the second day, I didn't think I'd ever see the light of day outside the tiny cubicle and the space they called the yard, but was nothing more than an enclosed area with high walls and no roof.

Then I finally got to meet my lawyer. I thought he seemed like any typical high-priced suit, and this one consisted of three pieces, gray jacket, shiny charcoal vest, and a dark tie that might have been blue or black. He sat on the opposite side of a plexiglas wall and had to speak into a phone receiver. I had to do the same on my side. I didn't want to touch the phone or the glass; it seemed unhygienic.

"Hello, Martin. I'm Bradley Kauffman. You can call me Brad. Your father hired me."

"Yes," I said into the filthy receiver.

"What can you tell me about what happened?"

"Nothing," I shrugged. I'd already said it all. "I don't remember what happened. We were at a party and I got drunk. Really drunk." I ran my hand over my face, feeling the scruff on my cheeks and chin.

"Wendy Fredericks and Alec Randall hosted this party?"

"Yes. Upstairs from me."

Brad leaned back in his little plastic chair, stretching out his legs and crossing his ankles. "They've been questioned and their answers don't look good for you."

"What do you mean?"

"They say you brought the drugs to the party. They say you always bring drugs and you fed them to Tia all night, ignoring their warnings."

"Bullshit." Why was I surprised? Hadn't I really known that Wendy and Alec weren't real friends? I'd known from the beginning that they'd eventually turn on me, yet I had chosen them anyway.

"Who else can help? Who else is a regular at these parties, Martin?" he asked, straight to the point. I appreciated that at least.

"I don't bring drugs to their parties. That's Seth's role. You know Seth Morgan? The guy they just let walk out of my apartment? Why isn't he here? He's her fucking boyfriend."

"Martin. Calm down," he said, but I hadn't even begun to get worked up yet.

I held up a hand to let him continue. I had to keep a straight head and think about this. Giving Brad the right information was probably the most important thing I had to do in my life up to this point.

Brad grunted and tilted his head, then disclosed, "We have his information, but he's siding with your other so-called friends."

"I'm sure." I wasn't any happier about that than my lawyer.

He rolled his hand in the air, gesturing for me to continue. "Who else?"

"Tad Ferretti. He's the drummer and singer for a rock band. He's usually there too. He may side with me if he's not worried about drug charges. He likes me."

"What do you mean? Don't all your friends like you?" he asked with raised eyebrows. He was fishing for more about my relationship with Tad, but I didn't want to give him much and I didn't want to talk about my relationship with Wendy and Alec either.

I shrugged, as if it were nothing, and to Tad it probably had been nothing. "We made out a little. You know? Nothing serious, but he likes me-likes me."

"Okay. I can work with that."

"He's in a band, though. You know? Drugs and sex are his thing."

"I get it. I'll look him up."

It wasn't enough to make me feel relieved. "What about getting me out of here. Can they really do this?" I held up a hand, ready to beg for help.

"I'm working on that too. I've ordered the transcript from the court. If the judge denied bail based on your lack of household goods, we may be able to overturn it."

"They also said it was because of my relations in New York. I only know one person in New York."

"Who's that?"

"Daltrey Boxbaum, and I would never involve him in this." I pointed to the tiny counter between us. "He's too important."

"Got it. I think I can get you released to your father's custody, anyway."

"And the charges? Can you get them dropped? They're bogus."

Brad offered a smarmy smile that said all it needed to about his character. "I'm working on it."

The conversation ended there.

##

I had nothing to do over the next few days aside from thinking since I couldn't very well escape myself. I kept going over how everything had happened and I wanted to blame either Wendy and Alec or my father. There comes a point in life though, when we all must embrace our adulthood and stop blaming others for our own actions and decisions. I had to take responsibility for it all.

Not that I'd killed Tia. I had nothing to do with that fuck up. She'd have to own that, even if she did it in the afterlife. Hell, I wasn't even that sad about her death, outside of the headache it caused me. I'd never cared much for her. Being arrested for it though, that was all on me. No one made me snort coke or take X. No one else poured all the beer on top of the drugs. No one twisted my arm to make me go to that damned party, or any of the others.

I blindly followed people I didn't know because I felt flattered. I never even liked Wendy, yet from the first time we met, I'd let her enthrall me. She got under my skin and I did whatever she wanted, just like I'd always done whatever my dad wanted. I'd become so used to the pattern, I'd never let my own wants and needs define my actions. What I wanted didn't matter, but what I wanted beyond reason was Daltrey and he should matter most, but I had acted like he didn't matter at all.

If I had even a small chance at any kind of future

relationship with Daltrey I needed to find a way to stand up for myself and stop following others. It wasn't high school and my life wasn't a popularity contest. In fact, I needed to man up to my entire life. It couldn't just be about Daltrey, as much as I loved him. I needed to do it for myself, otherwise it wouldn't mean anything and I'd probably just fall back into the same old habits.

I needed to start with my father. I'd thought I had stopped being his pawn, but that wasn't true. We had distanced ourselves from each other, but if he had ever called me, I would have dropped everything to do what he wanted.

I lived in an apartment approved by him; I drove a car he purchased for me; I even took a job he had referred me to. Nothing in my life had ever been what I'd chosen. Right down to my designer fucking underwear; I was nothing but my father's puppet. Where these thoughts used to anger me, drown me, I could no longer blame my father for it and getting mad didn't help either. A dark sadness sunk over me, digging into my chest. I named it remorse.

Finally, on day five, Brad Kauffman, attorney extraordinaire came through. He got me released. My body vibrated with the need to get out of this hell.

I waited and waited.

It took the paperwork most of the day to be processed and then once the CO came for me, I had to wait for my personal belongings. After hours of torture, dressed in my own clothes and holding the sealed plastic bag containing my wallet, I exited through the huge gray door as soon as the lock clicked it open.

I circled around the glassed in reception booth and made my way to the rows of plastic chairs where people waited for their own criminals to be released. I expected to see my dad waiting for me. Brad said he'd be there, but as my eyes fruitlessly scanned the room, I didn't much care about his absence. The need to escape overwhelmed me and I barged through the glass doors leading to the outside world, one I hadn't been quite sure I'd ever see again until I was out in it.

I took several deep breaths in the dry early evening air. The sun had started to hide over the horizon, sharing streaks of pink and purple and orange with me like a coming home gift. I had to put some distance between me and the building so I started aimlessly walking away, unsure of my destination, though I didn't really care much. I knew I wouldn't be going back to my apartment, but a nearby hotel might be an acceptable alternative. Before I could get far in my new plans, I heard my name called.

"Martin!" My dad. So, he'd shown up after all.

I turned to face him and waited. He beckoned me over to his car, a slightly more expensive Saab than my own. Dad wore his Ralph Lauren suite like armor, the dark brown emphasizing his brown eyes and light brown hair. His shirt was starched white and his tie a perfect match of brown with dark blue specks throughout. The classic single breast design was cut perfectly for his broad shoulders and narrow waist. Dad always took care of himself, barely looking old enough to actually be my father. He'd probably come straight from work.

"Get in," he commanded, barely acknowledging me.

I obeyed, silently, not wanting to start up the conversation that I knew I couldn't avoid. Even though I would have been happy enough to drive home in silence, the tension between us lingered heavy like mid-summer humidity, ready to explode in a wash of rain at any moment.

After a few miles, I couldn't stand it anymore. "Are you going to say anything?" I asked just to break that tension. I expected my dad to explode all over me like a water balloon, but he merely glanced at me with one eyebrow lowered over his dark eyes.

He made a few more turns before letting a huge sigh escape. "You look just like your mom, you know."

I did have her eyes and lighter, blond hair, and similar facial features, but my build generally resembled my father. "Nah," I said.

"You seem to be acting like her too. I'd hoped you'd take after me more."

"Are you fucking kidding me? I'm your fucking mini-me for Christ's sake."

"Martin," my father growled. "Don't speak to me in that tone of voice."

With my own sigh, I gave him a quick, "Sorry," that I didn't mean. "But, really I've done everything in my life to be just like you. The clothes, the job, the car. What more do you want?"

"I sure as hell don't want you in jail, Martin."

"Me neither," I scoffed.

"So, you want to explain yourself?"

Indeed. He wanted me to grovel, beg his forgiveness, and tell him how wrong I'd been about everything. Perhaps, he even wanted a promise to never let it happen again. I could go right back to being the good little boy. I didn't have it in me to give him what he wanted any more. I knew where I went wrong, but I wasn't about to share it with him. "When do we meet with the attorney?"

"Tomorrow morning."

"Great." I leaned against the door and closed my eyes, enjoying the California sun flickering across my face. The lull of the engine made me drowsy and I wanted nothing more than to sleep. I hadn't gotten any real sleep in the five days spent in lock up.

"Martin." Dad's voice woke me.

I moaned, still drowsy. "Yes?"

He pulled into the familiar drive way and cut the engine. "I called your work. Told them you needed an extended leave and they agreed."

"Thanks." Leave it to dad to try and fix everything for me, even though he was rightfully angry with me. I knew he loved me, but I shouldn't have to turn myself into a Xerox of him to get his approval. "You know I'm gay? Right?"

His eyebrows sunk over his nose and his lips pursed together. He grabbed the door handle and got out, leaving me sitting there wondering why I felt like I had to throw gas on the fire.

Reluctantly, I followed him in the house and looked around the open living room and kitchen with vaulted ceilings. "Where's Mom?" I figured she was already passed out in her room.

Dad crossed his arms over his chest and glared at me. "She's not here. She's. Uh, she's in rehab, Martin."

"What?"

"The world does not stop for you and your issues, Martin. I checked her in two days ago."

A million questions flitted through my head. I wanted to ask how it came about and whether my situation contributed to it. I guessed it might have though, so I kept my mouth shut. If dad wanted to tell me, he would. I nodded briefly.

"Look, you have enough to deal with. I'll order pizza. Grab a shower and relax, Martin."

I nodded and went to the room I'd used since I was a boy. It was difficult standing in the middle of that room, staring at the twin bed where I'd made out with Daltrey about a million times. I wished he was here with me, even if it didn't seem right to rely on Daltrey after how badly I screwed up.

I needed to call him. I noticed my phone sitting on the dresser when I tossed my still bagged up wallet on it. I opened the drawers and saw my clothes, underwear and T-shirts, a pair of jeans and sweats. The closet held three of my suits, including my favorite Hugo Boss. In the midst of dealing with my shit and putting mom in rehab, he still found time to make it back to my apartment and grab clothes and my phone. He'd even grabbed my charger. I went to plug the phone in, but it already held a full charge, so I tapped the screen, bringing Daltrey's number up.

"Hey, you!" Daltrey answered.

"Dal. Hey."

"You're out? Everything's cleared up? Your dad said they weren't giving you bail. What's going on?" His words came out so fast, I could barely understand them all.

"They didn't want to give me bail. I think Tia's family is behind that, but you know dad. He got a good lawyer for me."

"Oh, thank God. I hated thinking of you locked up like that, and those jump suites. OhmyGod!"

"Right, orange! Not my color," I chuckled and he giggled, making my heart a little lighter. "The whole thing is bogus, Dal. I mean, really. The only thing I'm guilty of is drinking too much and passing out. I don't know what happened to her or how she got in my apartment."

"She was in your bed?"

"Her and her boyfriend Seth, yes. I think they maybe were making sure I got home and then we all just passed out."

"Not good, Martin."

"I know. Especially with her dying. Then there's the gun. But, my prints aren't on it, so..."

"Are you sure? You don't remember anything else about the night."

"I think I would have remembered a gun."

"You didn't remember people in your bed!" he scolded me, and he was right.

"Well, I don't know. It was in my room and I didn't know about it. It must have been Seth's, but honestly, I don't remember him ever having a gun."

A soft growling sound came over the phone. Daltrey wasn't happy about any of it. "What's this Seth guy say anyway?"

"Nothing."

"Alec's mom—"

I interrupted him with a curse. "Fuck! They're fucking me over, Daltrey."

I listened to him breathe on his side of the world for a moment, laying back in the bed.

Abruptly changing the subject, I said, "I'm at my folk's house, in my old room."

"You are?"

"Uh-huh. Lying on the bed where we used to make out. Remember?"

Giggling that made my heart spin echoed through the phone. "Of course I remember."

That made me happier than anything. If I could just hear that giggle or see Daltrey's shy smile every day, I could be satisfied. I could do anything. "When I get this all worked out..."

My words hung out in the air like an invitation, but I didn't think Daltrey was ready for it.

"Never mind," I said, softly.

"No. We do need to talk about it. I just don't know. I don't have any answers. I don't know if I can trust you after all of this, Marty. Do you just settle for whatever's in front of you, Martin? For real? I need more than that. I wanted to have something more with you. God knows, I've loved you for so long and I've missed you, but since you've come back into my life, it's been nothing but issues. You, you. Ugh!"

"I know. Can you be my friend right now, though? I really need someone on my side." I had to fight back the tears that threatened and made my voice crack.

"I'm always on your side, Martin. I thought you'd know that by now."

"Okay, I know. Really."

"Let's not think about the future or make any decisions now. I'm here for you. Just get your shit together. Okay?"

I swallowed hard. "My dad put my mom in rehab. I think it's my fault."

A long exhale came across the phone. "Oh no, Marty. Don't blame yourself for that one. Your dad ignored her shit for too long. She should have gone to rehab years ago." I knew he was right. She'd been a drunk when we were kids, but back then we didn't understand it beyond how it made things easier for us to hang and make out. Horny teenage boys only cared about getting off together and that had been us. At least until Daltrey's father ended it all.

"You're right." I rubbed my hand over my face. "I have a meeting with my lawyer tomorrow. Can I call you after?"

"Of course. Yes." Daltrey's voice lowered, sounding sexy, but I couldn't focus on that. Not yet.

"Bye, Daltrey."

"Bye, Marty."

Chapter 23 - Crazy Is As Crazy Does

"Okay, Mr. Hannan, I'm going to lay it out for you," Brad, my lawyer said. He leaned forward, his elbows on his massive desk. "Now that our conversations aren't being recorded, we need to talk about this drug thing and I need you to be honest with me."

My dad hadn't come with me to the meeting. He dropped me off at my apartment earlier so I could get my car. No, I couldn't put him out by having him drive me around everywhere. I got in my car without going upstairs to my apartment and drove myself to the meeting. Along the way I thought seriously about trading my Saab in for something simpler, less expensive, and maybe compact like one of those hybrid models. It would certainly piss my father off, but that really wasn't my motivation for once.

I pressed my lips together and stared at my lawyer. Bradly Kauffman had perfectly styled brown hair and brown eyes with green flecks that reflected beneath the florescent lighting in his office. His jacket hung on the back of his chair and he'd rolled up the sleeves of his dress shirt to his elbows. Had I not Googled him and found out about his reputation first hand, I would have thought he represented the poor and downtrodden on a mostly pro-bono pay plan. I would have been wrong.

Brad happened to be one of the highest paid attorneys in L.A., representing the wealthy and the famous and getting them off more often than not. Most of his clients were similar to me, getting pulled into a system that wanted to see the high fall regardless of right or wrong and most of the charges had been blown up out of proportion, just like mine.

I sighed. "Okay. What do you need to know?"

"Were you doing drugs that night? What were you on?"

I was glad my father hadn't come. I didn't want him hearing how bad off I had been. "Beer, maybe a few shots of Jack Daniels, X, some coke. If there was anything else, I don't remember."

"That's, uh, that's." Brad leaned back, pushing his chair away from his desk and crossed his ankles. "I see why you didn't remember anything. Was Tia doing the same?"

I shrugged. How the hell should I know? I'd been too busy watching what Tad had been doing. "I wasn't paying attention to what she did, but it's likely."

"I'm expecting a full toxicology report on her later this week, so we'll know." Brad leaned forward again. "I still haven't spoken with the Ferretti kid, but I will. In the meantime, let me break this down for you." He took a sip of water from his bottle of Avian before continuing. "They've charged you with involuntary manslaughter, but the DA is talking about upping it to voluntary if they get proof you provided the drugs."

"What's the difference?"

"Doesn't really matter, I'm going to get it thrown out or dropped to accidental death. It's really all about your intentions. If they can show you meant to harm someone, they can get a higher charge, but even if you supplied the drugs, that doesn't mean you intended to harm anyone."

"I didn't."

"Didn't what?"

"I didn't supply the drugs. I got the X from Tad and I

don't know who brought the coke. It was just always there. Damn! The only person I intended to harm was myself."

"Seems like you did a pretty good job of it."

I rolled my eyes. "Yep. So?"

"Okay. That's all well and good, but the weapons charge is a completely different matter."

"Why? I didn't know it was there. I never saw it or touched it."

"You sure?"

"Pretty sure." I cocked my head to the side remembering what Daltrey had said the night before. What if I had seen it, touched it. How the hell would I know with how fucked up I was. "Not totally sure. I don't remember how Tia and Seth ended up in my bed. I don't remember leaving the party. So, what do I know? Maybe I did see it or touch it, but it's not mine."

"If your prints are not on it, that will help, and the burden of proof is on them, but it's still not going to be easy convincing the judge that you knew nothing about a gun being in your own home. Then, the no furniture deal."

"What?"

"The DA is trying to make it out like you didn't have furniture because you don't really live there and are a drug dealer."

"Listen, Bradley. I haven't lived there long. All my personal things are there and the furniture was due to arrive last week. They probably tried to deliver it when I was in jail. It's been ordered for weeks. I have a full time job as a programmer at Apex. I made the mistake of getting fucked up at a party. That's fucking it." My voice grew more intense with almost every word I spoke.

"I know," Brad said softly. "That's why I'm going to try and get the charges dropped or at least reduced to a simple misdemeanor. Trust me."

I ran my hands over my face. "This is all such bullshit."

"Don't get fucked up around people you don't trust. Your neighbors are the biggest issue here, Martin."

"Neighbors? Wendy and Alec, you mean?"

Brad gave me a curt nod. "I spoke to Wendy Fredericks early this morning. She is not a nice person." He closed his eyes and shook his head, leaving me to just imagine what she may have said. "I think they're just trying to protect themselves from garnering the same kind of charges you're now fighting, especially with the Witherspoons on a rampage." He huffed. "But, to say they aren't cooperating is not even an understatement. They're throwing your ass under the bus with dramatic flourish."

"That's bad. I never asked where the coke came from. Maybe they're dealing? Maybe you should talk to Alec's mother." I wrapped my fingers together into one solid fist and rested my chin on it, while my elbows angled into my knees.

"Alec's mother?"

"She doesn't have nice things to say about her son and his girlfriend. I'll get her phone number for you. She's some kind of social aristocrat, wealthy and established. Her word against her own son might help, huh?"

Brad grumbled under his breath a bit. "Why would she help you?"

"She likes Daltrey."

"Ah...the artist in New York?" He'd done some homework, but I should have expected that, especially since the prosecution had used my relationship with Daltrey to get my bail denied. "Okay. Get me her info." He waived his hand in the air, as if to say get on with it.

"That's all I have really. I don't know what else to tell you."

"Okay. I get the impression this wasn't the first party of theirs you attended. Ms. Fredericks made it sound like you were up there selling them coke twice a week since you moved in."

I snorted, loudly. "I've been to a few of their parties. I've even been to Tia's parent's house, but I never sold them any drugs. I never bought drugs or even brought any to their parties, unless you count a bottle of Jack or two. Hell, Seth was usually the one passing shit around." I looked up at Brad from beneath a heavy brow. Maybe Seth was the one behind all of this. His drugs, his gun. "Maybe they're protecting him."

"Hm, seems like nobody wants to talk about Mr. Morgan. Not the DA, not the Witherspoons, not Wendy Fredericks."

"Wonder why."

"I'm going to damn sure find out." He stood up and stretched his hand out for me to shake it, and I did.

I left his office and held my arm over my eyes to block the sun as I walked to my car.

"Martin!"

Seth leaned against the door of my Saab, his tanned faced set in a scowl. His shaggy blond hair brushed the tops of his shoulders. He wore flip flops, denim shorts, and a tank top with a surfer logo printed on the front, though it had faded. "What'd you tell your lawyer?" he asked with a smirk, nodding to the office I just came out of.

"What did you tell *your* lawyer?" I threw back at him.

He crossed his arms, tucking his hands under his biceps. "Right. I don't have a lawyer, man. Shouldn't need one."

"I think maybe you do."

"Fuck!" Seth reached behind his back and pulled out a handgun, flashed it at me quickly, then tucked it back in his shorts. "Get in your car and act normal. We need to talk."

I moved to get in the driver's side, and watched carefully as Seth walked around the back of the vehicle. I could get in and drive off, leaving him in the parking lot, but he could shoot at my car as I drove off. I didn't want bystanders hurt because I was being stupid. I popped the lock, letting him in.

"Good move, Martin." He pulled the gun out again and set it in his lap, where I stared at it. "Drive, Martin."

"Right." I put the car in gear and pulled out. "Where we going?"

"Doesn't matter. Just drive so we can talk."

I drove, but waited for Seth to continue. Did he really want to shoot me? Would he?

"I don't want to threaten you, man. I just can't be pulled

into all of this. It's bad enough that Tia..." he said, getting chocked up on her name. I thought for half a second that he really cared about her. He cleared his throat. "Dude, look. You don't know what it's like. You have everything. Please don't bring me into all of this. That's all I'm asking."

"How'd you even know where to find me today?"

"I followed you from your apartment."

Right. I stopped to get my car first. "Fine," I said.

"Is that fine as in you won't drag me into this or that I followed you."

"You're in it, Seth. God damn! What am I supposed to do? You were there."

Seth didn't say anything for a minute. Then he leaned forward and started mashing buttons on my dashboard. He turned on the CD player and flipped the discs until Tad's band started playing. "I should have known you'd have that," he chuckled. "I saw you two getting along for once." He must have been referring to the party.

"Not for long,"

"No," he said, turning the music off. "Look, man. You let everyone manipulate you, but when I ask for one fucking favor, you find your fucking backbone. What the hell?"

I tried to deny it, but he wasn't far off. I had nothing else to say.

"Just try to minimize it? Can you?"

"Your involvement, you mean?"

"Yeah, man."

"You were there. You were her boyfriend. I've already said that. To the cops. To the judge. My lawyer. I can't tell them otherwise now. But, that's all it is."

Seth blew out a long slow breath. "Turn around. Back to the parking lot."

I complied, watching Seth from the corner of my eye. His hands were shaking and his blue eyes were rimmed in red, but otherwise he seemed okay. When I pulled into the parking lot, he pointed his car out to me and I pulled up beside it. "Seth?" I asked as he opened the car door to get out.

"What?"

"I'm sorry about Tia. Sorry for your loss." I looked him in the eye when I said it. I thought I owed him that much, and if I didn't, well I said it anyway.

He pursed his lips together, turning them white. "Sure, man," he said softly and got out of the car.

I watched him drive away. I knew I'd tell Brad about the incident, but not yet.

##

I pulled into my father's driveway. I'd been looking in my rearview mirror like a paranoid spy or something, expecting to see Seth following me home. I sat in my car, waiting for him to pull up but I knew it wasn't going to happen. He'd said what he wanted to say. I wouldn't live my life looking over my shoulder.

Putting it behind me, I went in the house and plopped down on the couch. The silence felt wrong. I sat there listening to the strange clicks the house made.

I'd grown up right here, running in and out of that sliding glass door. Splashing around the pool in the backyard. Eating at the dining room table or the breakfast bar, depending on who was home. Dad always insisted on eating at the table but when he worked late, I generally ate at the bar alone while my mom drank her dinner in the bedroom. Sometimes we watched movies as a family here. Dad had switched out the old fashioned TV a few years back and now he had a giant flat screen hanging on the far wall. I bit my lower lip and sucked it into my mouth. Everything in this house was exactly the same and completely different.

I leaned back into the couch remembering my teen years, spent mostly with Daltrey. Could we have something real now as adults? We were only kids when we first got together, but it seemed neither of us could forget our first love. Maybe. Maybe we could be more.

I pulled my phone out of my pocket, it would be

afternoon in New York. I dialed, hoping he'd be available, and I couldn't help smile when he answered. "Hey you!"

"Hey, Dal-baby!"

"How'd it go today?"

I told him all the gory details and what happened with Seth afterward.

"Damn. You have to tell you lawyer, honey. Maybe get a restraining order or something."

"I know. I am."

"Don't wait."

"Okay, baby."

He gave me Rosalyn Randall's phone number and complained about Wendy and Alec. There wasn't much to say after that.

"So, what are you doing the rest of the day, Marty?" he asked.

"Nothing. I don't know. After five days in jail, I think I want to be outside. I might just hang around the pool. Ugh, wish you were here."

"Me too. I remember the fun we used to have hanging around your pool," Daltrey laughed. I remembered too. Mostly we just wrestled around, trying to touch each other as much as possible without being too obvious. Then, one time Daltrey had given me a blow job on the deck when my parents were both gone for the weekend.

"We had some really good times here," I said, looking around the house again. I expected the walls to start closing in on me, but with Daltrey breathing in my ear over the phone I felt nothing but hopeful.

"I have to go now, Marty. I have work to do."

"Okay. I'm sorry I interrupted."

"No, don't be. I wanted to hear how everything went. So, um, you know, keep me posted." I could almost picture his playful eye-roll.

"Will do, Dal-baby."

"Bye Marty."

I hung up the phone, but before I went out to the pool, I

thought I'd get in one more phone call.

"Hello?" a female voice answered.

"Wendy?" I asked.

"Is this Martin?"

"You know it is."

"Why are you calling me?" Her voice sounded afraid. I considered that Tia's death may have just scratched the surface open on a wound I had no idea had been festering around me.

"Why are you telling such outrageous lies about me?"

"Fuck! So, what? Are you recording this?"

"No. Just you and me. What's going on?" I asked, wondering if she'd confide in me at all.

"Look, Martin. Your daddy is a multi-millionaire or some shit. He'll buy you out of this mess. We don't have that luxury. So, just fucking go with it, will you?"

"Funny. Seth kind of asked me the same thing today. What exactly are you all expecting me to hide?"

"I'm not fucking hiding anything. Just fucking leave me alone." There was her anger.

I had to push for more, hoping she'd give me something useful. "Why?"

"Martin. You're such an ass. Alec's career is too important right now. He can't have any bad publicity. His mom will—Fuck! Please, Martin."

"His mom, what?"

"She threatened him. She's going to ruin him. Please, just let your dad buy you out of trouble and leave us out of it."

"You've dragged yourselves into it, Wendy."

"Fuck you!" she yelled. "You know how it is. You know how much I love him. I'd do anything for him...even you." It sounded like she was on the verge of tears, but I didn't trust that and couldn't let myself pity her.

"What exactly does that mean?"

"I thought it would be fun at first. You know? You're really good looking so right that's great. But it doesn't feel so good when I know he wanted you. Maybe more than he wanted me."

"So, this is all still about Alex for you?" Maybe I understood her motivations a little bit. What would I do for Daltrey?

"God. Fuck off Martin. It's never, never been about *you*." Then she hung up, making me think it was more about me than she wanted to admit. Despite how mean he'd been the first time we met, fooling around with me had to have been all Alec's idea. Hell, Wendy never wanted me. She'd tried to get me involved with other guys. Introduced me to Tad. Demanded I find a date. Why? To get me away from Alec? Maybe I had never thought enough about her motivations enough, merely assuming they were interested in me. They really weren't. Even now, that thought hurt.

She'd never been my friend. She didn't care that Tia was dead. This was all about protecting Alec's fledgling career. All about whatever Alec wanted. I still felt like I was missing something. Maybe calling Alec's mom would help, but I'd leave that up to Brad. I'd call and give the number to him along with everything that had happened since leaving his office.

Maybe he'd get more answers. I couldn't think about the bullshit anymore. My heart hurt knowing I'd given them so much of myself when they had never cared. I'd just been a plaything and so had Tia and she paid for it with her life.

I went to the bathroom to take a shower and wash off the shit I felt like Wendy had piled on me. I started the water to let it get hot and leaned over the sink to wait after taking my clothes off.

The steam fogged up the mirror and I wiped my arm across so I could see my blue eyes. I appraised myself in the mirror wondering if I looked like I'd changed at all. I felt like a totally different person now than I was when I went up to Wendy's and Alec's last epic party. I should look different, but I didn't think I did. Hating the irony, I got in the shower hoping to scrub that other person away from me.

Chapter 24 - You Can Never Go Home Again

Several days went by, and I'd hardly seen my father. I'd spoken with my lawyer more than my dad. I didn't care much about that, but I hadn't spoken with Daltrey either and the walls had finally started closing in on me. Part of me wanted to get out of there and do something, but another part wanted to just hide in my room, lingering on my memories of simpler times.

My father completely surprised me, tapping on the bedroom door. "Yes, sir?" I asked.

"I'm going to get your mom."

I got up and opened the door. "Want me to come?" I didn't want to join him on that escapade, but I felt obligated to offer.

"No. Just hang out here. Doing nothing with your life. That's fine." His voice dripped with sarcasm, which was so unlike him.

"Dad, that's hardly fair."

"What do you want me to say, Martin?"

I held up my hands. I had no idea where he was going with all of this.

"I don't know what to do with you. I don't understand you at all."

I couldn't help the snort that came out of my mouth. My dad gave me the evil eye, so I quickly added, "I don't understand myself most of the time, Dad."

"I only ever wanted you to be happy, Martin. I don't think you will be. I think you've made everything in your life just too damned difficult."

"What the hell does that mean?" I leaned against the door jamb and crossed my arms, defensively.

"You have to be gay. You have to be hung up on that artist kid. You hang out with drug addicts. You just seem to want to fuck up your life. You don't appreciate your own talents, what you have. You're just like her."

"Her?"

"Your mother. Who I have to go get now. Damn it!" He scowled as he examined his watch. Rolex. Of course.

I let my dad storm off, seriously too shocked to do anything else. He'd admitted I was gay and had some kind of relationship with Daltrey; though I really didn't want to leave that relationship where it currently stood. He'd been right-on about all of that. Finally, I walked out to the living room. "Dad! Hey!"

He stopped at the door and turned to look at me. His eyes looked sad and tired with bags under them. For the first time ever, he looked his age. For half a second I thought to tell him never mind, but then I didn't think I'd get the chance again. "Daltrey is special. Very special. Always has been and you're right. That isn't going to change. But Wendy and Alec and the partying. That was just to numb the pain."

"Pain?"

"Yes, the pain of having to live your life instead of my own."

He turned and walked out the door. I let him go. I'd said enough. I really wanted a drink, but didn't think that would be appropriate with Mom coming home from rehab, so I slunk back to my room to take a nap.

##

Dad brought Mom home along with takeout food that he ceremoniously dropped on the table. When we did Chinese, we put all the different packages in the center of the table and shared them. I piled my plate with rice and vegetables and pepper steak and then grabbed an egg roll and a Coke. I ate with a fork, refusing to fight my food with chopsticks, but it didn't stop my parents. I generally ignored them.

My mom ate quietly. She hadn't offered me a hug or anything. I didn't know what I expected. I think it was the first time I'd seen her sober in over ten years, and she didn't look good at all. Her once shiny blonde curls were dull and graying and she'd pulled them back into a pony tail that made her face look severe. Wrinkles were starting to show around the corners of her eyes. At least she didn't have bags like Dad's. I supposed for a moment that I'd helped put those bags there, but I couldn't focus on that.

"Martin," Dad finally broke the silence and I looked up at him, obediently. "Your court date isn't until next month. Perhaps, you should consider going back to work."

"Maybe, but I'm not ready yet."

Mom bit her lower lip, like I did sometimes when I had something to say that I didn't want to let out. I waited, giving her the chance, but she only eyed the food on her plate, stabbing at her sweet and sour pork as if it might get away from her.

"I'll think about it, though," I capitulated, but it wasn't what I wanted to say. Again.

"You do that, Son," Dad said, and I could hear his deep disappointment in his voice. I knew what that sounded like; it wasn't new.

"Dad? Can you just cut me a little slack? This has all been overwhelming."

"You don't think it's been hard on us? Your mother," he said, gesturing to my mom with his chopsticks. It seemed rude and disrespectful. He treated Mom and I just like Wendy treated others.

"I certainly didn't mean to imply it hasn't been hard on you, either of you. I didn't intend for any of this to happen."

"No. Of course not, but what did you expect? Seriously Martin, you have to realize that hanging around with the wrong crowd will get you in trouble. Hell, you were never like this. Not as a kid, not through college. What the hell?" he asked, dropping his chopsticks to the table next to his half eaten plate of food.

I got up and walked down the hall to my room, leaving my plate on the table and careful to shut the door quietly, not wanting to be accused of slamming it. I couldn't deal with them anymore, Dad's ironic accusations and Mom's silence. Would this push her to start drinking? What did my father expect? I couldn't change what happened; done is done. No, I'd never been in trouble during school, but I also didn't have friends or a social life—at all.

He opened my door and stepped into the room behind me. I looked up at him from where I sat in the center of the bed, waiting for him to start in on me again. I sucked in my bottom lip.

He ran a hand through his hair. "Martin," he started, then planted his hands on his hips, cocking out one knee. "Listen. Do I need to get rehab for you, too?"

"What? No. It's not like that."

"Then what's it like?" His voice wasn't disappointed or angry. I couldn't place the tone for a moment, and then I realized it was concern. I'd really judged him harshly, but having his concern now didn't change anything.

"My life is fucking miserable, Dad. You don't get it."

"Make me get it."

"I'm miserable because I've always done everything you wanted. I hate my job. I hate my car. Everything. I hated hanging out with those people. The only thing in my life that's meant anything to me is Daltrey."

My dad sat on the edge of my bed and ran his hand

through his hair again. He exhaled slowly and shook his head a little. "You said something like that earlier. I thought you were just mad at me."

"I'm not mad at you, but I can't be you."

"No, no you can't. You have to be you. I just want you to be happy, Martin. Whatever that is. Figure it out and fix it." He held up his hands in defeat.

##

The smell of coffee drug my sorry ass out of bed the next morning. Mom stood in the kitchen staring at the machine with a mug in her hand. "Hey," I said.

Her blue eyes that looked so much like my own came up and so did a quirky smile. "Morning. Sleep well?" she asked, as if we'd said more than two words to each other over the past few years.

I nodded. "How're you?"

She gave a soft laugh. "I'm okay. Better. I, uh, don't know how to do sober yet, but I'm going to give it a shot." She laughed again. "Shot!"

"Funny, Mom."

She bumped my shoulder as I poured myself a cup of coffee. "Come sit outside with me, Martin."

I followed her outside and we sat at the table near the sliding door.

"I've always loved it out here," she said. "Normally, it'd be a glass of wine or a mixed drink, but coffee works." She held up her mug. Joking about things had always been her coping mechanism, even when she was drunk. "You okay, baby boy?" she asked.

"No. Honestly. I'm scared."

"You have a good lawyer. You're not going back to jail," she said confidently.

"It doesn't always work out that way, Mom."

"Well, things never do. I never thought I'd be so shocked to be sober, but here I am."

"What's that mean?"

"Just that I never thought of myself as being a drunk, but I can't recall a lot of sober days over the years. It seems as if I fell into bad habits and life felt better when I didn't have to deal with anything."

Her truth felt heavy for the early morning. The sun played across the water of the pool, sparkling silver and white, and seeming like it should be hotter than it actually was. California mornings had a way of doing that. I sipped my coffee and gazed at my mother.

"I'm doing this for me. Don't misunderstand. I know you're having a tough time right now, and maybe you need me to be sober, but that's just a nice side benefit, really."

"I want you to be happy, Mom," I said setting my mug on the glass topped table. "You should do this for you."

She held her mug with both hands and regarded me over the rim. "Yes. So? Daltrey Boxbaum?"

I smiled, and asked, "Didn't you know what we were getting up to back then?"

My mother laughed hard until her eyes were watering and I couldn't help but join her. "No," she gasped. "I had no idea, Martin." After a minute, we both calmed down. "I'm sorry I didn't pay enough attention to you over the years."

"Well, most of the time we counted on that." I smirked, then wondered if that was a little unfair. Regardless, it was true. "He means the world to me."

"I get that. Listen. Most of my adult life has been spent in the oblivion of alcohol. Because I haven't been happy. Because I married your father thinking he was beneath me, but I did it because I loved him. So, that wasn't fair to either of us. Don't do that. You both deserve more."

"I don't know how any of this is going to turn out."

She put her hand on top of mine. "In rehab, I learned that happiness is worth pursuing. It's more important than anything. Sometimes thinking we don't deserve it or maybe we think it's too hard to keep after. I don't know. It should be everything. Why live this life at all if we don't try to be happy,

Martin?"

    Her words were both inspiring and terrifying on multiple levels. She sounded like she might kill herself if this sobriety thing didn't work out for her, and I was afraid it wouldn't. My father wouldn't change. He loved her, but it had taken him an awful long time to get her into rehab. If he didn't try to make her happy, would she give up? And what about Daltrey? Could we ever be happy together? Could I make him happy? I only had questions, no answers.

Chapter 25 - Lawyers Are People Too

Brad called me several times over the next few weeks. The court date rapidly approached and Brad had been negotiating with the DA. We'd hired a private detective to look into Seth Morgan. Brad had conversations with Rosalyn Randall and Alec's sister Joy, as well as Tad and other members of his band. He'd taken depositions from a few of them. They all testified that Seth Morgan was supplying the drugs and I had nothing to do with any of it. It all left Brad confident we'd at least get a plea bargain. The DA wouldn't really want to go to court with the evidence rapidly stacking up in my favor.

The day of the hearing, my father joined me outside the courtroom as we waited for Brad to show up. Five minutes before court was scheduled to start, he showed with a smile on his face. He shook my father's hand and clapped me on the shoulder.

"So, listen up. Seth Morgan was arrested last night," he said with a wink. "He had a lot of drugs on him. Coke and heroine and meth."

"Fuck!" I couldn't help but blurt out.

"I'd say," Brad chuckled. "So, I've been talking with the DA all morning. He agreed that the most likely explanation for all of this is that you got caught up in Seth's bullshit. But he still isn't happy and not willing to drop everything. He wants something for his trouble, so to speak."

"What the fuck does that mean?" I asked, not willing to give this guy his pound of flesh out of my own hide.

"He's sticking to the weapons charge. Everything else dropped. The gun was found in your apartment."

"What does that mean then?"

"It's a misdemeanor charge. He's recommending a suspended sentence and a fine. That's good though. Otherwise you'd get probation and you don't need that hanging over you. With this, you can go back to your life like nothing happened."

I scoffed, "My life will never be the same, no matter what happens."

My dad reached out and rubbed my arm from shoulder to elbow. It was the most positive affection I'd ever received from the man. I gave him a weak smile.

Brad blew out an annoyed huff. "So you want this deal then?"

"Yes." I couldn't see that I'd get anything better. Especially with Wendy and Alec still willing to testify against me, though I noticed they weren't present. "So, where are Wendy and Alec?"

Brad shrugged. "Don't know. I think they've dropped off the radar after I started talking to the mother."

"Who?" my father asked.

"Rosalyn Randall," I answered.

My dad broke out into a smile. "She's one of their mothers? God help the kid."

I didn't have time to ask what he meant by that because they opened the doors and we all filed in. My dad and I sat in the pew-like benches in the back of the courtroom where Brad indicated we should sit and then he went to speak with someone on the opposite side of the room who had already been inside when we entered. I presumed it was the District Attorney.

In a moment, he came back with a smile. "We're all good

then. The judge should agree, and then we sign off and go home."

At the end of the day, I walked away with a misdemeanor on my record and a thousand dollar fine that I paid up immediately. I also left that courtroom with some hard life lessons, all of which told me I needed to make serious changes in my life. I knew what I wanted, and I was damned determined to make it happen.

Chapter 26 - Change Everything Now

My stomach fluttered uncontrollably as I pressed the buzzer. I had no idea what kind of response I would get, or if he would even be home.

The door opened and Daltrey stood there wide-eyed, mouth open, wearing soft gray sweatpants and a bright yellow T-shirt. Both his face and shirt had been splattered with blue paint, looking oddly like an Easter egg, but still unbelievably gorgeous to me.

"OhmyGod! Marty!" he squealed and bounced on his toes. "I can't believe you're here. Why didn't you call me? OhmyGod!"

"Invite me in?" I asked.

Daltrey didn't disappoint me. He grabbed my arm, tugging me inside his loft.

The place overwhelmed me. The ceiling had to be three stories high, a huge wide open space with canvases and art supplies everywhere and two huge cabinets that appeared custom made stretched out on the wall next to the front door. A couch and chair lined up in front of the far wall that had a flat screen mounted on it. It was smaller than my dad's TV and seemed almost dwarfed against the bricks that traveled high above it. To the left of the sitting area, a breakfast bar separated a kitchen area from the main space. Beyond the kitchen area, a spiral staircase lead up to a second floor loft area that overlooked the expanse of the room.

"This is it," Daltrey squeaked out throwing his hand in the air as if to show me all of it at once.

"I like it. It suites you." I followed him farther into the space, lacing my fingers through his.

"So, like, how long are you here? In New York?" he asked, looking down at our hands, his smile dropping.

I tugged on Daltrey's arm, pulling him in against my chest, and I wrapped my arms around him in a tight hug. I couldn't help burying my nose in his dark hair. He smelled like turpentine and strawberries, an odd combination, but even that suited him.

"Listen. You were right about a lot of things. I've decided not to let anyone tell me what to do. I'm going after what I want most," I said softly, beside his ear.

Daltrey pulled back and looked up at me, his face questioning me wordlessly.

"Yes. That's you Daltrey. If you'll have me."

"I don't know."

"Shh... Let me tell you what's been going on first."

Daltrey nodded, but pulled out of my arms. "Coffee?" he asked, taking brisk steps away from me and toward his kitchen. I followed. I would have followed him anywhere, but I was okay with that because it was my choice and not anyone else's.

I watched him fiddle around with the coffee machine and pull out coffee mugs from a cabinet over the sink. "Sit," he ordered, pointing at the counter where two bar stools were tucked in. I pulled one out, following directions.

"I got a transfer to the Manhattan office," I said as I waited for him to get the coffee ready.

Daltrey leaned forward gripping the counter and locking his elbows. "Really?" His deep blue eyes called to me across the smooth gray countertop. I ran my palms across the soft, cool surface. "It's soapstone," Daltrey answered my unspoken question.

"Nice. Uh, I rented a tiny place close to work. Nothing near as nice as this, but it'll do. For now."

"Already?"

"Funny thing. My dad promised to back off. He's letting me do whatever I want. Then at the last minute he gave me back his AmEx card. I only used it for the apartment. Everything else has been paid for by selling my car."

"You sold your car?"

"Didn't think I'd need it in New York. Plus, I'm in walking distance to work."

Daltrey gave a nervous laugh. "Right, in Manhattan?"

"Yep."

Daltrey turned and busied himself with the coffee again, while I wondered what he was thinking. He hadn't said what he thought of any of it and I needed to know. "Dal-baby?"

He flashed his dark eyes at me, a quiver in his lip.

I had to ask, "What are you thinking?"

"Um, this is really fast, Marty. You know? Like, too fast. I don't know." He shook his head and closed his eyes. "I want to go for it, but still. I can't have, like drama, in my life now." He opened his eyes with a dramatic roll on the word drama and I laughed, unable to stop myself.

Daltrey's nose curled up. "This isn't funny. Gawd, Martin."

"Sorry," I said, trying to control myself. "I'm not asking you to marry me or move in. I'm okay starting slow. Dating. Maybe?"

A big white coffee mug was shoved in front of me and I grasped it, holding it as if letting go of the ceramic cup would be letting go of Daltrey. He cleared his throat and I lifted my eyes to meet his serious ones. "I don't, like, you know—I don't party."

"I don't either. I haven't had any drugs or alcohol since that night. And I don't plan to." That truth I could freely give him.

He smiled, sincerely. "Okay."

I sipped my cup wondering where everything was going next, when Daltrey walked around the counter and stood between my legs. He took the mug from my hand and set it on the soapstone counter. I immediately wrapped him up in my arms again.

"It's a start," he breathed into my chest. Having him so close and warm in my arms had me instantly hard. I wanted this man more than anything.

I pushed his head back and bent in to kiss him softly on the lips, hoping for more, and Daltrey didn't disappoint me. He opened his mouth, letting me plunge inside, his kiss more important than my next heartbeat. Daltrey's hands slid into my hair and tugged, as a moan broke from his throat, pouring into my mouth.

My hands moved of their own accord, finding their way under the loose T-shirt he wore and touching silky skin that burned beneath my palms. I needed him naked and closer. I wanted to rip his clothes off, but he pulled his own shirt over his head. "You sure?" I asked.

"Gawd, yes. Marty, I need you. I can't," he gasped and dove in for my mouth again. His tongue challenged mine and his hands roamed over my chest and back, tugging at my shirt. I let him pull it over my head and then it joined his on the floor. We pressed our chests together and I could feel his erection pushing against mine.

"Where's your bedroom, Dal-baby?"

He grabbed my hand and yanked me toward the spiral staircase and I followed him up. "Bathroom," Daltrey said, pointing to the double French doors at the top of the stairs. To the left, a hallway stretched out along the railing that overlooked the main room of the apartment. Daltrey had a small seating area there that backed up to a partition that blocked off the rest of the room. I stepped around it and saw his large king-sized bed stretching out into the space, diagonally from the far corner. The far wall was lined with tall closet doors. All of it looked sleek and modern. The bedspread shimmered a deep bronze.

Daltrey led me, our fingers entwined again, to the bed. He pulled the comforter back, revealing teal sheets. "My princess bed," he giggled. "I didn't expect company."

I wrapped him in my arms again. "I love it. Don't change for me or anyone. I love you for you." I kissed the top of his head and Daltrey made a purring sound I could feel reverberating through his chest. I liked it, but I wanted to hear that musical giggle out of him again. I tickled his sides below his ribs and just like that, he was laughing and pulling away playfully. I grabbed him, pulling him close again, then tossed him on the bed. I wondered if he knew what that giggling did to my heart.

I crawled across the sheets to him. He'd stopped running. "Daltrey."

"Yes, please. Marty." His breathy voice, high-pitched and demanding, called me to him.

We grasped each other's shoulders, holding on, kneeling in the center of the bed. Everything about this man made me want him more. How could I have ever doubted that or let anything come between us. "I'm not rolling over any more. Not for anyone. I want you," I said, looking into those dark eyes that I needed to see me.

"Good," he sighed, running his hand down my back, and tucking his finger into the waist band of my jeans at the small of my back. "I thought I'd lost you, Marty. Gawd, I want you too. Off," he commanded, tugging at my waistband.

I let go of him to unbutton my pants, and then let him shove them down my thighs. My underwear followed, making my dick spring out. Daltrey didn't hesitate to run his hand across my crown and then down the length of me, his fingers gripping and making me moan at the sensations of my Daltrey touching me.

"You. You too," I managed to say, though my intelligence level had dropped significantly in proportion to the hardening of my cock.

Daltrey made noises, grunted, and shifted, pulling his own sweat pants down. Our tongues met again for a moment and I didn't think I could hold back much longer, but then I didn't have to. Daltrey pounced on me, pushing me down on the mattress, rubbing his long cock against mine and making even more of those high-pitched noises that turned my heart inside out.

"I need more," he cooed, leaning over to the little night stand beside the bed. He pulled out a tube of Astroglide and shook it hard before popping the top and splattering what little was left in his hand. "Damn, I'm almost out," he muttered as he rubbed his lubed hand all over both of our hard cocks, making them slippery and sticky. "I have another in the bathroom and condoms," he said quietly.

The constant rub of our cocks and the sudden thought of being inside his hot channel had me gasping for air and praying I didn't come all over him right that second. "Stop, stop, stop," I moaned.

Daltrey pulled away and glared down at me with confusion. "What?"

"I want you. All of you. Go. Get them," I demanded. A part of me feared he'd laugh at me and maybe kick me out or tell me no. I didn't need to fear though. Daltrey's face broke open into a wide but still lustful smile. He tried to dash into the bathroom, but got tripped up by his sweatpants tangled around his ankles. He went down hard with a loud thump. "Daltrey!" I called out, rushing after him.

He giggled from the floor and kicked the sweat pants off his foot, tossing them up at me where I leaned over the bed peering down at him. "I'm good," he said, letting the giggling trail off. I shook my head and rolled off the bed to pull my jeans off before I ended up on the floor with him.

In a minute he was back, pushing me down again. "I haven't been with anyone since you, Marty." His words warmed my heart.

"I haven't either."

"You're sure?"

"Oh yes. I'm sure. Look. I know Seth and Tia were in my bed, but we hadn't done anything. There was no evidence that anything happened past sleeping. That, that wasn't even a question for me." Even if it had been a question, it wouldn't have counted. Sex you didn't remember didn't happen. I supposed that wasn't a great attitude, but it was easier to think that when I knew nothing had happened. If something would have happened, I'd have felt it in my ass. There would have been lube. I would have been naked, but I woke with boxers on and I was certain they'd stayed on.

Daltrey's expression on his face had me concerned about it. "Daltrey? I haven't. Whatever else, it's you. You're it."

"Okay," he said softly, and I wanted to know what was going on in his head, but he distracted me by dropping a condom on my chest. "I want to ride you, Marty." His voice dropped an octave, his eyes hooded over. He licked his lips, looking like the epitome of living breathing sex.

I opened the wrapper and rolled the latex down my shaft while Daltrey's sex-eyes watched me. They rolled back in his head as I leaned forward, realizing that he had his fingers in his hole. He was prepping himself, riding his own hand. "Oh fuck, Dal!" The sight of his lithe body undulating as he stimulated himself made me grip the base of my cock hard, trying desperately to hold off the impending orgasm threatening to burst loose.

Those little noises came again and I worried he was going to make himself come. "Dal? Now?" I begged. Daltrey responded by opening his eyes and looking at me hard before crawling over my body. "You sure? You're ready?"

Daltrey answered with a long moan as he slowly pushed his ass over my cock. He had a grip on it, all lined up, and he sat down slowly. He looked down at me, his tongue peeking out of the corner of his mouth. I couldn't have been more in love with him. I opened my mouth to tell him just how I felt, but then he started moving. His cock jutted out in front of him, hard and curving slightly to the left. I reached down to touch his muscled thighs.

He wasn't a big man, but his legs were incredibly cut and fit. His abs were a defined four pack only because he didn't have room for six on his slight frame. I didn't know how painting could keep him looking so great, but I was all for it. I rubbed the tops of his thighs, feeling the light dusting of hair, just enough to give a little friction.

He felt incredible, his tight hole radiating a scorching heat, gripping me and pulling on my cock as he worked himself up and down. His dick bounced against that four pack, long and lean like the rest of him. I couldn't resist it a second longer, so I reached out and fisted him.

He fucked up into my palm and down onto my cock and I knew I wouldn't last long. My hips thrust up, so I was fucking up into his hole, just as I'd imagined. "God. Daltrey! Grip my cock. Fuck!"

He squeezed his ass tighter and I felt it from the tip of my head, along the length, and down deep into my balls.

"Feels so good," he hissed, just before he started panting in a high-pitched moan like he could barely hold himself back. The tingling started in the middle of my back and traveled out all over my body and pooled in my balls, pulling them up tight.

"Now! Now!" I cried out. "Dal!" Electric shocks flashed underneath my eye lids.

Daltrey groaned, his body shook, and he fell forward as his own orgasm erupted, spewing his cum all over my stomach and chest. He lay on top of me, shaking, and rubbing his cum into both of our bodies. I wrapped my arms around his shoulders and kissed the side of his face and neck.

"Marty," he groaned out.

"It's okay, Dal-baby."

Then I felt cold tears splash on my shoulder.

"Shh. Daltrey. Everything's fine. I won't let you down, baby. I've got you."

"Thank you," he sighed.

I rolled over, pushed him on his back, and kissed his wet eyes and cheeks and lips. "I promise."

He smiled and drifted off to sleep. I lay beside him for some time enjoying the feel of his hot body pressed against mine. He rolled on his side away from me and I spooned around him, plastering my face into his back between his shoulder blades, feeling his sweat streak across my cheek. I needed to feel him against me, to know this was real.

I'd changed my whole life. Not just for Daltrey's sake, but I couldn't deny he was a large part of it. He gave me the motivation I needed to figure out what I wanted and to go for it. A new city, a new job, and all of it across the country from my dad. It really felt like I was on my own and I was determined to make it all work this time.

Soon the sticky became more uncomfortable and I needed to clean up. I moved slowly so I wouldn't wake Daltrey and made my way to his bathroom.

The glass door was trimmed with a thick black boarder and covered with a sheer curtain pulled taut from top to bottom. I pushed it open to reveal a sleek modern bathroom that was all tile and glass. Directly in front of the door, two big square sinks floated on the counter top. To the right, a series of narrow, floor to ceiling windows lit the room with sunlight, making it feel a little warmer. To the left, a glass wall and door separated the huge shower area with multiple shower heads. The entire room had been tiled with a gray ceramic. The room felt spa-like, modern, and masculine. I could probably live in that room alone.

I turned on the shower and adjusted the nobs until the huge rainfall shower-head turned off and the high powered one just below it turned on. I washed quickly and stepped out of the shower, not wanting to waste time away from Daltrey.

I found charcoal gray towels in the cabinet under the double sinks. I dried off and stared at the wall of mirrors above the sinks. I wiped a clean streak across them with the towel and looked at my reflection. My eyes seemed content. I sighed.

I'd come a long way and I still had a long way to go, but for the first time in years I could stand to look into my own eyes. I liked what I saw there: love, happiness, and hope for the future.

The end

Lines on the Mirror
Copyright © 2015 Maggie Chatterton

I stare at those lines
That I've drawn on this mirror
And I hate what I see.
I strive to be
Everything that they
Want me to be
Even if it is something
That isn't me...
There is an emptiness
Growing inside of me,
Slowly churning
Day after day
Burning away my insides
And I'm scared
That there's no cure.
I'm falling deeper
Into darkness.
With my reflection changing
Before my eyes
I fear that
My grasp on stability
Is slipping away from me.
With lines of muddy gray
And murky skies,
This darkness is consuming me,
Pulling me closer to rock bottom.
Lies are whispered behind my back,
But a hand is reaching out for me.
I feel almost hesitant to grasp it,
But the temptation is too great
And my neediness is consuming me,
Begging for the warmth
That his hand can provide me
As it draws me closer
To the light.

ABOUT THE AUTHOR

Lynn Michaels lives and writes in Tampa, Florida where the sun is hot and the Sangria is cold. Lynn is the newest addition to Rubicon Fiction, and she loves reading and writing about hot men in love.

Visit and LIKE on Facebook at:

https://www.facebook.com/pages/Lynn-Michaels/1450504665203028

lynnmichaels69@yahoo.com

http://rubiconwriting.com/lynn-michaels/

COMING SOON FROM LYNN MICHAELS

Corey has graduated from college and is trying to find his way, but when his Dom/boyfriend, Jack, demands that he move in with him, Corey loses himself in emotion, fighting Jack every step of the way.

Jack is a rich owner of a real estate investment firm and he's determined keep his submissive/boyfriend in line, even though Corey refuses to use his safe words.

Will their play become all consuming, or will they learn to trust each other enough to find love?

ALSO BY LYNN MICHAELS

In the world of Supercross, taking the holeshot means one racer leaps ahead of the crowd and into first place, leaving the rest of the pack behind. If Supercross racer Davey McAllister knows anything, it's how to take the holeshot. When the hot rising-star mechanic, Tyler Whitmore, shows up in his bed, Davey does just that.

But, dating a competitor's mechanic threatens to blow his ride if anyone finds out. With the fear of losing his sponsors, he has to keep his love life completely under cover, but Davey is in deep and wants to tell the world how much he loves Tyler.

Tyler Whitmore wants to be out of the closet, but dating the competition is a death sentence for his career. Overprotective of Davey's reputation and his own dreams, Tyler refuses to commit to his lover and is afraid of falling hard. Will they ever be able to find their way through the Premiere racing league pitfalls and acknowledge their love?

Now Available on Amazon or All Romance eBooks.

Made in the USA
Charleston, SC
06 November 2015